Allied at the Altar

When only a convenient wife will do!

The face of Victorian London is changing. Innovation and reform is the order of the day. At the heart of this new Society are Conall Everard, Sutton Keynes, Camden Lithgow and Fortis Tresham.

These four dashing heroes are determined to make their mark on the world. But what starts out as four convenient marriages will change these gentlemen's lives forever...

Don't miss this new sexy quartet from Bronwyn Scott!

Read Conall and Sofia's story in
A Marriage Deal with the Viscount

And look out for the rest of

Allied at the Altar

Coming soon!

Author Note

Welcome to the new series! Allied at the Altar is centered around arranged marriages and takes a look at various issues surrounding marriage in the 1850s. It also explores the subtle theme of change. The backdrop of the 1850s is very important to the series in a larger sense, as well. First, the 1850s mark an era of innovations of all sorts, including matrimonial innovations.

Conall and Sofia's story takes place at a time of marriage reform across Europe. Their union takes advantage of the 1836 Marriage Act, which allowed people to marry outside of the Anglican church through a civil license—the advent of the "town hali" or registry wedding.

Secondly, the story focuses on Sofia's status as a divorcée who hovers on the fringes of acceptable society, just before the new 1857 Matrimonial Causes Act is passed.

Conall takes advantage of this innovative era with his alpaca wool. His aspirations are based on the 1853 real-life importation of alpacas to Britain by Sir Titus Salt.

Sofia and Conall's story is innovative and risky. This is unapologetically not a story about virgins, shy wallflowers or spunky debutantes. By 1850, that world was beginning its slow fade. Sofia and Conall's characters reflect that in their personal choices, and in their struggle to let go of the past they know in order to embrace the new unknown. I hope you enjoy their story, and use it as your own clarion call to do precisely that.

A Marriage Deal with the Viscount

ISBN-13: 978-1-335-63486-3

A Marriage Deal with the Viscount

This edition published by arrangement with Harlequin Books S.A.

For questions and comments about the quality of this book, please contact us at CustomerService@Harlequin.com.

Printed in U.S.A.

Bronwyn Scott is a communications instructor at Pierce College in the United States and is the proud mother of three wonderful children—one boy and two girls. When she's not teaching or writing, she enjoys playing the piano, traveling—especially to Florence, Italy—and studying history and foreign languages. Readers can stay in touch on Bronwyn's website, bronwynnscott.com, or on her blog, bronwynswriting.blogspot.com. She loves to hear from readers.

Books by Bronwyn Scott

Harlequin Historical

Scandal at the Midsummer Ball
"The Debutante's Awakening"
Scandal at the Christmas Ball
"Dancing with the Duke's Heir"

Allied at the Altar

A Marriage Deal with the Viscount

Russian Royals of Kuban

Compromised by the Prince's Touch
Innocent in the Prince's Bed
Awakened by the Prince's Passion
Seduced by the Prince's Kiss

Wallflowers to Wives

Unbuttoning the Innocent Miss
Awakening the Shy Miss
Claiming His Defiant Miss
Marrying the Rebellious Miss

Visit the Author Profile page at Harlequin.com for more titles.

For Kathryn who wondered if llamas and alpacas
would make a good story. They do.
Now you know. And for Brony, my own "Alice"
and innovator who never hesitates to contemplate
"six impossible things before breakfast."

Chapter One

London—May 1854

Men reveal themselves the most in the least of their actions. In this case, it was the failure to offer a drink. On that omission alone, Conall Everard knew he was going to be refused. He'd learned to look for meaning in the smallest of gestures—or the lack of them. Today, he'd been in the Duke of Cowden's study for precisely one and a half minutes and he already knew the interview would go poorly. This afternoon, the Duke had not offered him a drink, only a seat in a maroon, Moroccan-leather chair designed for style over comfort, a sign he was fortunate to get an appointment with the Duke at all no matter how short the audience. Longer audiences got more comfortable chairs. It affirmed his earlier assumption of bad news. The Duke was a busy man. Most of *ton*nish London wanted a moment of the man's time, a place in his deep pockets or a whisper of his wisdom. This audience had been granted out of remembrance for the Duke's friendship with Conall's father rather than any desire to do business with his late friend's son. Unless…

Unless Conall could change the conversation. The Duke might intend to refuse him, but Conall had persuaded hard hearts before, usually of the feminine variety and usually for business of a different sort, but, none the less, persuasion *was* persuasion and Conall Everard, the newly inherited Viscount Taunton, was as persuasive as they came. Conall leaned forward, as if he were oblivious to the Duke's oversight on the drink. 'I appreciate your time today, your Grace, the alpaca has much to recommend it: the waterproof layering of its wool, even the feel of the wool, which is far softer than our sheep.'

The Duke cut him off with a wave of his hand and the tired sigh of a man much beset. 'I read the report, Taunton.'

'Alpacas can be raised in England,' Conall pushed on, ignoring the pain that still stabbed at him whenever someone called him that. *Taunton.* The title was his now and with it went the reminder that his beloved father was dead. After a year, he was starting to think he might never recover from the blow. He might not have if it had been up to him. But it wasn't up to him. Nothing would ever just be about him again. A viscount had to put his family first, his people first, all of whom who were counting on him to make the Viscountcy viable again. He'd had to shelve his grief and shoulder his responsibilities. He could not fail today. 'Imagine what it would mean, your Grace, if we had direct access to the wool source without the complications of importing.'

'We know what it would mean.' Cowden's patience was thin. 'The *board* read the report, all seventy-two pages of it.' The board being the Prometheus Club, a group of wealthy, titled gentlemen with a knack for profitable investments—such a knack, in fact, that a single word from them could make or break an entire venture. A word would be nice, as long as it was the *right* word, Conall thought. A word would be imperative, even. But today he was here for much more than garnering verbal endorsements. Before words could matter he needed money and a lot of it. *Soon.* His alpacas were already here. It was a gamble he'd had to take to have them here before the summer shearing. But it had cost him the liquidation of every asset he'd been able to lay his hands on. Now there were no funds to develop the project. What good would the alpaca be to him if he could not buy the mill? He pressed on, ignoring the warning signs from Cowden.

'Then you already know how immediate access to the wool could reduce costs by having the supply for *our* mills on *our* own land.'

The Duke's greying eyebrows lifted as his gaze flicked to the long wall of windows revealing the outside, no doubt imagining alpacas with their shaggy coats trotting around his immaculate gardens. Conall stopped, recognising his mistake. It was a poor choice of words. 'Figuratively speaking, of course, your Grace,' Conall hastily amended. 'Americans dominate the cotton market at present and, by doing so, they hold us hostage. We have to pay their prices in order to meet our mills' needs.' He shook his head. 'That situation can't go on for ever. The slavery issue will tear that country apart in a few years, mark my words, and then where will we be? Our supply will be cut off. But if we had alpacas, now that would be real leverage, real control.'

Cowden was not impressed. 'We have Scottish sheep and we are developing cotton in our other colonies like Egypt. I think we will survive if the American market goes under.'

'We should strive to do more than survive, your Grace. Alpaca wool is better quality in all ways.' Warmer and softer, it lacked the itchiness of sheep's wool. Surely, the Duke saw the benefit in that? Women would go wild for it. It would make beautiful scarves, blankets, and shawls, to say nothing of its practical uses. As a luxury item alone it would command a certain market.

The Duke leaned forward and fixed him with a warning stare that said the time for argument was over and *had* been over before he'd even walked into the room. 'Taunton, I do appreciate you coming to me and to my club first. However, on a majority vote, we have decided to pass on investing in your alpaca syndicate.'

He was sunk, then. His great gamble had failed before it had even really begun. Conall let the full import of that rejection sink in. He had not just come to the club first. He'd come to the club first *and* last. There was nowhere else *to* go. Banks had turned him down. Did Cowden know that? No lender had been willing to loan him money on the risky venture of shipping alpacas from Peru to England for fear the cargo would die on the voyage or wouldn't acclimate to England as well as Conall proposed, especially with the cloud of debt hanging over the Viscountcy already. He had no collateral should the venture fail. He had no other avenues to pursue besides banks and the Prometheus Club. No other investment club had ties with him that obligated them to hear him out on his father's behalf.

And yet, up until this moment, Conall had been so certain it wouldn't matter. He'd been sure the Prometheus Club, named for the Titan god of foresight, would see the opportunity behind this, if not the genius. Now, by a majority vote, his one hope had been cut, his one grand plan for resurrecting the failing coffers of the Taunton Viscountcy.

His mind tripped back to that one word and what it meant. *Majority. The vote had not been unanimous. There had not been consensus.* Hope surged, once more. Maybe surged was too optimistic. It flickered, a last ember among the ashes.

'I do wish I had better news for you.' The Duke was a shrewd man, sharp-minded and blunt when needed, but he was not an unkind man. Conall had known Cowden most of his life, had grown up with his sons, and he knew the Duke believed the moment of crisis had passed, the bad news delivered, the rejection accepted, the dirty work of refusing the son of an old friend done. Conall smiled. That was the Duke's mistake. This wasn't over, not yet. This was where he'd take his advantage. He waited patiently for the expression of sympathy sure to follow.

'I understand your father's passing revealed some difficult circumstances. I am sorry for it. If I had known there was such distress…' He spread his hands in an expansive but helpless gesture as if the words 'difficult circumstances' or 'distress' adequately encompassed the amount of debt Conall had discovered after his father's death. Indeed, none of them had known. Conall's father had kept the shocking financial reality of their lives well-hidden from even those closest to him.

'I appreciate the sentiment, your Grace. Perhaps there is something you could do? You mentioned the decision was not unanimous. Might I ask for the names of those who are interested in investing? I would like to contact them on my own. Perhaps they would like to invest privately, outside the club.' If there were three or even four men who'd expressed an interest it would be enough. His blood started to thrum with possibility, his mind already running the numbers. 'And yourself, of course. I would entertain a private partnership with you.' It was a bold move to put the question directly to Cowden, to call out his vote explicitly with the assumption that Cowden had voted affirmatively.

Cowden steepled his hands, his hazel eyes soft with something akin to pity, and Conall felt his stomach plummet. 'I am too old for such adventure, Taunton. I want to bask in my profits and let the club work for me after all the years I've worked for it. I want to enjoy my grandchildren and my sons while I have the vigour left to do it.'

Conall supplied the requisite chuckle, masking his own disappointment. One *did* need a certain amount of vigour to keep up with Cowden's family. The Duke had managed three sons, his eldest had married seven years ago and seen to it that his wife, Helena, promptly produced four sons, one every two years like clockwork. Now, Cowden's second son was set to marry and there was no doubt in society's mind the Cowden cradle would be full this time next year and the year after that. The Cowden males knew how to do their duty. Except for Fortis, the third, the one closest to Conall's own age. But despite his wildness, Fortis had still managed a brilliant military career, as youngest sons should, and an acceptable society marriage, even if he hadn't seen his bride since the honeymoon six years ago.

Conall cleared his throat. 'I certainly understand, your Grace. But the other members, perhaps?' He knew he was pressing, but he could not let the opportunity go.

'There was only one, Taunton.' Ah. The Duke had meant to spare his feelings with the rather liberal use of the term majority. A minority of one was not much to go on. The Duke blew out a breath, debating with himself. 'I'm not sure I do you any favours by revealing the name to you. The investor is not a "usual" member. I originally had misgivings about allowing them to join, but they have proven reliable thus far even if they are a bit of a phantom.' The Duke speared him with a sharp hazel gaze. 'I want the very best of investors for you. I would not want to set you up for failure.'

Dear Lord, the Duke had withheld a drink and now he was withholding a name. Today was definitely not his day. 'I am already set up for failure. In fact, failure is a surety if I maintain my present course,' Conall said bluntly. The Viscountcy could not last more than a few years at the given rate before it gave into genteel poverty. There was his sister, Cecilia's, Season to manage next year and hopefully her dowry the following, his brother, Freddie's, schooling and an endless list of repairs for the estate. He could not leave this room without a name, without hope that he might be able to meet those obligations. 'Give me the name and let me assess the quality of the investor myself.'

Nothing persuaded like a direct order. Usually people didn't refuse if not given the option. Although the Duke's warning was making him uneasy—an investor who never attended meetings, who voted by correspondence, who only had the quality of their name and the depth of their bank account to recommend them. It was not like the Prometheus Club to be so lax in their standards. This member must be a paragon of investment intuition to have his eccentricities tolerated.

The Duke's hazel eyes showed another debate. 'It's not only for you that I hesitate.' He took a small piece of notepaper from his desk, reached for a fountain pen and wrote four words. He pushed the paper across the desk. Conall read the name: La Marchesa di Cremona. 'A woman?' And a foreigner at that. No wonder the Duke was hesitant to reveal the potential investor. 'I thought the Prometheus Club was only open to titled men?'

'Yes.' The Duke gave an elegant shrug. 'She does business under the name of Phillip Barnham.'

'And you keep her secret?' Conall probed, understanding the depth of trust the Duke displayed in telling him. It was the kind of confidence entrusted to family.

'She is a woman who has led a gilded but unfortunate life. Society has not judged her kindly for it. If I do not keep her secret, if *you* do not keep her secret, she would have no honourable recourse for supporting herself.' In other words, the board didn't know.

'The Great Exhibition owes its success to the efforts of many, not the least of which were her contributions, under her alias, in bringing certain key inventions from the Continent to be displayed here,' the Duke explained, perhaps to build her credibility with him. Conall knew Cowden had been heavily involved in the Great Exhibition. No doubt he'd been impressed. La Marchesa's connections and business acumen had been recommendation enough to take her on as a secret partner to the club. 'I would not want her exposed, Taunton, nor would I want you misled. You see why I hesitate on both your behalves?'

And yet, Conall could not do the same. He did not have the luxury of hesitation, not with seventy-five head of alpaca and his people waiting on him. If Cowden trusted La Marchesa, that would have to be good enough for him. He had no choice but to go forward. 'How shall I contact her?'

Cowden smiled broadly. 'You're in luck. She is here for tea today. She's in the drawing room with my wife and daughter-in-law.' Conall wondered how much luck had to do with it. The Duke cleared his throat, perhaps sensing the question of coincidence. 'She's here for Ferris's wedding, nothing more, as a favour to my daughter-in-law.' The daughter-in-law with four sons, Conall reminded himself.

The Duke dropped his voice. 'There's something else you should know. La Marchesa has something of a reputation. But the two of them go way back to finishing-school days.' He splayed his hands in a gesture of happy surrender that Conall surmised to mean daughters-in-law who'd birthed four grandsons and ensured the succession deserved to be indulged, especially when it came to their friends who made the Duke money.

Well, the woman's reputation was nothing he could afford to be concerned about either. Nor was it his business. His business was to secure a loan for his mill. When he'd come to London he'd promised himself to use any and all means possible. He'd just not imagined such drastic measures. Conall rose and took his leave, shaking hands with the Duke. 'Thank you for your assistance. I'll look in on the ladies before I go.' That was his first rule of any persuasive encounter: he never left until he got what he came for. He might have been rejected by Cowden and the club, but he had been offered a consolation prize. He was not leaving here today until he had the next meeting secured.

'Of course, her Grace would scold me if she knew you hadn't stopped in.' The Duke was more jovial now that business was truly done. 'I hope we'll see you at the wedding?'

'I plan to be there. Will Fortis get leave to come home for it?' Conall enquired. It would be good to see his old friend again. The wedding was at the end of the week. Fortis might already be en route.

The Duke gave a short shake of his head. 'He's with the allied forces in the Danube, headed for Sevastopol the last I heard.' He smiled, but Conall detected the worry behind the Duke's eyes, a reminder that for all his wealth and power, Cowden was just a man, a father worried about his son. And with Fortis there was always a reason to worry. Fortis Tresham was far too brave, far too reckless for his own good. It was what made him a good friend, one of the best Conall had ever had, and what made him a brilliant officer. But perhaps not the best of husbands. He hadn't been home for years. Conall wondered how Avaline was holding up under her husband's prolonged absence, but he didn't dare ask. A man's marriage was far too personal to discuss between third parties as small talk, even when those third parties were fathers and best friends.

'Fortis is a good soldier, your Grace. I am sure all will go well.' Conall smiled. 'Besides, Camden Lithgow is with him. Cam is cool-headed enough for both of them.' Lithgow was another friend, the grandson of an earl looking to make a name for himself that went beyond resting on the laurels of his family's antecedents. 'Again, thank you for your assistance.' Conall took his leave and found his way down the hall, family enough not to need a footman's announcement or direction.

Conall didn't kid himself that circumstances were ideal. The possible investor was an unorthodox choice— a woman, who apparently operated on the fringes of the *ton* except for her connections to the Duke's family. She was not what he would have chosen, but a lot had happened in this past year that he would not have chosen either. Feminine laughter met him at the drawing-room door, each laugh distinct, indicating the smallness of the gathering. This was not a large tea, but a quiet, intimate affair for three. Two of whom he knew. The other was riveting. Conall's gaze lit on the stranger immediately. How could it not?

She was the sort of woman a man noticed even in a room full of people. Her blonde hair carried the sheen of platinum mixed with gold, a striking complement to the alabaster cream of her skin which was tinged with the faintest shades of pink. That tinge gave her the appearance of youth, of freshness, as did the crisp lavender muslin of her gown.

She might have been springtime personified if not for her eyes which were blue and hard as sapphires. They told a different story. This was a woman of some worldly experience. Those cool blue pools of knowledge held his with a boldness not often encountered at an English tea. Had she been expecting him? Was she prepared for this meeting? Perhaps she'd even asked for it? Conall had the unnerving sensation that she knew him. He didn't know her. He was certain of it. He would remember her even if he'd seen her only once. She was not a woman a man forgot, more the sort other women remembered with jealousy. No wonder society had judged her harshly.

The Duchess came forward, taking his arm. 'Taunton, what a pleasant surprise.' Was it, though? He felt as if he was the only one surprised by his arrival, that they had been anticipating him all along, the tea a mere ploy in order for La Marchesa and he to meet. 'Come, let me introduce you to our guest. You already know Helena, Frederick's wife.'

Helena rose to kiss him affectionately on the cheek and Conall saw the reason for the intimacy of the gathering and for the Duke's permission to bring Helena's special but potentially scandalous friend to tea. The future Duchess of Cowden was pregnant again. It was a good thing Ferris's wedding was this week. Any later and she'd be too obviously *enceinte* to attend. 'You look beautiful,' Conall assured her. And she did. Pregnancy agreed with Helena as much as family agreed with Frederick. Frederick was a lucky man. A stab of sad envy went through Conall. Frederick had everything to offer a wife, to offer a family. Conall could offer none of that security, only a debt-ridden title and a failing estate. He had nothing to pass on to one son, let alone four.

Helena turned to the other woman with a soft, warm smile. 'Sofia, let me present Viscount Taunton, a friend of the family. Viscount Taunton, my dear friend, La Marchesa di Cremona.'

'*Buongiorno*, Marchesa.' Conall bent formally over her hand, careful not to take his eyes from her face. The use of her title brought a shadow to her eyes for the fleetest of moments. Had he been looking down he would have missed it. Did she prefer not to use her title? A wry smile twisted at his mouth, struggling to get out. He knew a little something about that.

She gave a light laugh at his Italian. 'There's no need for that. I am as English as you.' Her smile deepened. 'I can see you are surprised, which is all the more reason to dispense with the title. It only serves to confuse people.' She slanted a playful but scolding look at Helena. 'I would be Sofia here, dear friend, just plain Sofia.' Her voice elongated the 'I' with exquisite precision. 'Just as you are Helena and not Lady Brixton when you are among friends.'

Conall doubted this woman could be plain anything. He cast a swift, hopefully surreptitious glance at her hands. There was only one way an English woman acquired an Italian title. They were long, slender hands. Elegant. And empty. Devoid of a ring. But she was not devoid of a title. It did make for a bit of mystery and perhaps therein lay the whiff of scandal the Duke alluded to: an Englishwoman married to a foreign marquess.

She folded her hands, covering her empty finger as she spoke. He hadn't been as circumspect as he had hoped. 'I am told, Lord Taunton, you are interested in importing alpacas.' Her eyes were steady on him as he took his seat and accepted a cup of tea. She was assessing, studying, her gaze as bold as her question. What did she see in that raking inquisition of a gaze? A man she could trust with her money? A man with an enterprise worth investing in?

Well, two could play that game. Conall returned her gaze with an inspection of his own. He would make it clear from the start he would not be intimidated. He might need investment money, but that didn't mean he'd play the sycophant. Nor did it mean he'd take funds from just anyone. This had to be a good fit for him. His reputation and that of his family were on the line.

They finished their tea and the conversation flagged for the slightest of moments. The Marchesa smiled expectantly at him, a hint of challenge in her blue eyes. 'Perhaps you would care to take a turn about the gardens with me and explain your venture further? We can spare the Duchess and Lady Brixton our boring business talk.' She rose, her confidence in his acceptance obvious. She knew he wouldn't or couldn't refuse the request. It was the whole purpose he'd come down the hall, after all, and they both knew it.

'I would be delighted.' Conall understood perfectly well this was his audition. What he said and did in the next few minutes would determine the future of Taunton. He offered the Marchesa his arm. 'Shall we?'

Chapter Two

She should not have touched him. The arm he offered her was firm and steady beneath her fingers, sending an unlooked-for warmth to her stomach. She'd been on her own too long, defending herself against lechers and men like Lord Wenderly, who'd made her the most indecent of offers, men who were too ready to objectify her simply because she was beautiful and alone—easy prey in their minds. As a result, she'd not been prepared for her body to react this way. She'd not been prepared for *him*, the handsome Viscount in his prime, with intelligent eyes and a certain energy that filled up any space he occupied. He was electricity personified. At some point when the alpaca investment had been under consideration by the Prometheus Club, her mind had decided viscounts interested in alpaca farming were portly, short, middle-aged eccentrics with rather less hair than more. After all, that description represented in some part all the men in the Prometheus Club and it stood to reason that like sought out like. But Taunton defied expectation. She'd been entirely unprepared for the man who had sauntered into the Duchess's sitting room full of masculine charm and confidence.

Looks and charm should not have affected her like this. If anything, those attributes should have put her on edge. She'd fallen victim to looks and charm before. She thought she'd become immune to handsome faces a long time ago, once she'd figured out handsome faces did not necessarily indicate handsome intentions. And yet, Taunton had a dangerous magnetism to him, a charismatic edge.

Sofia gave him a long considering look, tallying his assets in what she hoped was a more objective sense as they walked the gardens of Cowden House. Forewarned was forearmed. She would study him, discover the source of his charm and he would not catch her by surprise again. As a male, he did not disappoint. He was young still, but not too young, in his late twenties, possibly early thirties. He was grey-eyed and dark-haired and had a face that was saved from chiselled sternness by his smile—something he brandished often, a charming weapon of sorts. It would be interesting to know if he used it offensively or defensively—to engage or to hide. He had height and was elegantly built for fashion, a tailor's dream without being foppish, while still maintaining a certain breadth of shoulder and an athletic trimness of waist. She noted the excellent cut of his blue morning coat and the expensive wool of his cream trousers, cut narrow in the latest fashion.

Those were just the top notes. She'd wager the pristine white linen that peeped above the layers of his coats was fine Irish and the ankle boots that emerged from beneath his cream trousers were expensive Italian leather. No wonder he was interested in alpacas from Peru—wool from halfway around the world. The man was a walking calling card for international trade and a very handsome one at that. But his best feature was how he sounded, the most sibilant of tenor baritones, a murmuring quicksilver stream of words that matched his eyes.

She could have listened to him all day. As it was, she didn't need to. She'd read the report, of course. Much of what he shared wasn't new information to her. The purpose of this walk was to learn about *him*. What sort of man was asking for her money, for her partnership? If this were to be done without the backing and comfortable insurance of the Prometheus Club, it was imperative he be a man of great integrity—an asset, unfortunately, not many men of her acquaintance possessed. Misjudging a man's character wasn't a mistake one could afford to make twice. If the Viscount fulfilled this first requirement, there would be time for discussing alpacas later.

At the end of his exposition, Taunton's grey eyes crinkled at the corners as he gave her a friendly smile. 'Do I pass?' They'd reached the end of the garden where a small, round pergola, more decorative than useful, adorned the far corner by the high fence that kept aristocrats in and street riff-raff out, a discreet reminder of power and who belonged inside its circle.

She'd straddled that fence quite precariously since her return to England. One wrong move and she could be entirely on the other side. Her presence on this side of the fence was accepted by very few like Helena Tresham, tolerated by some—namely those who wished for Helena's favour—and considered downright dangerous by many who worried what would happen to their womenfolk if she was allowed to run amok among them with her ideas of freedom and equality. She wondered where the Viscount would land on that scale of tolerance if he knew just how many scandals were attached to her? Or did he need her money badly enough to ignore them?

Sofia met the Viscount's gaze with a light laugh and a tap of her fan on his immaculate, expensive sleeve. 'Have you passed? So soon? That would be a rather hasty decision made on limited acquaintance.' Perhaps he was used to women making impulsive decisions where he was concerned. He was good looking and affable, easy to be with and easy on the eye. Women probably poured their hearts out to him regularly and much more. She was not foolish enough to trust a handsome man with her secrets or her heart, or the contents of her bank account without further investigation. 'Such action would be rather impulsive, wouldn't you agree, my lord? I don't think you would want to do business with an impulsive investor who threw money around indiscriminately to any who asked.'

She smiled to lessen the scold. She wanted to be sure of him, not alienate him. She needed him as much as he needed her, perhaps more. His need was simple: money. For him, money was the end goal. She, however, needed more than money. For her, money was the means to other, grander, ends. She needed the things money could buy, but only if she had a lot of it and relatively soon. Freedom and financial security were expensive commodities these days and she needed both for her own well-being and for the well-being she wanted to ensure for others.

'*Touché*, Marchesa. You are quite shrewd. I can see why Cowden trusts you.' He inclined his head in a nod to her reprimand, his grey eyes becoming serious, and she recognised she'd been wrong about part of her earlier assumption. Women might be imprudent around him, but he was not impulsive. This was not a game. She knew, too, in that narrowing grey gaze of his he was vetting her as much as she was vetting him. The realisation gave her a moment's anxiety. She did not like to be scrutinised, talked about, guessed about, as if her life was a trivial game. Sofia usually tried to prevent such speculation by taking the upper hand first.

'What else would you like to know?' His voice was quiet now, sterner. The easy fluidity with which he'd spoken of his alpaca project was gone, replaced by something sharper, the tone of a man who had something to lose. Good. She didn't want to do business with a man who could afford mistakes, or who embraced projects on a whim only to tire of them halfway through. She needed this to matter to him, as if it were life or death. For many reasons. Most obviously for the making of money. Less obviously for the distraction his worry would create. The more he worried about alpacas, the less time he'd have to be curious about her.

'I want to see timelines for importation, for profit yields. How soon will there be any return on the investment? I want to see the facility where they will be kept. I want to read the sources you used for your research and draw my own conclusions.'

'I am afraid that will be somewhat difficult, given that the facility and the other materials are not in London.' His tone implied they would simply have to do without those key facts. After all this time, she was still amazed at the innate confidence of the aristocracy. The Viscount simply expected her to hand over a significant amount of money on the merits of a short conversation and one report. Then again, aristocrats had a very different sense of money from the rest of the world. Even noblemen with debt—and that was nearly all of them—seldom understood the value of a single pound versus a hundred pounds. Perhaps if they did their debt would be less? She'd not understood the reference to spending money like water until she'd married, even though her father had lived well above his means. Life with the Marchese had been illuminating in so many ways.

The Viscount smiled, perhaps to appear less argumentative, but she didn't miss the faintest hint of agitation in the Viscount's quicksilver tones. He did not like the idea of waiting. A bit more desperate than he let on, was he? It was good to know he had a sense of immediacy as well, although she wasn't sure what a handsome viscount might be desperate about. 'Marchesa, the materials you seek are in Somerset, at my home,' he explained as if distance eradicated the need for research.

Somerset, in the south-west. Twenty hours' carriage ride from London via the mail coach with fast horses, good roads and little luggage. The train would do better at four hours even with several stops along the way. She fixed him with a pleasant smile and a direct stare that brooked no rebuttal. 'I hear Somerset is lovely in the early summer. We can go after the wedding festivities. I shall make the arrangements and send you the details.' She held out her hand for him to shake, the masculine gesture catching him off guard.

There was the slightest of hesitations at her bold gesture and then he smiled, taking her hand with a firm grip. 'Somerset it is, Marchesa. I will send word to my staff to expect us.'

She left him then, with the excuse she needed to send notes of her own and to make arrangements for their departure. In truth, now that next steps had been laid out, she did not want to spend any more time in the Viscount's company. He would have questions about her; he would want to know what a married woman with a foreign title was doing here in England alone.

Those were questions she preferred not to answer. The less he knew about her, the better. The sooner they were away from London, the less chance there was of him discovering her sordid past.

Sofia let out a breath. This was not going as planned. She would have been content to stay hidden away in her Chelsea terrace home, conducting business by letter behind the façade of Barnham's name, making money and pursuing her own dreams, her own plans. She wouldn't have participated in the Season at all if it hadn't been for the wedding and the lure of the alpaca deal.

That wasn't quite true. Those were *lures* that brought her out into society. But there'd been a *threat*, too, that even now under the warm spring sun brought a chill to her bones. Sofia pressed a surreptitious hand to the hidden pocket of her skirts, feeling the folded sheet of paper within: Il Marchese's latest letter and least friendly to date. It had arrived on the heels of Helena's invitation to the wedding, an invitation she'd thought to refuse. But the letter had changed that. It was a reminder that for all of her careful plans, a formal divorce sanctioned by the Kingdom of the Piedmont and the distance of three delicious years of freedom, she was still not beyond

Giancarlo's reach. Il Marchese di Cremona, her husband, wanted her back.

It wasn't the first letter in the last six months, but it was the darkest. The first letters had wooed her with apologies and testaments of reform. He wanted to try again. He would be a better husband this time. She did not believe those protestations, not with ten years of infidelity and cruelty to weigh against his words. Nor had she given them any credence. Why should she? She was here and he was a continent away and unlikely to bestir himself to come after her. She knew him. But those letters had invoked a tremor of subtle fear. He'd found her. The address on the envelope proved it right down to the number of her row house—not that she'd ever taken pains to hide her location. She'd not thought she needed to. She was here in England with a choppy Channel, a continent and the legal assurance of their dissolved union. She had every security that Piedmont no longer recognised her marriage.

But times had changed, it seemed. This letter no longer cajoled. Giancarlo's patience and the King's was running thin. Piedmont might recognise her divorce, but the Kingdom of Piedmont no longer *approved* of its existence. The King himself wanted Giancarlo to reclaim his wife, and Giancarlo, wanting the King's favour, was willing to do so.

Sofia drew a deep breath against the panic such a thought raised. She wouldn't go back, not even if the King of Piedmont required it, which it seemed he did. This time, Il Marchese was not the only one with money. She had money, too, a lot of it, and that was the most important weapon of all. With money, she could fight. She could raise an army of solicitors and barristers, she could tie up proceedings in Chancery for years with appeals.

The comfort in that idea was short-lived. Of course, Il Marchese wouldn't fight fair. If she took it to court, there were things he might accuse her of, things that, even though untrue, could cast a poor light on her scruples and cause people to question her morals. Should that fail, what he couldn't force legally, he would force practically. He would simply take her, kidnap her and drag her back to the Piedmont. Then, a piece of paper regarding the dissolution of their marriage would hardly matter. There was no one to stop him from taking her except herself.

Il Marchese would have to find her first. Money meant she could fight. It also meant she could run. Money was portable. She would go to ground in the most obscure parts of England if need be. The trip to Somerset was a start. Would the Marchese give her fair warning? Would he come himself or would he send his minions to negotiate?

No. She wasn't going to think about it. She would not worry over it. He wanted her to worry. This letter was the beginning of the torment he'd designed for her, part of his game, lest she forget who really held all the power. She entered the house, her head high, a smile on her face. Helena must not know about this new threat. Helena would want to fix everything, would want to use her father-in-law's influence to protect her without realising the consequences of stirring that pot. Sofia could not allow her friend to be dragged down into the mire of her life. She'd not told Helena everything, could hardly bring herself to give words to her marriage, not when Helena's was so blissful.

This was her battle and she'd wage it alone as she'd waged so many other campaigns in her life. Alone, victory was possible, escape was possible, freedom was possible. With others involved, there could only be…complications. In two days, she could leave London behind her and vanish into the west. Like a good general, she would retreat, regroup and fortify her new position. There was only the wedding to get through and then the ball. She'd survived worse.

Chapter Three

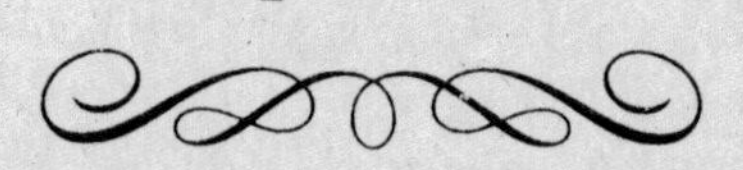

Conall shifted uncomfortably on the hard seat of the pew. He'd survived worse, but there was no doubt weddings made him edgy. They were reminders of the passage of time and the pressing need to do his duty for the Viscountcy; a duty he could not afford without a wealthy bride, which placed him in a rather contradictory position. To marry money, one needed to have money. Unless one wanted to marry a wealthy Cit. No woman of good birth wanted to marry an impoverished title. Olivia de Pugh had reminded him quite coldly of that axiom when she'd broken off their pending betrothal right after his father's death when Conall had gone to her in good faith with the financial details his death had revealed. She had not been impressed with his honesty.

Weddings were also reminders that marriage was the greatest business risk of all, one that came with no safety net, as his mother had discovered. Her lifetime of security had been an illusion maintained only as long as his father had lived. Even his death proved that forever was for ever—the choices made in that marriage would follow his mother always. When it came to matrimony, there was no getting out of it, there was only tolerating it.

Conall took his seat five rows back from the Cowden family pew and looked around St George's. There were plenty of people here who were doing just that—tolerating it. Behind him sat Lord and Lady Fairchild, who both gambled copiously, but never together, perhaps to recoup the excitement their marriage lacked; to his left was Lord Duchaine, who had come alone as he usually did. Lady Duchaine was in Paris, staying longer with each annual trip to the Continent. There were rumours she kept a lover in a grand apartment in the Faubourg, a lover ardent enough to override the pleasures of the London Season.

There were others, too. All decked out in high fashion, all with false smiles and similar stories. Duchaine and the Fairchilds were by no means anomalies. How ironic they'd all come to celebrate another couple being consigned to their ranks. Conall thought it more appropriate if they'd come to mourn or at least warn the couple. It seemed hypocritical for the noble masses that filled St. George's to smile and shed a 'happy tear' when they knew from experience just how elusive marital happiness was.

Across the aisle, Olivia de Pugh, golden and

lovely in a pale-yellow gown specked with tiny primrose flowers, entered with her family and the very wealthy Baron Crossfield. She spied Conall and gave the slightest of nods and an I-told-you-so smile. Another time, he might have felt the intended sting of her gesture, but today, Olivia's traditional English beauty left him empty. Perhaps he'd had a narrow escape, after all. What man wanted to be loved for his income or title alone? Wasn't this room full of people who were testament to how unsatisfying that premise ultimately was? And yet the practice of matching title to fortune persisted as if by doing it over and over again, it would suddenly come out aright.

Or maybe the room was full of people, like him, who'd once hoped they'd be different, that for them, marriage might work out. After all, it had worked out for the Treshams. That family was renowned for their love matches. Conall focused his gaze on the Cowden pew, where there sat two generations of exceptions. The Duke and Duchess of Cowden were already in place, hands linked, heads bent towards one another. Beside them sat their two daughters-in-law—Helena valiantly hiding a six-month pregnancy beneath crinolines to avoid censure and Fortis's wife, Avaline, her blonde head held high against gossip about her absent husband. Conall made a note to speak with her at the wedding breakfast, to offer her the consolation of his presence. At the front of the church, Ferris Tresham waited for his bride, his older brother at his shoulder in fraternal solidarity. Ferris's eyes were riveted on the back doors, but Frederick's gaze was for Helena. Anyone could see that after seven years of marriage, he was still mad for his wife.

Once upon a time, that had been Conall's dream, too—a love match with a woman who inspired such loyalty and affection in him. His father's death had changed all that. His hopes for a marriage were different now. These days, a good marriage was defined for him as one that would secure his mother's future, his sister's dowry and his younger brother's education, along with the upkeep of the estate. He would gladly set aside his personal affections to achieve those things which his father had failed to guarantee. That failure tainted his grief, mixing anger with an overwhelming sense of loss when he thought of his father.

Around Conall, people began to shift in their seats, heads craning to the back doors. Murmurs escalated to barely suppressed whispers. Time to start? Conall turned in his seat to catch sight of the bride and the signal to stand, but there was no one. 'False alarm, eh?' He elbowed his friend, Lord Hargreaves, good-naturedly.

Hargreaves, blond and young, with a nose for gossip, arched his eyebrow. 'Hardly a false alarm, old chap.' He lifted his chin with a discreet jerk to indicate the back rows of the church where a woman sat, square-shouldered, and dressed in lavender. Conall chuckled at that—lavender was a colour for half-mourning. Perhaps someone else understood weddings as he did. The woman's face was veiled by a fetching lavender creation atop spun-gold hair, but it could not entirely obscure her identity.

She was not the sort of woman a man forgot.

Even veiled, there was an allure to her. She could not hide in a crowd even if she wanted to and apparently today she wanted to. The veil was doing La Marchesa di Cremona no favours. If anything, the mystery it created made her even more conspicuous. Some people were just made to stand out.

'I wouldn't have thought she'd dare it,' Hargreaves went on. 'Then again, she's dared so much already, one wonders if another dare matters.' Hargreaves narrowed his gaze in mild disgust. 'Lady Brixton's affections tolerate much. Although I wonder if Lady Brixton actually thought she would come?'

La Marchesa chose that moment to lift her veil and settle it atop her hat, revealing the refined alabaster features of her face. In her eyes was a quiet fire that challenged the guests to look their fill. She sat still, the very rigidity of her posture a defence against the murmurs flying behind fans. Hargreaves leaned close with a whisper. 'It was all around White's yesterday that she refused Wenderly's offer of carte blanche. Slapped him for it, in fact.'

Conall stiffened at the callous treatment of her reputation, not caring for the way Hargreaves dissected her, although he'd be hard pressed to explain why. 'Is there a reason she should have accepted?

Wenderly's over fifty, nearly old enough to be her father.' It wasn't just the age. Wenderly had peculiar tastes. The thought of her with such a man put a cold pit in Conall's stomach. He told himself the compulsion to defend La Marchesa was for Helena's sake.

Hargreaves raised an eyebrow. 'One wonders what she has to live on if she refuses men like Wenderly out of hand.' The implication was crassly clear. A woman alone required a protector. 'Her refusal cost Wenderly the loss of several hundred pounds and his pride at the betting book. Everyone is speculating about who she's angling for if she feels she can disregard such a generous offer. Wenderly's pockets are deep. He'd have kept her in jewels and gowns. She'd be striking on his arm, with her height and her hair colouring,' Hargreaves hypothesised with shrewd calculation. 'She could have been set for some time.'

Ah, so that was the root of Cowden's remark about honourable recourse for supporting herself. Cowden feared without the outlet for business investments, La Marchesa might be 'inclined' to take a less honourable offer of support. What else remained for an Englishwoman who'd been away so long she'd become something of a foreigner to her own people?

The realisation that other men coveted her, that they reacted to her in the most carnal of ways, sat poorly with Conall. He told himself it was for business reasons. If she chose to invest with him, his family would be linked with her. Perhaps he should consider if there was truth to the rumours before rushing to champion her simply on Cowden's hesitant word. He'd spent less than an hour in her company. What did he know of her tastes and associations? Perhaps she *was* deserving of the speculations being whispered around him. And yet his conscience whispered another message: *perhaps she was not*. Simply because her husband was not with her shouldn't make her a target of vicious gossip. But he knew better. A woman alone who also had the audacity to be beautiful could not escape notice or censure. She was a creature who defied the natural laws of society.

He'd been out in society long enough to know he shouldn't be surprised by the stir she caused. La Marchesa had an incomparable elegance and maintained a freshness about her that *made* a man want to stare, want to imagine tracing his finger along the delicate line of her jaw, across the pink of those lips, down the slim column of her neck to the discreet décolletage of her lavender gown. She certainly didn't *dress* like the demi-monde. Her gown today was all that was proper, as was everything about her: her posture, her tasteful, quiet jewellery. Without the whispers, she might have been any gentleman's wife.

How many other gentlemen were sitting here nursing the same idea? *Could* she be theirs? Conall's own speculations stirred to life. He gave a deprecating chuckle at the direction of his thoughts. He was lowering himself to society's level with such base thoughts. Why did the presence or absence of a man at a woman's side define her? It was a thought worthy of his sister, Cecilia, who believed herself to be a grand proponent of liberated womanhood.

La Marchesa lifted a hand to play with the pearl necklace that lay at the base of her throat, the only sign that she was uncomfortable in her surroundings, or that she might possibly be privy to the things whispered about her.

Hargreaves tilted his head in frank appraisal. 'She's a beauty and now, with her European seasoning, she'll bring a delicious *je ne sais quoi* to a sophisticated man's bed.' The last did it. Conall rose. He would not sit there and be party to sordid gossip about a woman who had no opportunity to defend herself against rumours, deserved or not. A woman, without a man to defend her, had no recourse and this was the result. She made herself an easy target for society's sharp arrows.

'Where are you going, Taunton?' Hargreaves looked aggrieved at his departure, then caught the trajectory of his gaze. 'Oh, you think to try your luck?' He chuckled knowingly. 'Be careful. Wenderly isn't the first to fail. I hear she's a man-eater, like one of those flowers that lure insects and then shuts its petals around its victim. Not that I'd mind having those petals wrapped around me and squeezing hard, if you know what I mean.'

Conall swallowed, his words terse. 'I do know *ex-*

actly what you mean. If you'll excuse me?' He made his way back up the aisle and slid into the empty space beside her, just as the doors of St George's opened and the bride sailed forth on her father's arm, white, pure and unsullied, drawing attention away from the Marchesa.

'What are you doing?' La Marchesa whispered as the crowd surged to their feet in a loud rustle of clothing.

Conall smiled. 'Weddings are best enjoyed with a friend and you seemed in need of one.'

'Thank you, but for the record, I was perfectly fine on my own.' She smiled back, the briefest of expressions. 'I hope you don't regret it. Rumour has it I'm a dangerous woman to know.' Then in quiet undertones, she added, 'Don't think for a moment this will help you get your money. You can't flatter or flirt your way into my finances.'

Conall kept his gaze straight ahead, politely fixed on the bride's progression. 'It never crossed my mind.' It truly hadn't. He'd looked to the back and seen the determined expression in her eyes. That had been enough. She was a warrior among foes here. For reasons he couldn't fathom, and didn't *want* to fathom, he hadn't wanted her to be alone. For all the strength and sharpness she'd exhibited, there was vulnerability in her, too.

Perhaps it was his fascination with that vulnerability, with her mystery, that had prodded him to the back. Perhaps it was sheer chivalry that demanded he stand up for the Treshams, who'd taken her in, or maybe it was simply because he knew what it was like to be alone in a room full of people. There'd been numerous occasions after his father had died when people hadn't known what to say, or how to say it, so they'd said nothing, but gone about their conversations with others, talking *about* him, not *to* him, just as they were doing to her today. No one acknowledged the Marchesa directly. Even in the crowded church, the spot beside her had remained pointedly empty. But everyone knew she was here and everyone had decided it was best to treat her as if she were invisible or inanimate, a *thing* that couldn't be hurt by their darts. All except for him.

Sofia worried the hem of her handkerchief with fingers hidden in the folds of her skirts. She'd be damned if she'd let anyone see how the wedding discomfited her. She'd provided them enough sport for the day simply by being there—something she was regretting in hindsight. It was true: weddings always made you remember your own. Her own was something Sofia would rather forget. As a result, she did not enjoy the marital celebration. Specifically, she did not enjoy the way it made her *feel.*

The bride passed, radiant and innocent in white, and Sofia's stomach clenched. She'd been radiant and innocent once. Her own wedding had been much like this: pews filled with people, flowers and ribbon festooning the aisles and the candelabra, a dress with yards of satin and lace, and a blushing bride beneath the sheer tulle of her veil. She'd been as eager as this girl for the adventure of marriage.

The adventure had not gone well. It should have, and that it hadn't had been a surprise. Her husband was handsome, wealthy, well-travelled and titled. He lived in a grand villa in Piedmont, had expansive apartments in Turin, the capital of the Piedmont kingdom, a lodge in the Dolomites, a summer palace, and had showered his bride with enough jewels to turn a young girl's head. He spent his summers at the villa on Sardinia, his winters gambling in Nice or in Venice amid the festival of Carnevale. For a girl fresh out of finishing school, it had been a fairy-tale come to life. She should have looked closer. She should have refused. *Her parents* should have refused. They should have known better when she did not. They had of course known, that was the rub. They simply hadn't cared. They'd needed the money badly enough to forgo looking beneath the Marchese's glamour.

She was wiser now. When something looked too good to be true, it probably was. Even this attractive man, who stood next to her thinking his station beside her would put a stop to wagging tongues, was likely riddled with secrets. How like a man to believe his presence was all that was required to make a woman decent. Did he ever stop to think his presence might have made things worse?

She'd hoped to be inconspicuous today with a veil

of her own lending anonymity, but it had done just the opposite. Neither had her bid for discretion been helped along by the man beside her. It was hard to hide when one was seated by the handsomest man in the room. Every woman's eyes in the church had followed his progress back up the aisle to the empty seat beside her and the whispers had started again.

Sofia slid Taunton a covert look. Did *he* realise his efforts had only made her more obvious? Had only intensified the talk about her? His gesture had likely only served to link him to the chain of sordid speculations made about her. She'd bet the contents of her reticule the guests behind them were thinking he'd come to try his luck in winning her intimate attentions much as Wenderly had. Maybe he had. Perhaps he thought his looks would stand him in better stead than Wenderly. Perhaps he even thought to woo the money out of her.

His efforts might have worked on another woman. As for her, she had no intentions of making the same mistake twice. A man needed more to recommend himself than his good looks. If that was behind his reasoning in coming to her side, he would be disappointed in the results. She wouldn't thank Cowden for it, if he turned out to be the same as other men. She employed the guise of Barnham for precisely that sort of protection when it came to business dealings and she'd trusted Cowden to vet this family friend of his before revealing her situation.

The bride reached the front of the church and everyone took their seats. The service began and Sofia pushed away the rituals and the memories as best she could with thoughts of the upcoming enterprise. If Taunton was right about alpaca wool being as lucrative as his research indicated, she could double her profits, eventually. However, funding the loan for his mill came with a certain amount of risk. Mills were far more expensive than a cargo of silks. The mill loan required focusing a large portion of her funds on a single venture instead of spreading them out among several as she preferred. Diversifying was a much safer investment strategy in case one of the deals didn't turn out; loans were also paid back slowly, over time. There was little help for her in that.

In the background of the wedding, she was mildly aware of Ferris Tresham's voice affirming his vows, 'For richer or poorer…' A loan certainly was the poorer of the investments. She wasn't looking to make a loan. She was looking to make money. She had her own causes to pursue, her own dreams about making the world more equitable for women and children, those who had no voice. She'd often thought of building a mill town herself where that could be possible. But she was years from such a goal. Why buy her own mill, why wait until she had funds to do it on her own, when she could do it through the Viscount? She could build her mill town through his mill, through his alpaca-wool industry in exchange for funding his venture. But before that she had to make sure, first hand, the venture was sound. There was no sense in investing in a mill that created a product for which there was no market.

The Dream, as she liked to call it, kept her busy right up to the kiss. Her stomach slowly started to unclench as the bridal couple passed by on their way out of the church. Sofia drew a deep breath. She'd survived, but not unscathed. 'Are you well?' Taunton solicited, offering his steady right arm as the guests began to exit. She needed that firm arm more today than she had yesterday. She hated needing it, hated relying on him, a virtual stranger who'd decided to play the hero. Today she was prepared for him, but that didn't stop the warm strength of him from travelling through her again at his touch.

'You're pale.' There were questions in his grey eyes when he looked at her with concern. But she didn't want to answer questions today.

'I'm quite fine. Just a bit tired.' She lowered her veil as if the fabric could hold the questions at bay a little longer. There would be a consequence for not answering them, though. In her absence, others would respond in her stead with their own speculations. How long would it be before Taunton heard the rumours, before he wanted to know who she was?

Out of doors in the bright sunshine, she released his arm. 'If you will excuse me, I think I will forgo the wedding breakfast. I've a bit of a headache. Will you give my regards to Helena and to the bride and groom?' She moved into the crowd of guests before he could protest. She had her reprieve—until the next time. And there would be a next time. There was the honeymooners' ball to get through and, heaven help her, the four-hour train ride to Taunton where they'd have hours with nothing to entertain themselves except each other and her past.

Chapter Four

He would get her back even if he had to cross the Channel to do it. He hoped it wouldn't come to that. He didn't much care for England. Giancarlo Bianchi, Marchese di Cremona, surveyed the view of Piazza San Carlo from his *palazzo* window; the famous statue of Emanuele Filiberto on horseback, flanked by coffeehouses and aristocratic *palazzos* like his own, was a far cry from the stolid square town houses of London. What a filthy city London was with its soot and litter in the streets. For all its innovations, London could be improved. It couldn't hold a candle to his city, to Turin, the centre of the Risorgimento, with its fine universities, scholars, artists and musicians.

He brushed at the sleeve of his coat as if removing a fine sheen of street dirt. He'd not set foot on English soil since he'd claimed his bride thirteen years ago. God willing, he wouldn't have to go back. Andelmo, his most trusted minion, would bring her to him. His wife was proving to be more problematic than he'd originally anticipated, a concept that both irritated and aroused him.

His valet entered his suite with the trunks containing his new spring wardrobe, his secretary following close behind. It was time for the morning reports although it was well after noon. Giancarlo motioned for his secretary to join him at the desk in the window bay. 'What news do you have? Is there any word from London?'

The secretary handed him a telegram. 'There has been no sighting. The house remains empty, as it has since your man's arrival.'

'What else? Is that all?' Giancarlo frowned at the note. Time was money and he was growing impatient. He tapped his fingers on the surface of a side table. She had not responded to his earlier letters. He couldn't even be sure she'd received them. Because of that lack of response, he'd sent Andelmo weeks ago to track her down, to verify the address, to put the offer to her and wait for an answer. If the wrong answer came, Andelmo was to drag her back by her hair if that was what it took. That had been several weeks ago—time enough for travel, time enough to arrive and conduct reconnaissance. The only word he'd received since then was that his man had arrived and had found the address, but seen no sign of her.

Giancarlo blew out a sigh. 'We have to flush her out. We have to make her come to us.' He snapped his fingers. 'Get some paper and take notes. Here are new instructions. Tell Andelmo to go through the house, look for any sign that it's hers and if so, leave a "calling card", of sorts.' If she was in London, the act would flush her out. If it didn't, they would have to start the search anew. If she wasn't in London, it would mean one of two things: she hadn't received the letters or she had received them and they had frightened her, perhaps sent her to ground. He hoped for the latter.

Giancarlo folded the telegram and tucked it into his pocket. Already, just the thought of her sent twin rills of lust and desire through him. He flicked his hand at both the men in dismissal. 'Leave me. I need to think. Go downstairs and arrange for my supper, and find me some company for tonight, preferably company that comes with a sister.'

Giancarlo took a seat behind the desk, steepling his hands in thought as he looked out over the *piazza*. Would it be enough to flush her out? Sofia probably *would* come home, eventually. The question was, how long did he want to wait? It might be a while. By all reports her London home was small. His secretary had overlooked the significance of that detail. Small homes were efficient, the means to the end of providing shelter, but nothing more. Small homes inspired no owner loyalty. One did not entertain in them, one did not put them on display for others to see. One could forget about them.

He scoffed at the notion. Her choice was so disappointing. A row house? Truly? When she was used to *palazzos* and rich apartments? He'd provided better for her. Row houses were the milieu of middle-class families, tradesmen even. Perhaps she would be missing the luxury he had showered her in by now. Perhaps a row house was all that was available to her. She was too ruined for Mayfair society to receive her. Either way, one thing was certain: she wasn't entertaining in it.

Giancarlo chuckled to himself. He'd warned her London would turn its back on a divorced woman. No decent home would receive her, not even her own. Perhaps in Chelsea she could be anonymous, or perhaps Chelsea was willing to lower the bar. What did she think about her freedom now with three years of ostracising? Any other woman would have begged him to take her back by now.

He'd misjudged her there. He'd only let her go because he hadn't really believed she'd leave for long and he'd enjoyed the thought of how he might make her beg to return. Then again, his Sofia never had been the usual woman. He shifted in his seat, arousal growing as he thought of her—all that magnificent spun-gold hair falling loose about her shoulders, her eyes flashing defiance as he delivered his dictates.

Bend over and bare yourself for my crop, Sofia, unless you'd prefer Andelmo to assist you. You know the penalty for my displeasure...

No matter how many times he'd attempted to bring her to heel, she'd resisted.

She'd left him before he'd broken her. She hadn't

merely left him, she'd *defied* him. She'd dared to run away—twice—despite the punishments he'd threatened to mete out. It certainly upped the stakes of the game. He hadn't had such delicious prey in years. Who would have guessed the young schoolgirl he'd married would have turned out to be so delightfully appealing? He smiled to himself, imagining Sofia. What would she do when he caught up to her? When he had her cornered? Would she fight? Would she beg? Would she plead for mercy? Would she cry? Giancarlo twisted the heavy signet ring on his finger.

He'd wager his ring his Sofia would fight. His surety in that belief was what gave him patience. He *would* find her and it *would* be worth the wait. Capturing her would be glorious, a prize equal to his efforts. Razing the house at Margaretta Terrace would let her know she'd best gird herself for battle.

He would not lose her this time. He had too much on the line. The new Piedmontese King, Victor Emmanuel II, was disappointed in him, didn't trust his judgement as a divorced man. One of the first things the new King had done was outlaw the divorces approved by his father. He wanted the noble men in his kingdom to be upright, married men. Giancarlo had been overlooked for riches and plum opportunities since Sofia had left. The new King had made it plain that favour would smile on him if he were to bring his wife to heel.

It wasn't enough to offer to simply remarry, to

take another bride, even of the King's choosing, which of course Giancarlo had offered to do as the most expedient means to the end. The King was heavily religious, devoutly Catholic, and he felt that a divorced man marrying another was compounding the original sin with the sin of adultery. Only Giancarlo's first wife, his *only* wife, would do. The wealth promised was enough to send him haring across the Continent to England to retrieve her and then to punish her into submission so complete this truancy of hers would not be repeated. This time he'd be successful. It was a rare woman who wasn't frightened by the consequences he'd impose for her betrayal.

Sofia was afraid. It was that simple. She stared at her reflection in Helena's long pier glass. She had not looked so fine in ages—her hair done up in an elegant braided coronet, the discreet glitter of diamonds at her ears, her figure shown to advantage in a silk gown of deep sky-blue cut in the latest fashion with its low-swept, off-the-shoulder bodice. The gown was the way she liked them—minimalist in adornment. There was a delicate overlay of lace and ribbon at what passed for sleeves and that trim matched the inset of the bodice, but otherwise, the gown lacked flounces and fussiness. And yet, for all the fineness of figure, or perhaps because of it, she was afraid.

'I can't go to the ball, Helena, I simply cannot.'

She made a slow, rueful twirl in front of the mirror, liking the susurration of the fabric against her ankles. It would be a shame not to waltz in this gown. She used to love to dance. But the cost of a dance was too high. This woman in the mirror would be noticed and remarked upon. Men would want to possess her. When she refused, they'd make crass comments among themselves and perhaps crasser wagers as Wenderly had. Women would hate her. They would say she'd come on purpose to put them all to shame, to tease marriageable men away from marriageable girls who deserved gentleman husbands. They'd call her a Delilah, a Jezebel. There would be no refuge for her. She'd had a taste of that at the wedding. She was not eager to repeat the experience.

Helena merely smiled from the *chaise* and absently rubbed her belly, unconcerned with the outburst. 'Don't tell me you're afraid after all these years. The girl I went to school with didn't care what anyone thought, least of all a room full of old peahens.' Helena knew how to throw down the gauntlet.

'I still don't. I'd just rather they keep their thoughts to themselves instead of talking about me as if I'm not there, as if I cannot hear them when I'm standing right in front of them.' Sofia unfastened the diamond-and-sapphire choker at her neck and set it reluctantly on the vanity. She might not have made it through the wedding if it hadn't been for Viscount Taunton. He'd left her no choice but to endure. After he'd dared to sit with her, she couldn't have paid back his effort by running out. And in truth, it had been easier to endure with an ally beside her.

Sofia reached for a hairpin, determined to take down the elaborate coiffure. The sooner she was undressed the sooner she could put this pretence that she was going to the ball behind her.

'Taunton will be there,' Helena announced as the maid moved through the chamber laying out her own finery for the ball.

'Of course. He is a close family friend,' Sofia replied coolly, careful to show no reaction. She eyed her friend in the mirror. What was Helena up to?

Helena rose a little clumsily from the *chaise* and began her own preparations. 'Taunton will dance with you, Frederick will dance with you. With the notice of two decent men, others will come. You won't be alone. I thought you liked Taunton?'

'I am considering conducting business with him on your father-in-law's recommendation, that is all.' Sofia didn't like the look in Helena's eye. It wouldn't be the first time Helena had tried to play the matchmaker. The maid slipped a green-silk gown with large painted roses patterned on the fabric over Helena's head.

'Taunton's a good man. Frederick will vouch for him.' Helena's dark head popped through the dress.

'We'll see if he has any business sense. Alpacas aren't the norm when it comes to investing.' Sofia watched Helena smooth her skirts over her belly and turn in front of the mirror, critically eyeing her growing silhouette. She felt a stab of envy for her friend. Helena had the perfect life: a loving husband, domestic comfort and security, children and another baby on the way to love. It was only natural Helena would want the same for her. But it couldn't be that way for her; she'd lost that chance the moment she'd married Il Marchese and she'd sealed any hope with her divorce. No decent Englishman married such a ruined woman due to the legal implications alone.

There were other, more emotional implications, too. She'd never give her freedom, her very life, to a man again. But how did one make a woman like Helena, with everything she could wish for, understand that?

'I do not think dancing with Taunton is a good idea.' He was exactly the sort of man the matchmaking mamas coveted for their own daughters: handsome, well-mannered, pleasant and titled. They would hate her especially for taking up the attentions of such a specimen. To make her point, Sofia pulled out another pin, feeling the coiffure loosen.

Helena speared her with a stern look that said she was done cajoling. This was serious now. 'If not Taunton, who? When? It's been three years, Sofia. Surely, you don't mean to entomb yourself for the rest of your life?' Helena's eyes flashed, reminiscent of the tenacity that had won her a duke's heir.

'Surely, I *do* mean just that and the sooner you accept it, the sooner we can move past this,' Sofia replied with the determination that had seen her through four years of a finishing school that had thought a country gentleman's daughter beneath them and ten years of a marriage marked by darkness.

Helena softened. 'You're too young for such absolutes, my dear friend. You're also too young to be alone. You should remarry and start again.'

'Not with a man like Taunton. He can't afford me.' They both knew she didn't mean the reference monetarily. A titled Englishman with any ambition socially, politically, couldn't afford the scandals that came with her.

Helena averted her gaze and fussed with her skirts. Even Helena couldn't deny the truth in that. Perhaps there was a quiet country widower out there who could take her on without damaging the back half of his life overmuch, if she was ever interested in marriage. But a titled man? No. Helena didn't go down easy, however. 'Taunton isn't much for town. He's only up a few weeks a year to look after paperwork. He much prefers country life at the family seat.'

'He's inherited the title now, that's bound to change whether he wills it or not.' Sofia turned aside Helena's subtle riposte.

'Taunton is a man not easily swayed in his convictions.'

A knock at the door interrupted whatever offensive manoeuvre Helena was mounting. 'Guests are arriving, my lady,' a footman informed through the door.

Helena gave her appearance a final look. 'It's sure to be a girl this time. I'm carrying high, unlike the boys, and I'm so much bigger than usual for six months.' She held out a hand to Sofia. 'It's the very last of the wedding festivities and my last outing for a while. After tonight, I'll shall be too large to escape notice. Please come, dear friend.' She gave a soft, irresistible smile. 'You and I have nothing to lose, not when we stand together.'

Sofia felt her resolve weaken. She'd never been able to refuse Helena anything. 'All right, I'll come for just a bit. Let me fix my hair and put my necklace on.' She would go and support Helena against the gossips who were bound to say she should have retired from society weeks ago. And why not? If she'd meant to baulk, she should have baulked far sooner than this. She'd let things get out of hand. She should not have accepted Helena's invitation to play the companion during the weeks leading up to the wedding, to attend the wedding, to stay with the family and now to dance at the honeymoon ball before Ferris and his bride set sail for a few months in the Greek isles.

Helena smiled her victory. 'Try to have a good time tonight.' Sofia fastened the necklace, hearing the unspoken message. It was the last thing Helena could do for her for quite some time. She should make the most of it before she returned to the anonymity of her Chelsea row house and its middle-class neighbours. She'd not been home in a while and she missed it. No one in Chelsea really knew who she was and they didn't care. She'd found a bit of happiness there, rebuilding and reshaping her life. She had her work behind the façade of Barnham and she had the charity work allotted to women as well. She helped at the orphanage and at a small school. It was a start towards her larger dreams.

Ready at last, Sofia looped her arm through Helena's and leaned close as they headed out on to the landing. 'You've been the very best of fairy godmothers to me, Helena, and I *do* know it.'

But tonight at midnight, the fairy tale of belonging to Cowden's exclusive world would end. She'd always known it would. Like so much else, it had been an illusion only and a thin one at that. There'd been *no* illusion about the reception she'd receive and she'd not been wrong. The only surprise had been her reaction to Taunton. But she had herself well in hand and he would not sneak past her guard again with his looks or with his kindnesses.

Chapter Five

He had to stop being surprised by her beauty. Conall had seen her three times now, twice in a crowd with plenty to distract, yet he'd failed to be distracted. Each time she took his breath away. Even here, amid the sumptuous glitter of the Cowden ballroom, surrounded by London's most beautiful women and a most elegant setting, she claimed all his attention the moment she entered the ballroom, her arm tucked through Helena's. 'Stunning,' Conall murmured, hardly aware he'd spoken aloud until Frederick chuckled beside him.

'Yes, indeed. I didn't think Helena would persuade her.' Frederick leaned against the satin-swathed pillar and joined him in watching the two women across the room, his gaze riveted on his wife.

Conall cleared his throat to cover his slip. 'Yes, of course, an absolute coup on Helena's part,' he said rather too enthusiastically.

Frederick wasn't fooled. 'Oh, you mean *her*, as in

"*Sofia* is stunning". Hmm,' Frederick mused, a studied eye fixed on him before returning to peruse Sofia's blue ball gown. 'Yes, I suppose she is if you like the blonde, dazzling sort.' He laughed good-naturedly. 'And do you? Do you like the blonde, dazzling sort?' Frederick relieved a passing footman of two glasses of champagne. He handed Conall one. 'Cheers, old chap. It was good to have you here this week. We don't see enough of you.' He nodded to the two women making their way towards them. 'Do you think that might change?'

'I'll have my father's seat in the House of Lords to look after,' Conall replied, obliquely pushing aside Frederick's none-too-subtle fishing expedition.

'That's not what I meant.' Frederick sipped at his champagne thoughtfully before adding, 'She doesn't care for town much either.' Frederick slanted him a look and it occurred to Conall that Frederick could easily oblige him on the account of solving the mysteries of the Marchesa di Cremona. It was certainly a temptation to take the easy route and one he could justify on the basis of the potential of doing business with her. There would be instant gratification, but such a temptation had the reek of gossip about it. Conall had always believed if one wanted to know another, one should ask that person instead of gathering information from secondary sources, even sources as reliable as Cowden's heir.

Conall took a swallow of his champagne. 'It's purely business.'

'It's all business right *now*.' Frederick finished the rest of his drink and passed off his glass. 'You could change that, to the benefit of you both. I think she's a person very much alone in the world, not unlike yourself,' Frederick said pointedly. 'Your father's death has changed you. You've set yourself apart.'

Conall shook his head. 'I am not alone. Besides, I have my family: Mother, Cecilia and Freddie.'

'Again, that's not what I meant.' Frederick raised an eyebrow. 'We are not designed to be alone, old friend.'

Conall gave Frederick a hard look. 'Let me be blunt. I haven't anything to offer any woman at the moment. You know that better than anyone.'

'Marriage is not only about money and you have more than money to offer a bride,' Frederick warned. 'You didn't use to be such a cynic. You were going to marry for love like your parents.'

Conall frowned. 'Not any more. I can't afford love and, as it turned out, neither could my father.'

'Your father did the best he could,' Frederick said in defence of the deceased, his own tone matching Conall's in sternness, then suddenly his face changed, his gaze going past Conall's shoulder.

Conall watched his friend's face light up as his wife approached and gave a friendly laugh. 'We can't all be you, Brixton.' That didn't mean the hunger wasn't still there, the hunger to have what Frederick had. He'd always thought he would. The past year had shown him how flimsy that assumption was and how out of reach. He would need more than luck to reclaim the notion of a love match. He would need a miracle.

They bowed to the ladies and Conall watched with the usual sense of envy as Helena slid her arm through Frederick's with familiar ease. 'My dance card is empty,' she flirted with her husband. 'Perhaps you might oblige me?'

The five-piece orchestra was tuning up, a ballroom's subtle call to arms. Around them, matchmaking mamas began to marshal their troops as Ferris and his bride swept out on to the floor to open the dancing. A few turns on their own and then the guests would join the dancing. Helena caught his eye and Conall knew Frederick wasn't the one doing the obliging. It was *him*. She'd timed this perfectly, knowing very well he was too much the gentleman to leave a lady standing alone while her friend was dancing and he had no other partner.

'Marchesa, would you do me the honour?' He bowed to her and offered his arm. If he waited too long, his gesture would look like an offer of charity.

'I think Helena has manoeuvred you into this.' Sofia blushed prettily as he led her on to the floor. The first dance, at Ferris's request, was most untraditionally a waltz, but the whims of besotted bridegrooms were tolerated on such an occasion as a honeymoon ball.

'Do you mind? I certainly don't,' Conall assured her. He fitted his hand to her waist and took her other hand in his as the signal came for guests to join the dancing. He swept her into the pattern with a wide smile. In truth, he enjoyed dancing and to dance with a partner who was his equal was a rare pleasure. Tonight, he had both the opportunity *and* the partner with which to indulge himself. She was exquisite in his arms. Her movements answered the slightest direction from his hand; her eyes were alight with a joy that matched his own and he realised that it wasn't simply the cut of her clothes or the attractiveness of her features alone that gave her beauty. Her beauty came from a well somewhere deep within her. It was an intoxicating well to drink from and one he was in no hurry to relinquish when the dance came to an end.

'Come outside with me,' he issued his abrupt invitation with a hint of breathless anticipation. Even without the possibility of a business connection between them, she was captivating. He had not been captivated like this for years, not since he had first come to town, fresh home from his Grand Tour of the Americas and his eyes had lit on Lady Francesca Wheless. Of course, he hadn't known her. Lady Francesca had turned out to be less perfect after he'd spent three months in pursuit and learned the truth of her. It would likely be the same with La Marchesa, given enough time, but for tonight he wanted to enjoy the illusion of perfection wrapped in sky-blue silk and perhaps she wanted to enjoy the illusion of him. Lord knew *he* wasn't perfect, not once one got past the handsome exterior.

The Cowden gardens were well-lit against anyone falling prey to the inherent temptations of a honeymoon ball, but due to the earliness yet of the evening, the gardens were relatively empty. Conall had them—and Sofia—nearly to himself. 'Are you packed for tomorrow?' he asked as they strolled, making small talk of their impending trip to Somerset in the morning.

'Yes.' She gave a light laugh. 'The Treshams will be robbed of all their company at once, I fear. Ferris and Anne will leave in the morning, too, as will Helena. She can't stand to be away from her boys for too long, although Frederick plans to stay a while longer.' They were doing it, the classic trend of small talk between acquaintances who were neither strangers nor friends; talking of mutually held acquaintances so they didn't have to talk of themselves. They could talk all night in this manner and never once speak of themselves in any meaningful way.

'And what will you miss? Unlike the rest of us, you are not going home tomorrow. You are being dragged away on business,' Conall reminded her in an attempt to redirect the trajectory of the conversation. Tonight, under the moonlight and paper lanterns, he was hungry for a connection based on something more than acquaintance. He wanted something more for them than unpacking their friendship with Brixton and Helena.

She paused thoughtfully. 'I'll miss my projects. I help at an orphanage and do some teaching for them.

Just little things like basic reading and numbers.' But it wasn't little to her, Conall thought, noting the soft smile that took her mouth when she spoke of it. She found meaning and purpose in it. It spoke of a kind soul and Conall thought once more of the inner well of her beauty. The Marchesa was becoming quite a paragon.

Conall tried one more time to learn something uniquely personal about her. 'You must miss Italy, Marchesa.' The enquiry was a misstep.

She fixed him with a hard, polite smile. 'No, my lord, I do not miss Italy at all. In fact, I try not to think about it.' She was daring him to ask the next question. So intuitive was it, that it was already framing itself in his mind: *And your husband? Certainly you must miss him?* Conall tamped down hard on the temptation. Tonight was for enjoying illusions, not truths. There'd be time enough for truths in Somerset, for both of them. She was not the only one being careful.

Conall retreated, withdrawing his conversation to safer ground. 'I've never been to Italy, so I have nothing to compare it to, but I've heard the weather is temperate, much nicer than here, and the food is delicious.'

'We lived in Piedmont, in the north-west, surrounded by lakes and the Alps. It was hardly anything like Rome or Florence. The climate would surprise you, I think.' Conall recognised a bone when he was tossed one and that was what this was—a brief look into her life, albeit a very safe, very narrow slice. It was her way of saying thank you for the retreat, for understanding she didn't want to disclose any more.

'Shall we go back in?' Conall offered as they turned at the end of the gardens. If they were gone too long, Helena would think her matchmaking efforts were successful.

'Yes, I suppose we should.' But she sounded reluctant. 'We wouldn't want to give Helena any encouragement.' She smiled, luminous and radiant without trying.

Conall laughed. 'Those were my thoughts exactly.' The garden was filling with couples now, the first foray of dancing over, and people were heated, except for the frosty glares women shot Sofia's way. Some of the men nodded to Conall and stopped to exchange a few short words, but he saw the speculation rife in their eyes. That speculation asked the same question: did he mean to try his luck with her now that Wenderly had failed? He knew Sofia saw it, too. She was tense beside him, her laughter gone, her luminescence shuttered.

'Perhaps a walk on the terrace?' Conall offered, sensing her reticence to return inside where the gossip was bound to be worse.

'I shouldn't keep you.' He felt her hand start to pull away from his arm and he trapped it with his other hand. He would not let her slip away this time as she had at the wedding.

'I am in no hurry.'

'You will be missed,' she protested, raising an eyebrow to indicate by whom as a pair of young girls passed, their eyes on Conall and then narrowing at the sight of her.

Conall shrugged. 'Girls such as they hold no charms for me.' He had no intentions of filling his evening with empty-headed debutantes, not when there was this charming woman who so obviously needed him. For the first time, he saw a glimpse of her fragility. Perhaps Frederick was right and she was quite alone despite her usual vivacious show to the contrary.

He led her to a quiet corner of the veranda where they might have some privacy at least from prying eyes. 'They aren't worth your notice. They're silly girls with nothing else to do.'

'I know.' She managed a smile. 'I've never been good enough for them, not this crop of debutantes or any other. I've never paid them any mind. Not even in school.' It was a brave statement, but Conall heard the courage it took to utter it.

'In school? Didn't you and Helena go to school together?'

'Yes, but I was always beneath the other girls. My father was gentry, hardly the same calibre as earls and dukes.' She tossed her head in defiance at the memories. The diamonds at her ears sparkled. 'I never came out, you know. I married the Marchese straight out of finishing school. I went from Finlay's Academy directly to the chapel and then on to Italy. One day I was a mere schoolgirl and the next morning I was La Marchesa di Cremona. I'd traded my schoolgirl aprons for trunks and trunks of fine clothes.' There was no gloating in her tone, no sense of victory in triumphing over the girls who'd teased her. There was, however, a wry sense of regret.

'It must have been a difficult transition,' Conall probed carefully. He could imagine just how alone she'd been at the time, a young, sheltered girl who'd never been anywhere suddenly off to Europe, to a place that didn't speak her language, where she had no family, no friends, only a husband to rely on for everything, even basic communication.

Sofia gave an elegant shrug and turned away. 'I'm home now.'

Conall was about to ask where home was—surely she had parents and perhaps a family somewhere—when the words floated up to them from down below in the garden, two young women gossiping in the dark, away from the watchful eyes of their chaperons. 'She's not received in any decent home. Only Lady Brixton takes her up, but Lady Brixton is nearly a duchess so she can do as she pleases.'

'I think it's more than that,' came the spiteful whisper. 'I think Lady Brixton owes her something fierce and she holds it over the poor lady.'

The girls laughed.

'Received or not, it doesn't stop her from gathering all the men's attention. First Wenderly and his money, and tonight she's stolen away handsome Lord Taunton,' one girl said with a pout.

'It's easy to steal a man when one has loose morals. All the Italians do,' the more worldly girl responded with derision.

'She's English,' came the reminder.

'Not really. My mother says she's been gone for ten years.'

'I wish she'd go back. She already has a husband and a title. It's not fair for her to ruin our chances.'

'She can't go back.' The girl's voice dropped to indicate the degree of scandal in what she was about to say. 'My mother says she's divorced.'

Divorced. The word shimmered in the night, nearly a palpable ghost between them. The scandal was revealed. The veil of illusion torn. Her blemish was exposed.

Conall could see Sofia pale with mortification in the moonlight. 'Perhaps we should go in and find Helena.' Although he was torn between doing that and vaulting the balustrade and taking those girls in hand. They needed a scolding.

Sofia shook her head and said quietly, 'No, don't bother Helena. I think it would be best if I just went home.'

'Of course. I'll call for my carriage and have it out front,' Conall offered.

'I can find my own way, it's not necessary.'

'No.' Conall stalled her with a hand on her arm. 'I will see you home safely, end of discussion.'

* * *

The ride home was a silent one. What was there to say? Her secret was out. Sofia was mortified, not only at the girls, but at her own foolishness. How quickly she'd bought in to the illusion she'd created, the pretence that she could belong for a night! And how glorious it had been to live in that illusion, to feel lovely in her blue dress, to dance with a man who treated her like a princess. Her first instinct had been right. She should not have come.

She'd not realised how hungry she'd been for that kind of contact, for connection. He'd asked for nothing except her company. She'd been able to forget for a little while about business, about the obstacle of her past, until those two girls had brought it all back to her, a reminder that she could never truly forget. Society wouldn't let her. To be fair, even if the girls hadn't been so blunt, the damage had already been done. She'd seen the looks from the strolling couples and Lord Taunton had, too. This was the second time in his company that scandal had found her. Tonight, however, he was playing the gentleman, allowing her silence, as he sat across from her in his immaculate dark evening clothes, every bit as handsome as the rumours gave him credit for, and a symbol of all she couldn't have even if she wanted it. She did not wish to marry again, she reminded herself firmly.

The carriage came to a stop in the narrow street before her home. Conall leapt down and halted.

Something preternatural in his posture had her on alert. 'What is it?' She moved to the carriage door, determined to get out.

'Stay inside the carriage, Sofia,' he urged, waving her back with his hand while he moved forward towards danger. 'Something seems amiss.'

The clouds parted and the moon shone through, confirming Conall's suspicions. A window pane was broken, the moonlight reflecting off its jagged edge. 'No!' Sofia climbed down, racing along the walkway to her door. Conall grabbed for her, catching her about the waist, but she would not be set aside.

'It's my house,' she ground out. But her fear was rising. There was more than one broken pane and the door she'd firmly locked when she'd left to join Helena looked ajar.

'If you won't stay in the carriage, then stay behind me,' Conall instructed. 'Whoever did this might still be here.' Gingerly, he pushed the door open and Sofia gasped. Inside, furniture lay broken, shards of glass and porcelain peppered the floor. Drawers were pulled out from cabinets, their contents strewn about the front parlour.

She should have come home sooner. A hundred recriminations went through her mind. This was her fault. She might as well have hung a sign on her door. Chelsea wasn't unsafe, exactly, but it wasn't Mayfair either. Thugs could have been watching the house and, knowing she was gone, taken the opportunity to break in.

Conall stepped forward, footsteps crunching on the glass. He grabbed up a chair leg, brandishing it like a club. Methodically, he went through each room, broad shoulders filling each doorway, makeshift club at the ready to deal out justice. At the stairs, she watched him go up, her own hands trembling as they fumbled to light the remnants of a lamp.

Light only made it worse. Her favourite tea cup, smashed. A sweet porcelain statue of a dog, shattered. The cushion of her favourite chair where she'd sit by the window and sew, ripped apart, the stuffing littering the floor. The pages of her books torn out. Nothing remained unsullied.

Conall came downstairs, his expression grim. 'It's the same throughout.' He let out a breath. 'Does anything seem to be missing?' he asked hopefully.

'No.' Her hand shook hard as her brain began to register consciously what it already knew. This was more than a break in. It was wanton destruction. Thieves *took* things. Thieves didn't risk breaking into a home to take *nothing*. She felt faint, numb with the realisation. The lamp slipped from her hand.

Conall rescued the lamp before she dropped it, all efficient action. He took charge, or was it that he stayed in charge? He'd been in charge since the moment the girls had whispered about her in the bushes at Cowden's. He got her through the next horrible minutes. He found her the remnants of a chair to sit on with its ruined cushion. He lit a fire from the furniture shards. He rummaged in the kitchen for a pot and her bottle of medicinal brandy and put it over the fire to warm. He put the little pan of brandy in her hands, lacking a cup. 'Drink, you will feel better, I promise. Milk would be best, but at least you'll be warmer.' He squatted beside her, steadying the pot in her hand with his own wrapped warm and firm about hers.

'I haven't been home. Milk would sour. This is my fault. I left for too long.' She'd left and far more had gone bad besides milk.

Conall took the pan from her. 'No, Sofia, this is not the work of thugs. You know that.' Ah, so he'd come to the same conclusions, too. 'Whoever did this was looking for something, or someone, and when they didn't find it, they wanted to make sure you knew they'd been here.'

And so they'd destroyed her life, the precious life she'd built so carefully, piece by piece, dish by dish, cup by cup, for three years. There was only one man who would do such a thing, who would take *joy* in such a thing. Sofia began to shake again. There wasn't enough warm brandy in the world to comfort her now. Giancarlo was actively hunting her. His patience with his unreturned letters was wearing thin. How thin? Was he here already? Or was this the work of his minions? Of his personal manservant, Andelmo? Just the thought of the name caused her to shiver. How many times had that hulking thug of a man been a witness, a participant even, in her humiliation? If Il Marchese had sent him, it was serious.

Conall shrugged off his coat and put it around her. 'Let's get you back to Cowden's. In the morning, we'll sort all of this out and see what can be saved and then we'll start looking for who did this.' He held her gaze with his steady grey eyes, his hands running up and down her arms in an attempt to warm her, soothe her, this man who knew her scandal, who owed her nothing. 'There will be justice for this.'

Sofia's brain started work again. They could not stay here. They could not come here again. 'No. There is nothing to save and we have train tickets tomorrow for Somerset.' It was suddenly imperative to her fear-driven mind that she get as far away from here as possible. Giancarlo, or whoever had done this, was probably counting on her to come and paw through the rubble. Perhaps they had stayed too long already. Was he watching the house even now? How long had they been here? Twenty minutes? She shot a glance at the unguarded door, half-expecting to see Giancarlo come through it, pistol waving. He would shoot Taunton for the sport of it. She'd seen him do it before, to a poor boy who'd had the misfortune to look too long at her at a picnic. He'd ended up with a knee that would never bend quite right again and she'd ended up with a riding crop across her backside for having supposedly enticed him.

Sofia struggled to her feet, lurching unsteadily in her fright and shock. Conall caught her and she resisted the urge to fall into his arms entirely, to lay this whole mess on his broad, willing shoulders. 'Just take me back to Cowden's, *please.*' She couldn't keep the urgency out of her voice. She had to get them away. She would grieve for the loss of her sanctuary later. Right now, all that mattered was getting to safety and then getting on the train and out of London.

Chapter Six

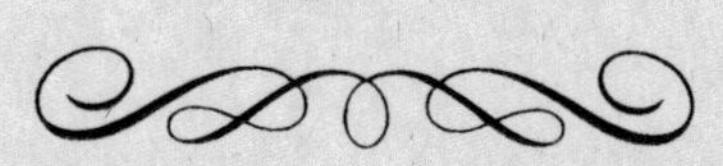

The Flying Dutchman chugged out of Paddington station promptly at nine-fifty the next morning for its four-and-a-half-hour run to Exeter, stopping at Taunton, Conall's family seat, along the way. Conall slid the door to their private compartment closed, shutting out the noise of happy travellers making their way to the spas and seaside of the south-east as the train lurched towards full speed.

'It's not called the Holiday Express without cause,' he joked, trying to instil some of the outside levity into the decidedly more sombre atmosphere inside their compartment. 'It's Bedlam out there. You must have worked magic to get private accommodations on short notice.' Then again, the holiday revellers hadn't had their homes destroyed or their darkest scandal exposed in the most public way possible.

'It was nothing a smile and kindness couldn't achieve.' Sofia glanced up from her efforts to settle in. 'You're happy to be going home,' she observed with a smile that was over-bright and did not match the shadows beneath her eyes. Conall saw her game too easily. She wanted to pretend last night hadn't happened, that the girls' words didn't matter or exist between them. But this time a smile would not achieve her aims. He would not be distracted.

'Are we not to speak of last night, then?' Conall asked bluntly. Sometimes it was best to address the elephant in the room. He had four hours to learn her secrets. It had been a blow last night to hear the word 'divorce'. For a man who had strict criteria about whom he needed to marry, it was a firmly pounded nail in the coffin of his nascent fantasies. Part of him didn't *want* to know empirically that this marvellous creature across from him was unattainable. There was a certain freedom in not knowing the precise scandal attached to her. With precision came limitations, boundaries that could not be crossed.

'Why? It has no bearing on your business with Barnham.' Her response was politely cool. Her gaze was steady, but her façade was no longer foolproof. 'I assume Cowden told you about my alias? I instructed him to use it if it became necessary. It will protect you from any association with me if it comes to that.'

'You needn't hide your divorce from me for that exact reason. You're right, it has no bearing on our business. I am perhaps the one person you *can* talk to about it, if you would like?' He watched her process that bit of information, her hands tight in her lap. Today, she wore a pale-blue travelling costume with lavender accents that brought out her eyes—eyes that bore the shadows of a sleepless night. Despite the shadows, she was still lovely. Her colour had returned and she was valiantly trying to put the terror of the burglary behind her. The burglary had shaken her deeply, far more than she liked to let on. But he'd seen her in the immediate moments after the discovery, he'd seen her hands tremble as they held the pan of brandy. He knew better than to believe the calm outward demeanour she wanted to present this morning. 'Secrets only have power *because* they're secrets; things that have to be hidden.'

'My divorce is not a secret, as last night so clearly demonstrated. Even the newest of debutantes knew about it. It's a scandal. If you must know, Il Marchese di Cremona and I divorced three years ago. Ever since then, that particular distinction has followed me with the dogged tenacity of a loyal hound, only less welcome.'

'I am sorry,' he said carefully into the silence between them, although he thought the words might be wrong. What did one say to a divorcee? It was a social death. It put a woman into a half-life. It separated her from her husband and thus from society. No one would receive her, but what was the point of being received anyway? She might not even be eligible to remarry, legally or socially. Some laws forbade a divorced spouse to remarry.

'I am not sorry,' she answered plainly. 'It was not a happy marriage and I was glad to be rid of him at any cost. He is in Italy; I am here. I have the freedom to do as I please as long as I don't offend society with my presence. It's a fair trade.'

'Freedom at the price of isolation?' Conall prodded. Socially, there were very few who could take on a wife with that stigma. An *affaire* would be her only recourse for an intimate relationship. In short, divorce forced a woman to choose to live as a nun or, by social standards, as a whore, going from affair to affair, or perhaps becoming a man's mistress. No wonder she was lonely. No one but the Wenderlys of the world could claim her. No one else would dare defy convention.

She smiled coldly. 'Is this to be a four-hour interrogation?' The smile didn't quite conceal the bite of her words. 'I wasn't aware I needed to be interviewed.' It was a reminder that *he'd* come to *her*. He had sought out the one investor who had not voted against his proposal.

'And *your* approval is all I need,' Conall answered with a smile of his own. They could make a war out of smiles if she wished. He had no intention of backing down, gentleman or not, no matter how badly he needed the money. 'I merely wished to know more about my travelling companion and potential business partner. That hardly qualifies as an interrogation, Marchesa.'

'It is hardly necessary, is what it is. My divorce does not define me,' she reprimanded sharply, taking no pains to soften her blows in her rejoinder. She reached in her travelling satchel for a book. 'My personal life is hardly worth your concern. I am an investor, just like any other.'

'If you're just an investor, you are the most intriguing investor I've yet to meet—burglaries and blue ball gowns notwithstanding,' Conall mused.

He couldn't resist goading her—perhaps if she were goaded enough she might reveal a bit more of herself. He began to enumerate her points of intrigue on his fingers. 'A woman using a man's alias to conduct business, a woman who—'

'A woman? Is that all you see?' she interrupted. 'Cowden led me to believe I might expect better of you. He said your sister was quite a proponent of women's rights,' she scolded. 'I *am* a woman. A divorced one. Do people tally *your* assets starting each sentence with "a single, unmarried man"? An *unmarried man* with a business plan to raise alpacas and buy a mill, an *unmarried man* with an English title?' she mocked. 'What makes me interesting shouldn't be my sex or my marital status.'

Conall nodded, conceding that part of the argument. 'Point taken. However, you cannot deny there is a certain mystique about you. One might argue you even cultivate it with your veils and seclusion.'

'It is not my intention to cultivate anything, my lord.' Apparently that extended to a relationship with him, although last night he'd thought differently when they'd danced. There was a chemistry between them.

She opened her book with an exaggerated show meant to imply the conversation was over, but Conall was not willing to be dismissed so easily. 'You cultivate nothing? Not even carte-blanche offers from one of the *ton*'s richest peers?' He might be the one needing money, but he was not going to pursue it blindly. Who wanted to do business with a spineless turnip of a man?

She snapped her book shut with a loud thump, her eyes flashing as they fixed on him, blue eyes meeting grey. 'Certainly not. Why is it that a woman must always belong to a man in order to define her place in the world, Lord Taunton?' Gone was any hard-won familiarity—he'd been downgraded to Lord Taunton, a title he still wasn't entirely comfortable hearing in relation to himself.

Conall leaned back in his seat, hands folded above his head, studying the virago that was the Marchesa di Cremona. 'You do indeed sound like my sister. Are you always this argumentative, or just after weddings, balls and break-ins?' He regretted the words immediately, mostly because in hindsight he knew them to be true. He understood better how difficult the wedding must have been for her, conjuring up images of her own, less-blissful marital state.

She opened her book again and said firmly, 'I hope you brought something to read, Lord Taunton. It will make the time pass more quickly.' She was working hard to defend herself with that sharp tongue today, using it to keep him at a distance.

Conall reached for his own bag and retrieved a treatise on alpaca wool. He brandished it in one hand as evidence. 'I have all the entertainment I need right here. "The clipping and shearing of Alpaca".'

Usually reading about the alpaca absorbed him. Usually the clack of the carriage wheels on the steel tracks lulled him to sleep. Under the right circumstances, he found train travel soothing—a quiet compartment and time alone with his ideas. Today, the usual conditions of rail travel were not enough to soothe his mind and calm his thoughts. His mind wanted to think about her, the Marchesa di Cremona, Sofia of no last name. He wanted to think about her marriage, what sort of a man had her husband been to make her seek divorce as a preferable option?

Conall turned a page in his pamphlet and gave her a covert look. She was intelligent, sharp-witted, lovely, and she would be a trial to the wrong sort of husband. Goodness knew she wasn't the sort *he* was expected to marry. Is that what had happened? Another disaster of a *ton*nish-style marriage of title to money without consideration for temperaments?

He directed his eyes back to the pamphlet with a firm scold. This had to stop. He could not continue obsessing about her. It was bound to be bad for business between them if he allowed her to affect his objectivity. He was becoming as bad as Hargreaves, sniffing out gossip. What did the state of her marriage matter to him? As they'd both affirmed, this was about business only. And yet his eyes kept slipping over the edge of his pamphlet to take in her face: the curve of her jaw and the pert snub of her nose, the tiny dimple on her left cheek.

His mind slid to wonder all nature of things, not the least of which included the errant thought that if he had such a wife, he would not let her get away. If she were his, he would find a way to tame her— No, that wasn't the word for it. She would not want to be tamed. She would want to be accommodated. He tried his thought out again. If he had such a wife, he would find a way to accommodate her. The word wasn't perfect, merely better. Accommodation would be a place to start.

A sixth sense told him she would want to be more than an accommodation. She'd want to be a partner; she'd want to be a man's equal. Most marriages weren't built for that. Hell, the legal system wasn't even built for that. His parents' marriage had been, though. Once, it had given him hope that it was possible to have more than the empty beauty of an Olivia de Pugh. Maybe it still was. Maybe somewhere there was a woman who aspired to be more than an ornament on a husband's arm, who would want to build something with him from nothing. He just had to find her. Next year perhaps, or the year after that, once things were settled with the alpaca.

* * *

The train made its first stop in Didcot an hour out from London, an hour closer to home. Even under the circumstances, the thought of home brought a smile to Conall's face. He'd sent a message earlier in the week to tell his family to make ready. Right now, they'd be rushing around to put all the final pieces in order, to stage the greatest play of their lives; laying out the fine china he'd managed to wheedle out of a distant cousin since he'd sold the family china months ago, moving the good furniture into the public rooms and library where the Marchesa would see it, making up her bed in the Dower House with the last of the pristine Irish linen they kept carefully locked away in a cedar-lined trunk, laying in food worthy of a house party so their guest would never guess just how much he needed the money.

Desperation did not breed confidence in an investor. However, part of him felt guilty over the deception, especially when it was being perpetrated on a woman whose home had been all but destroyed. Still, his more practical side argued, business was business. He'd offered last night to delay the trip and she'd insisted they keep the appointment. He had to be satisfied with that effort and, if the appointment was going forward, then he had to move forward with his plans, too. Time waited for no man.

Conall rose and took the opportunity to excuse himself to the club car. He would have better luck reading and shaking this newfound obsession of his if he was surrounded by the manly presence of brandy and cigars. He wasn't even sure La Marchesa heard him leave, so absorbed was she in her novel, making it clear *she* wasn't plagued in the least by errant thoughts regarding *her* travelling companion.

Her polite coolness was something of a novelty in itself. Conall usually had little trouble holding a woman's attention—an innate talent that had both its assets and disadvantages. After all, he didn't want or need every woman's attention. But he found he wanted hers—a disturbing thought all its own. What would he do with that attention if he had it? Perhaps it was just the challenge of achieving it that had him provoked. It had been a long time since he'd been motivated in that regard and he was a man who didn't take defeat lying down, although, he mused with a smile, sometimes he took victory that way.

His departure was a hollow victory. There was little to be proud of in it. She'd driven him from the compartment quite deliberately by being difficult. But it had worked. He'd asked his questions, as she'd known he would. What man with money on the line wouldn't have? And she'd evaded him by going on the offensive, by turning each of his statements into an argument. Politeness would not have achieved her ends. If she'd given him an inch, he would have taken the proverbial mile.

Sofia set aside her novel and stared out the window, watching villages slide by in a series of hills and valleys. She did not need to pretend she was reading now that he was gone. He had not shunned her. Quite the opposite—he wanted to know her. He'd been generous in that regard, too generous. Or perhaps it was just a ploy to win her approval.

She could not afford to oblige him. Objectivity was crucial for making good business decisions. If that were to be compromised by liking him, the quality of her judgement would be compromised as well and that served neither of them.

It wasn't his good looks that threatened her objectivity. She was far too jaded to be persuaded by a handsome face. It was *him*: his genuine manner that made a woman feel comfortable in his company as if they were old acquaintances, the concern in those grey eyes. He *had* been worried for her at the wedding. He'd been willing to protect her with his social countenance, just as last night he'd been ready to defend her with his physical countenance. She would not easily forget the speed with which he'd drawn a weapon, searching her destroyed home for signs of a lingering intruder. Nor would she forget his tenderness as he'd lit a fire and warmed the pan of brandy. She'd been surprised by his efficiency. Since when did viscounts know how to perform domestic chores?

He was attracted to her. She was used to recognising the signs and he had been from the moment he'd walked into the Cowden drawing room. It was there in the flare of his grey eyes, the way his gaze lingered on her face. And yet, she would wager all she had that at the end of the day, he was a gentleman far out of Wenderly's league. Wenderly's eyes had lingered on her and he'd immediately thought such beauty could be owned for a price. There was no respect in Wenderly's wandering gaze. She was an object to him. She knew that sort of man well. They populated her husband's circle.

How much will you take for one night with her? She must be incomparable nude. I will draw her for you.

There'd been no such crassness in Taunton's gaze. It had lingered, appreciated, but it had not coveted, had not assessed her, had not sought to acquire her. Yet his gaze, the one he tried to hide behind his pamphlet, said the man in him contemplated the wanting of her. The gentleman in him had found the thought unseemly and so he'd removed himself.

It was for the best. Taunton was a good man. But for all the respect he accorded her, she was not a good woman. She was an outcast by English standards, a woman of no virtue, of no standing. She had neither a husband nor children. She was the very worst of fallen women: a divorcee, a woman who had failed in the two tasks society assigned to her.

The train chugged on towards its destination, making stops in Bath and Bristol as the morning fell behind her. The door to the compartment slid open as the conductor called out the arrival in Taunton. Conall Everard had returned, his presence dominating the compartment. He reached above her to take down the valises from the corded nets meant for luggage. He smelled faintly of tobacco and brandy as he stretched overhead.

'I owe you an apology for this morning,' he offered solemnly after the bags had been brought down. 'I put my nose where it ought not to have been and I made you uncomfortable with my questions and my insinuations.'

'I am not easily intimidated.' Sofia rose and shook out her skirts. She was more discomfited by the apology, in truth, than she had been by their argument. When was the last time a man had begged forgiveness from her?

'Whether you are or not does not excuse my behaviour. Perhaps we might start again?' He smiled then, his eyes crinkling at the corners into their well-worn tracks. The train chose that moment to set on the brakes. Sofia lost her balance in the disruption. She fell forward, straight into Taunton's quick arms and steady grasp, her face crushed against his chest.

'Ow!' She rubbed at her nose. Sweet heavens, the man was made of steel beneath his coats.

'Are you all right?' He steered her to her seat and sat her down before tipping her head up as he peered at her nose. 'No blood, you've not broken it,' he cajoled. 'But perhaps I should send for a cold compress?'

She shook her head. 'I'll be fine in a moment. Besides, we've arrived. I don't want to hold you up.' She laughed, feeling faintly ridiculous over this handsome man staring up her nostrils. 'Welcome home.'

Taunton smiled, an unaccustomed warmth taking up residence in her stomach. 'I will take that to mean "apology accepted".' He ushered her through the narrow corridor of the carriage, signalling for a porter to follow with their valises. At the door, he handed her down into spring sunlight nearly as bright as his smile. 'Welcome to Taunton, Marchesa.'

'Northcott,' she corrected suddenly before she could think better of it. 'My name is Sofia Northcott.' She had not used that name for years. It was the name of her youth, before marriage, before she'd become the Marchesa. It was *her* name.

The Viscount smiled. 'Very well, then, welcome to Taunton, Sofia Northcott.' He made a wide gesture with his hand towards a long-bed wagon where men were loading their trunks. 'Come this way. Your carriage, such as it is, awaits.'

And maybe more, Sofia thought. She shielded her eyes and took it in, her breath catching. The medieval tower of a church loomed at the far end of a neat kept street full of half-timbered Tudor shops. It might have been any of the myriad towns and villages that dotted England, but this one tugged at her heart. This one was where she'd make her fortune. Maybe this would be a place where she could reclaim the rest of her freedom.

Chapter Seven

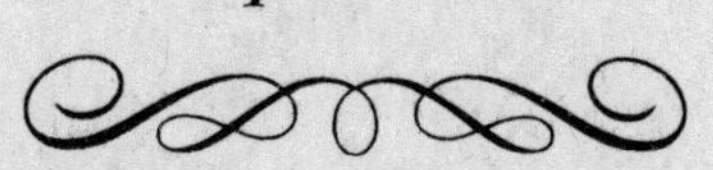

The drive to Everard Hall was animated and pleasant. Conversation flowed easily around points of interest. Gone were the sharp tones that had edged their morning. Sofia had questions about everything she saw and Taunton had answers. This was the home of his boyhood and he was proud as he pointed out highlights. The town sported a hospital, he boasted proudly. He pointed out the medieval church she'd spied from the station as well as many other smaller, newer churches. There were schools, too, she was delighted to see, although not a school for girls. Not yet. But that was putting more than one horse before the cart. Before she could do anything, she had to gather her resources and decide if anywhere in England was safe for her now that Giancarlo was threatening. The mere presence of his threat put her grand dream on hold. She couldn't very well go building schools and safe factory towns if she had to look over her shoulder every day to make sure the past wasn't catching up to her.

Once they were out in the countryside, Taunton's animation grew. 'We've had mills since the thirteenth century, thanks to the Tone,' he told her, nodding towards the sparkling ribbon of river. 'It's good for fishing, too. I'll take you one day.' His pride was infectious and Sofia found herself enjoying every word of his recitation. 'By the fifteenth century, we were exporting our wool all the way to France. But I am thinking alpaca wool can go further than France,' he added. 'There are markets to tap in Italy and Flanders, all the great weaving capitals of the Continent. Alpaca wool can create a luxury item sheep's wool cannot aspire to. It can also create jobs, which we need a great many of these days in Taunton. Not everyone can be a farmer any more, not profitably anyway. The old life is fading. We are all affected by it.'

Sofia was already thinking of ways to expand on his marketing plan. It was easy to get caught up in his excitement. It was too bad the Prometheus Club had not asked him to present. They'd have been stuffing cheques into his pockets before he'd even made it out the door. Then again, that was precisely why the club only reviewed offers in writing. She'd do best to remember that. Emotional attachment didn't guarantee profits. Logic guaranteed profits. But there was logic here, too. She *was* impressed. The infrastructure was in place. There was a river and there were mills, and a convenient means of transport by rail to Bristol and from Bristol there were ships to anywhere in the world. Wool was also a proven market.

Taunton and the Somerset region had thrived on the wool trade for centuries.

The Viscount turned off the main road on to a narrower one. 'We're almost there. In a mile or so, the house will come into view.' She heard the wistfulness in his tone. He was eager to be home. Pleased, in fact. She envied him that sense of place. After last night, she was literally rootless with nowhere to go, the security of the last three years destroyed. Another person would run home, but she didn't have that option. Running home would be tantamount to running back to Giancarlo. Her family had knowingly sold her into a marriage she hadn't understood. But Conall had it all—a home, a family.

A thought occurred to her, underlain by a *frisson* of panic. 'Is your family at home?' Surely, he didn't mean to take her home to decent folk, not after last night.

Taunton nodded. 'They are. My mother, my sister, Cecilia, and my younger brother, Alfred. We call him Freddie. You will be well-chaperoned.'

Sofia looked at her hands, the old shame she'd fought so long to repress starting to surface. No one had concerned themselves with her reputation for a long time. Mostly because no one believed she had a reputation left to guard. Sofia gathered her courage. 'It wasn't my reputation I was worried about.' She paused, hoping the implications of her words would make the problem clear. When he said nothing, she tried again. 'I am not sure your mother and sister will find me appropriate company, or that you should find me appropriate company for them.'

She met his gaze and he slowed the horses. 'Why is that, Sofia Northcott? They don't go about in society often. You needn't fear they'll have heard of Wenderly's proposition. They know only that you're a friend of Lady Brixton's.'

'I meant the divorce.' He was making her spell it out.

He smiled. 'I thought divorce did not define you?' He clucked to the horses. 'You may put your concerns at ease. I have you lodged at the Dower House, although I think that will be horribly inconvenient between walking up to take your meals with us and going over my research.'

She cut him off with a smile. 'The Dower House would be lovely, although I don't need a whole place to myself. An apartment over a carriage house would suffice.' She wanted him to know she would not abuse his hospitality. The less time she was on the estate, the less damage she could do the family.

The Viscount scoffed at the idea of the carriage house. 'I am hardly putting you up in the carriage house apartment. Who knows how long you'll stay? You may fall in love with Somerset and never want to leave.' He gave her a grey-eyed wink.

Sofia laughed, but she knew she *would* have to leave, no matter what the proposition she put to Taunton. With luck, she could come back time and again to check on the mill, but for the most part she'd have to direct business at a distance. At some point, no matter how appreciative of her money, Taunton would recognise his reputation couldn't afford her. He would be glad for her alias.

They came around a bend in the road and the house came into view, so quintessentially English with its Georgian façade and square portico, wings on each side flanked by towers from a bygone age. It was a delightful hotchpotch of architectural styles and history that made her gasp and then it nearly made her weep. How would she explain that a house had almost moved her to tears or that in the three years she'd been in England, she had not left Chelsea except for a few shopping expeditions behind a veil and a rare tea or two with Helena? She had no reason to move beyond the confines of Chelsea. Her business was handled through a solicitor who thought he worked for Barnham and by correspondence. There was no family to receive her and certainly no one in London who was interested in entertaining her. She was invited nowhere. And now, she didn't even have Chelsea.

'It's exquisite,' she managed to say as they drove beneath the wide, square portico. 'Charming, really.'

Taunton laughed and came to help her down, his hands firm at her waist, a reminder of his easy confidence. 'It's a lovely old pile. Charm leaks in the winter, but it's home.' More importantly, it was *his* home and, despite his protests, she could see he was proud of every inch of it.

Up close, however, she could see the flaws he alluded to. The bricks were chinked in places and the heavy wood door at the entrance was faded and scarred with age. But the imperfections merely added to the character. Inside was much the same. Unlike the pristine marble-floored hall at Cowden House with its crystal chandeliers and polished banisters, this home was lived-in. Thick oak banisters marched up the square staircase with its comfortably worn runner. To be sure, Everard Hall was not without elegance. An intricate lattice-worked wainscoting lined the hall walls and a crystal-cut vase filled with long-stemmed gladioli in pinks and whites decorated the console. But Everard Hall knew what it meant to be lived-in.

'Shall we go through? My mother will be out in the gardens.' There was no avoiding it. She'd rather go to the Dower House and hide away with the research, but the Viscount had a light hand at her back, ushering her through the halls and talking affably about the home and his family. Taunton treated her as if she was an honoured guest instead of a business acquaintance, or worse. Outside, his family took their cues from him. His mother and sister greeted her with the same warmness, and she found herself relaxing in their company, able to lay aside at least one worry.

There had been no censorious looks, no coldness or polite reserve. Tea had been a lovely affair in wicker chairs set amid the rose garden, his mother and sister charming, feminine versions of the Viscount with their dark hair and grey eyes. Taunton had taken her on a tour of the extensive gardens, which he argued were the estate's best features. She met Freddie at dinner and was coaxed into playing backgammon with him afterwards, beating Freddie soundly, which earned him a great deal of teasing from his siblings. It wasn't until she'd looked around at the smiling faces that she'd realised how much she'd enjoyed the evening and it made her wary. She hadn't *enjoyed* much of anything for a very long time. Not even her freedom. She spent an inordinate amount of time hiding away, constructing façades and lies to hide behind in order to protect that freedom. When she did go out, she was constantly on alert. That had not been the case tonight. Tonight she'd been part of a group.

Sofia rose and smoothed her skirts. 'I should be going. It's been a long day.' It had been a wonderful day, too, once she'd gotten past the morning quarrel. Already, that seemed ages ago. 'My lord, if you wouldn't mind showing me the way to the Dower House, I will go and get settled in.'

The Viscount offered her his arm, his grey eyes merry. 'I will do better than that. I will take you there myself.'

'Your family is lovely,' she said once they were out of doors. The spring evening was just past dusk and little lamps lit their path. Bullfrogs from one of the ponds croaked nearby.

'They liked you, too.' He laughed. 'You were so worried they wouldn't. But,' he said with utter seriousness, 'we have to get one thing straight before any of this goes further. No more of this "my lord" business. Here at Everard Hall I am Conall. My title is for London, not for home.' He slid her a sly look. 'You can relate, I am sure, Sofia Northcott.'

They laughed together over the little joke and she was struck again by how easy it was to be with him. He was affable without being silly, intelligent without being stuffy—that much had been evident today in his description of the wool industry. It was a potentially intoxicating combination. A woman might waltz with the affable gentleman, but she'd marry the man who knew how to run his estate. There was more security in intelligence than there was laughter. This man had mastered both. If she was ever looking to marry again, she would look for such a man. But she wasn't looking for marriage. Besides, what man would want to marry her? No man of quality married a woman as ruined as she.

'Tomorrow I will show you my sources for the research,' he offered as they reached the Dower House. A homely lamp burned within, bathing the night in a soft, golden light and a footman opened the door as they approached.

'Welcome home, ma'am. Your trunks have been unpacked and your bed has been turned down.

Annie, the maid, has seen to it.' It was about as perfect as an evening got, right down to this.

She turned to her escort and tried it out, finding it came naturally to her. 'Conall, thank you for today and for this evening.' The words seemed inadequate. How could she possibly convey to him how touching it was to be part of a family again, if only for a short time?

He left her then and she made her way upstairs to find everything as expected: the soft linen sheets turned down on a sturdy, carved-oak tester bed, her cotton nightdress laid out, her brushes set out on the dressing table and the young maid waiting to help her. They were simple pleasures, to be sure, for a *marchesa* who'd had a whole complement of servants to wait on her and a suite of rooms done in enough gilt to rival Versailles. Those luxuries had paled against the cost extorted from her to have them. In the end, they hadn't been near enough compensation to make her stay.

Sofia dismissed the maid and took up a vigil on the window seat, savouring the quiet sounds of evening. Tonight had been full of other, less tangible luxuries: the luxury of honest companionship, laughter among people who cared for each other, time spent without worrying over judgement. And it couldn't last. Today had been a fantasy. She could not forget that. She'd been brought here for a purpose: to assess the wisdom of backing the importation of alpacas. She was *not* an honoured guest, no matter how Conall Everard's family treated her. They didn't know her. If they knew the depth of scandal that surrounded her, they would rethink their welcome. She knew that to be empirically true. She'd watched it happen in London. Even her own family had washed their hands of her. In the three years since she'd been back, they had not sought her out once. After their first refusal to see her, she had not bothered to give them her Chelsea address.

And yet Conall had not been thwarted by her past. He had brought her home, introduced her to his family, shown her every courtesy of manner a gentleman showed a lady. He'd given her the perfect day. Her conscience began to stir, her sceptic's armour began to rouse. It whispered a reminder: nothing was perfect. *No one* was perfect, not even Conall Everard. When something looked too good to be true, it probably was. Why had he gone to the bother? Why had he given her the perfect day? Why was he willing to overlook her shortcomings? Certainly the money was part of it. He wanted an investment partner. He needed her money.

Sofia twisted a strand of hair around her finger. The best way to solve puzzles was with questions. What happened if he didn't get the money? Would his experiment simply be tabled for a while? What would tabling the alpaca experiment mean for him? Noblemen dabbled in all sorts of whims. But being knowledgeable about the alpacas suggested this was more than a whim to Conall and she'd noted his commitment to the project before when they'd talked at Cowden House. But how much did he truly need this deal to succeed? What happened if it didn't? Did he simply move on to the next item that interested him?

Sofia shut the window, her hand lingering on the latch. Her instincts told her that wasn't the case. He needed this desperately. She shut her eyes and sighed, seeing now in hindsight what she hadn't seen earlier, perhaps because she simply hadn't wanted to. Illusions were potent that way. Conall Everard needed the money enough to put on quite a show today with his exposition of Taunton history, tea with his mother, a tour through the gardens and a memorable evening. And he'd been very persuasive doing it: catching her eye over dinner, offering her a smile when no one was looking, a light touch here, a hand at her back there.

It wasn't just the charisma of himself that he'd harnessed. There were other things, too. The setting. Had he guessed how such a day would affect her? She'd like to think not. She'd like to think Conall hadn't orchestrated the day and she'd like to think she wasn't so easily read or manipulated. But two things were clear as she headed off to sleep on sheets of finest Irish linen, sheets that didn't come cheaply. Conall Everard was wooing her approval with all the resources at his disposal from smiles to Irish linen and crystal vases. And, he was using the same strategy to hide something.

She'd nearly overlooked it amid the little treats of

today, all the gifts he'd put in her path. But tonight, with the clarity that came from being alone, she saw it plain. Today had been *too* perfect, Conall had been too affable, his family too accepting. They'd asked her none of the usual questions. She knew what secrets looked like. She had them herself and she hid them in the same ways, secrets that went beyond the shame of her divorce. Secrets she'd go to great lengths to hide and to protect. They were dangerous to her freedom, her Achilles heel. Everyone had one, of course. The question was, what was Conall's? What was it that he didn't want her to see?

Chapter Eight

Conall paced the wide bay of the library window, watching the rain dissipate and trying *not* to watch her with her pale-gold hair put up in a twist that left a few wisps to frame her face. It was a rare woman who pored over reports about alpacas for hours and jotted notes in the margins with the same enthusiasm his sister, Cecilia, devoured the latest feminist tracts from London.

Conall could not recall reacting to a woman so thoroughly in ages, maybe not ever. Certainly he'd not reacted this strongly to Olivia and certainly he'd not expected to still be reacting to Sofia Northcott this way after so much time spent in her company; fourteen days in all if he counted London. One would have thought the newness of her presence would have worn off by now. Wasn't familiarity supposed to breed contempt? If so, it had failed miserably in his case.

If anything, familiarity had enhanced the sensation of her. He was keenly aware when she entered a room. Her presence electrified the space, gave it energy. Even his family noticed. Evenings were more entertaining with Sofia among them. She played backgammon with Freddie, sang and turned pages at the pianoforte with Cecilia, when they weren't avidly discussing women's rights. She stitched with his mother. She fit in very well among the Everards. Of course, that had been the plan. She was supposed to. But it didn't seem like artifice to Conall. He had to tread cautiously here and not get sucked into his own illusion.

As for himself, he spent his days with her in the office, watching her go over the alpaca research while he pretended to conduct estate business from his desk. He might be behind on answering correspondence, but he had her face memorised down to the most intimate details of its design: the delicate curve of her jaw, the pert snub of her nose with its faint freckles across its bridge, the curved pink shell of her ear, the ashy sweep of her lashes.

He'd had a lot of time to notice. She had been at those papers every day since they'd arrived. She came up to the main house in the morning after breakfast and left in the evening. He'd done well the first day, giving her the space and privacy she needed to explore his sources and his conclusions without crowding her. But he'd not been able to stay away.

He attributed it to the suspense. What did she see in the reports? Was there something he'd overlooked?

Was there something that worried her, that might affect her decision to fund the mill? He wanted to be on hand if she had questions. She had very few and he hoped that was a good sign. It was really too late for doubts. The alpacas were here, tucked away in his fields, waiting for the summer shearing, which would be meaningless if he didn't have a mill. It had taken everything he had to get them this far.

The clock was ticking, bringing with it a bittersweet conclusion to their association. Sofia had worked at a feverish pace to assimilate the information. He should want her haste. The faster she invested, the sooner he could breathe easier and the sooner Sofia could leave Everard Hall before she detected the ruse or before her scandal could touch Cecilia's chances for a good Season next year. He should want all those things, but he resented the cost at which those things could be obtained. Once this was settled between them, she'd leave. The thought left a hollow feeling in his chest. Evenings would be less merry without her.

There was a rustle of papers and skirts, a sound that carried a sense of finality to it. She was done with her perusal. Conall turned from the window with a smile, hoping to look relaxed and confident. 'Well? Is all in order or is there something else I might provide you with?'

She laughed and rose, stretching. 'I don't think I could read another page.' She tucked a loose strand of hair behind her ear. 'I think I know everything I need to. You were very thorough.' Her gaze went beyond him to the windows. 'What I do need, though, is fresh air. I think the rain has stopped long enough to permit it. Why don't you show me the alpaca?'

Conall had the gig out front by the time she'd gathered her gloves and hat. He would take her further interest as a good sign. Surely, she wouldn't be asking to see them if she thought the animals were a poor investment.

'I have acreage enough for seventy-five alpaca,' he told her as they drove. 'That amounts to one acre per five animals. There is more land available if this proves to be a success.'

'Seventy-five?' The surprise was evident in her voice. 'Isn't that a bit ambitious?'

Conall shrugged, trying to appear unbothered by the hint of alarm. 'Hardly. Alpaca can be sheared every two years, so my thought is that a herd should be sheared in a staggered rotation. There has to be enough wool every year. Otherwise, production of alpaca woollen goods wouldn't be consistent. There'd be an on year and an off year.' He furrowed his brow, puzzling through the logistics. 'It could be done, I suppose. The mill could alternate the wool it processed every other year.'

'But the profit wouldn't be as great,' she concluded for him. 'With seventy-five alpaca, you'd have the chance to turn a profit within the first year.'

Conall nodded, relieved that she saw the merit in

his strategy. Still, he was asking for a large sum in order to take a large risk, a mill devoted to the production of alpaca wool. They reached the fields and he put on the brake. 'The estate has five fields left over after some tenants moved on to greener pastures, shall we say?' He chuckled. 'We will be able to rotate the herd between them. There should be plenty of grass for forage and it's supplemented with hay and grain.' The dream was near, he could almost touch it. To be foiled now would be devastating on multiple levels. He'd gambled everything on this.

Was this how his father had felt? Euphoria at the prospect of success mixed with gut-clenching worry over the possibility of failure? And then those ventures had failed, over and over again, each one eroding the family coffers a bit further. Was this how it had started for his father? One gamble that was sure to pay off? Only it hadn't. Instead, it had created a need to seek another investment and then another.

Conall flexed his hand at his side, reining in the emergent panicked anger that so often accompanied thoughts of his father these days. He was not his father. He had done his research. This was a safe bet. He hoped Sofia didn't see through him, through the carefully constructed ruse of financial solvency. They'd put out every luxury to show Everard Hall and the family at their best. Would it be enough?

Sofia smiled at him, her blue eyes thoughtful. She was contemplating things, weighing the costs and benefits of all she'd read and all she'd seen. 'Help me down, I want to walk and while we walk, talk to me about the alpacas. Can they only be used for wool?'

'You're thinking of supplementing our income.' Conall came around to swing her down, aware of how light she felt in his arms, the faint scent of basil and thyme in her soap, fragrant and sophisticated, but not heavy like the floral scents worn by other women of the *ton*. This scent was uniquely her.

'There's the milk, which I believe is similar to camel's milk.' Conall offered his arm as they strode through wet grasses. 'I have a friend, Sutton Keynes, with whom I've been corresponding. He has a small camel dairy. The milk is good for young thoroughbreds. Alpaca milk would be a similar product we could market to the racing stables. There would be the alpacas themselves once the herd is established. They can be bred and we can sell alpacas to other interested buyers.'

He paused to sneak a glance at her. He was using 'we' on purpose, already assuming she would come alongside. It was usually a good persuasive strategy. How was it working today? 'And, of course, we could always set up an alpaca syndicate. I had hoped to use the Prometheus Club to do that, but after we've established our base and people see how successful it is, we can run our own syndicate of investors. Cost and profit sharing benefits all parties involved and it's more efficient than one man on his own.'

'You're a man with vision. I like that.' She gave him another of her smiles and it warmed him. He was enjoying this, talking with her, discussing business.

She made a man feel comfortable in her presence, like he could be himself as opposed to a pattern card of some outmoded notion of a gentleman. Was that ease what had drawn Wenderly, or had he seen only a beautiful woman alone?

A loud bray interrupted the conversation as they approached the fence. 'I think we've been spotted.' Conall nodded proudly towards his herd, placidly spread about the acres, grazing.

'What is that sound supposed to be—a baa or a neigh?' Sofia laughed at the noise.

'They sound a lot like camels, actually. At least they look a lot cuter than camels.' Conall grinned. 'All seventy-five made the voyage successfully.' Voyages were hard on animals. His alpaca had arrived underweight, but he could fix that with a few weeks of extra grain.

'They are adorable.' Sofia studied them, her head cocked as she took in their long necks. 'I've never seen anything like them.'

'I want you to meet one.' Conall pulled her forward, pouring some grain into her hand. 'Cup your palms like this,' he demonstrated, holding them up to the fence rail.

She followed suit, laughing when a few bold alpaca pushed their soft noses into her hand and nibbled. 'They're like horses and camels and sheep all rolled into one, maybe a giraffe, too, with those long necks.'

'They are. The ancient Incas used them as pack

animals in the mountains. They're sure-footed like Scottish mountain goats. But their species is related to the camel. They're both camelids.' He laughed. 'And you're not wrong about the giraffe part either. All three, the camel, the giraffe and the alpaca's ancestor, the guanaco, are from the order of mammal, artiodactyl.' He was waxing scientific in his enthusiasm. Was it the alpaca that brought it out or was it Sofia? The way she listened, the way she laughed, as if this was the most enjoyable experience she'd ever had, walking the meadows and talking of alpacas.

She slid him a teasing, sly look. 'Is this what you read about in your pamphlets and treatises? Artiodactyls?'

'Why, yes, it is. Pigs are artiodactyls, too, so it's not just exotics,' he informed her with a playfully exaggerated air of a scholar. 'Do you want to know what else I learned?' He slipped between the rails of the holding pen and took an alpaca by its rope halter. He led it up to the rail where she could pet it. He ran his hand down the alpaca's side. 'Feel here. This outer layer is coarse, it's the guard hairs. Now feel here…' He dug his hands into the thick coat a bit deeper. 'This is the fleece we want. Do you feel how soft it is?'

'Oh, it's wonderful!' Sofia sighed, then frowned, worry in her eyes. 'It doesn't hurt them, does it? To lose their coats?'

'No,' he assured her. 'It's healthy. Carrying around a full, thick coat in the summer can lead to heat complications. That's why England is such a prime location. The climate doesn't get too hot for too long. We'll shear a third of the flock this year. June is the best month for shearing, that way there's time for the coat to grow back before winter.' Conall sobered. There would be a 'we'. He and his tenants and Freddie. But she would be gone by then no matter how this deal went.

Sofia stroked the soft side of the patient alpaca. 'Tell me again, how much did you want?' It was the merest of whispers, as if asking too loudly increased her level of commitment.

Conall's answer came back in a whisper only slightly louder. 'Fifteen thousand pounds.'

Sofia let out a low, unladylike whistle. 'Are they worth it?'

'Wool is life,' Conall answered without hesitation. 'Wool brings work and regular wages that aren't reliant on the caprices of a good harvest or weather, it brings industry and progress, not just with factories and mills but with roads and transportation, both of which are needed to get products to market.'

'Taunton already has mills,' she ventured in quiet rebuttal. But he was ready for her argument. He grinned and opened the bag he'd slung over his shoulder and pulled out a blanket.

'Madame, I give you exhibit one.' He shook it open and laid it out on the grass.

'No! Don't do that,' Sofia protested quickly. 'The grass is still wet from the rain, it will get soaked.'

He gave her a game smile and did it anyway. 'Please, sit.'

Sofia looked at the square sceptically, unwilling to get her skirts wet. For encouragement, Conall sat and patted the space next to him. 'You won't get wet, I promise. Trust me, Sofia.'

Trust him. She wanted to, Sofia realised. It had been a long time since she'd trusted anyone. It would be nice, just this once, to be able to trust someone; to trust that he spoke the truth, that he wasn't hiding something from her, that he wasn't just after the money or her body. And maybe she could trust him. Since she'd been here, he'd not importuned her in any way, he'd not made suggestive remarks, had not treated her the way men usually did once they knew of her divorce.

Sofia gathered her skirts and prepared to sit. She would put Conall to the test. If she was wrong, she'd only have wet skirts. She'd paid higher prices. Did Conall realise how much more than money was riding on this? A verse from childhood surfaced. *A man honest with little, is honest with much, but a dishonest man with little, is dishonest with much.* It was the smallest of tests, but for her it had become a defining moment that would mark the quality of Conall's character. Sofia sat, fearing that she would find the very flaw she'd been looking for, that all along Conall Everard had been nothing but a handsome, charming, overly optimistic viscount with no head for business.

Her skirts were dry! Sofia let out a breath she hadn't realised she was holding. She knit her brow, running her fingers along the surface of the soft wool in puzzlement. 'How can this be? Wool absorbs water, it gets wet,' she argued against the proof of her eyes.

Conall gave an enigmatic smile. 'Alpaca wool is waterproof. Look.' He reached into his bag again and brought out two samples. 'This is alpaca wool. Do you see how the fibre is hollow? Now look at the sheep's wool.' He held out the second fibre. 'There's air pockets. It's not entirely hollow. Here's what that means. The hollow alpaca fibre traps heat better and, thus, it has better wicking capabilities.' He flipped up a corner of the blanket and exposed the underside. '*This* is wet. But *we're* not. The alpaca fibres keep it from our skin. The wetness never reaches us.'

Sofia fingered the wet wool, deep in thought, seeing the possibilities: mountain climbers, travellers, explorers would want this product. Even the day-tripper on a picnic would want this given the rather fitful quality of English weather in general. The Royal Geographical Society would be interested in including it on expeditions, there would be prestige in that. Carriage makers could include a blanket with purchase. Perhaps they could design a crest to go in the corner of the blanket, make it a status symbol. *They.* She'd best be careful with her pronouns. There would be no 'they'.

'Is it a better insulator, too?'

'Absolutely. Again, all thanks to the hollow tube,' Conall replied.

She could see the possibilities, his vision, her dream, all rolled into one neat package. It was time to gather her courage. 'Very well, then, I've made my decision. I have a proposition for you.' She could feel Conall's body tense in the space between them as he waited for her verdict. 'I don't want to offer you a loan. I want to offer you a partnership.'

Chapter Nine

To his credit, Conall took the offer thoughtfully. 'What are your terms of partnership?'

'I'll purchase the mill. You may have daily oversight of the mill, but I will decide how it's run. There will be no employing of children, no long hours. The mill won't run on Sundays and only a half-day on Saturday. There will be a decent wage. There will be a school for the children whose parents work there.' She outlined her terms, her eyes steady on his, watching to see if he'd flinch, to see if she'd misjudged him.

She'd never met a man like him before—a titled man with a selfless vision. She'd been touched by his talk of jobs, to build something useful for the region. *When it sounds too good to be true, it probably is.* Except when it was.

She'd been persistence itself these past weeks, digging through research, looking for a flaw, for his flaw. Surely, there had to be one. There always was. She'd worked with enough men to know and yet she hadn't found one.

Conall had questions. 'What of the profit, then, if you're giving it all away in wages and infrastructure? Wool will only sell for so much.'

'*Sheep's* wool will only sell for so much,' Sofia corrected easily, unbothered by the debate. 'Alpaca wool is a luxury, as you've pointed out. It's new. It can command any price it wants if we market it right.'

'We? Where will you be in all of this? Do you mean to stay indefinitely?'

What did she hear in his voice? Worry that she would taint him by long-term association? Or did she hear something different? Intrigue as to what the possibility of staying might hold? He *did* like her. Of that, she was certain.

She'd seen the signs, been aware of his gaze lingering as they worked. Her conscience was quick to play the pessimist. *Of course, he doesn't know what you're running from. If he did, he wouldn't like you so much. He couldn't. Viscounts aren't made for social lepers.* But this one needed money and she needed protection. He'd protected her once already. Perhaps he would do it again. Protection seemed to come to him innately. In exchange for investing, he could protect her dream. He would oversee the mill and its development according to her plans. He could be here when she could not. That was what this proposal was about—protecting her dream of building a safer world from Giancarlo. To do that, she needed Taunton to be her steward in her absence.

That was all. *It was most definitely not about her.* Sofia's ever-present conscience put a fast halt to that line of thought. She wasn't going to marry again. She wasn't ever going to give a man that kind of power over her. It made no sense to marry one man in order to escape marriage to another. She'd fought for her freedom for too long. Besides, Conall would never forgive her for the scandal, for tainting his family if she stayed. It was too much to ask of any man, even a good one. So she said simply, 'I will check in from time to time, but I have other business interests to look after as well.' But she wasn't sure if that was regret or relief she saw on his face.

Instead, she determined to make the most of this glorious day. The sun was warm on her face and the blanket was dry. There was no better place to be than right here, in this meadow, right now. She leaned back on her hands, contemplating the man beside her. 'How is it that you know so much about alpaca? I think it must come from more than reading tracts.'

'Is this an interrogation, Miss Northcott?' Conall teased, accommodating her change of conversation.

'I like to call it curiosity.' She laughed. She was curious about him in a way that went beyond business, a way in which she'd thought she might not ever be curious about a man again. Perhaps it was good to know she wasn't dead inside, that Giancarlo hadn't destroyed that part of her. But it was terribly inconvenient. She'd grown used to complete objectivity. One could not be objective while mentally stripping one's client out of their clothes.

'Well then, for the sake of curiosity.' Conall indulged her with a smile. 'I did my Grand Tour in the Americas. While my friends were sightseeing in the great museums of Europe, I was hiking in the Appalachians, sailing in the Caribbean and climbing the Andes in South America.'

'Why did you go to America?' Sofia picked at a blade of grass, suddenly self-conscious of their proximity on the small blanket in conjunction with her earlier thoughts. Conall Everard had been one surprise after another from the moment he'd walked into the Duchess's sitting room and these revelations had only heightened his appeal.

'My father preferred it. He told me once that this world of ours was dying. How long did we think the aristocracy could hold out against technology if we didn't adapt? He always encouraged me to look ahead. He believed we couldn't afford to live in the past.' He chuckled and gave her a stern look. 'I spent three years over there, arguably the best three years of my life, to date.'

'A very different three years from mine,' Sofia mused. That explained why he did not recall her—more specifically, why he didn't recall the scandal of her. 'While I was being hustled out of the schoolroom and into a hasty marriage, you were packing your trunks for America. Yet another difference between English men and women. At eighteen, a woman is deemed ripe for marriage. At twenty-one and unmarried, she is deemed nearly ready for the shelf.'

Conall laughed. 'You and Cecilia think alike.'

She gave him a coy look and continued her argument. 'Perhaps because it's true. A man at eighteen is continuing his education and at twenty-one is on a Grand Tour, still transitioning from adolescence into adulthood, a role, by the way, which society doesn't expect he'll fully take on until his thirties while a woman in her thirties is well past her prime, her children nearly grown themselves.'

'I won't say you're wrong, or that the condition is right,' Conall acceded graciously and then asked solemnly, his eyes meeting hers, 'Was your marriage awful?'

She looked down at the grass. They'd not spoken of anything personal; not her marriage, or the burglary, since the train. But the desire to travel a little further down those paths lingered despite their best attempts to ignore it. What could it hurt now that business was nearly concluded? She would be gone in a few days, vanishing into England, somewhere Giancarlo couldn't find her, somewhere no one could find her. It was a condition of the latter. To escape Giancarlo, she had to give up the few friends she had for fear he might find her through them.

'Yes,' she said after a while. 'I would not leave my

marriage on a whim. No woman would choose this if there was anything to redeem in her marriage.' Sofia waved a hand to indicate the half-world of divorce.

'I didn't mean to imply you would,' Conall said softly, waiting for her to continue.

She picked at the grass again. 'There was nothing to redeem. No children, no affection. Nothing that mattered. He was unfaithful, but that was the least of his failings.' Towards the end she had welcomed his infidelities, as long as they kept his attentions elsewhere.

Against her better judgement, she let her eyes drift to his face, her gaze lingering on his mouth—on the thin, sensual aristocratic line of his lips, the straightness of his teeth, the slight crook of his smile. What would it be like to kiss a good man? They were so close, nearly touching, their fingertips inches from each other on the blanket. All she needed to do was lean in and she could taste that mouth, taste *him*—his trust, his goodness, his truth. Maybe she could taste him, as long as she was the one doing the kissing, as long as the kiss was her choice. That was the one thing her marriage had taken from her. She'd had no choice, no consent in what was done to her and all else had crumbled from there.

Sofia leaned in.

His lips were there, as if they'd been waiting for her, warm and welcoming. She'd meant for it to be a light buss, but she couldn't resist the temptation to sink into the invitation of his mouth, into the strength of him for the briefest of moments. He smelled of starch and sunlight, the scents of spring and clean man.

'What was that for?' Conall breathed the words against her lips, his mouth hovering just above hers. He was in no hurry to move away. His hand was at the nape of her neck, tangling in her hair, keeping her close while letting her drive the interlude.

'An apology.' She sighed. 'I was wrong about you. You could have charmed me, flirted my approval out of me, or at least tried. A lesser man would have.' She kissed him again, slowly, deeply, wanting it to last.

'And this kiss?' She could feel Conall's smile against her mouth.

'That was "thank you". Thank you for not lying. For telling the truth about what I'm investing in,' she murmured, her body wanting more; one kiss might have given her a taste, but now she was hungry for the feast.

Conall let her take his mouth in a third kiss, as if he understood the kiss had to be hers. But the response could be his. He answered this kiss with an assertiveness that surpassed the previous kisses. Where they had been gentle, this kiss was insistent. Where they had contained an element of the tentative, this was all bold certainty. She knew the message. Here was a man who knew the pleasures of a kiss, who wanted to share those pleasures with her. For a moment, she let him. It was her decision to relinquish the kiss to him, to see where he might lead them.

He drew her with his tongue, his hand at her nape guiding, his mouth deepening the kiss until it became a languid duel between them. She answered, letting her body be swept away on the current rising between them like the lazy swirl of a summer river.

Her own fingertips found his face, they traced his jawbone. This was what afternoons were for: long, slow kisses of exploration. Now she knew what it felt like to be kissed by him and that had to be enough. She pulled back slowly, unwilling to relinquish the moment, but knowing that if it continued it would lead to a place she did not want to go. This could not happen again. It could go nowhere. 'My apologies, I should not have,' she said. 'Sometimes it's hard to remember there are good men in the world, that not everything has a rotten core.'

She gave a tremulous smile and took one last look at his face. It was time to end this foolishness. She stood up and brushed at her skirts. 'Thank you for indulging me. You needn't worry this will get in the way of our business. I will write the necessary letters tonight.'

Conall gripped her arm gently, as they walked to the gig. 'But first, we'll celebrate.' He grinned. 'You never did ask me if I accepted your terms. Were you that sure of yourself?'

'Is that a yes?' She gave him another smile, one meant to be brighter. She hoped it succeeded.

'It is indeed. I'd suggest we seal it with a kiss, but it seems we've already done that.'

Tonight they would celebrate. Then she'd be free to leave. He would have his mill and her dream would have its steward. They'd both be safe from her fantasies. It was too bad the solution didn't make her feel happier. Deep down, she had to admit she was in no hurry to go for reasons that had nothing to do with business and everything to do with their kisses. Today she'd invested fifteen thousand pounds—nearly all she had—in those reasons, perhaps both business and pleasure. It was a small fortune. A woman could live comfortably off that sum for years. Or, she could build a future. She'd decided to build a future for herself and for others. It was a great gamble, trusting this man. But even if he failed, she'd still have the mill, still have some semblance of her dream intact. It was as safe as gambles got.

Sofia shielded her eyes against the brightness of the afternoon sun on the drive home. She could see the house from the top of the hill. At a distance, Everard Hall was the embodiment of security. It was impenetrable, as if nothing bad could touch it. And it might even be true, Sofia thought. She'd gone through the papers and the research on alpacas, looking for some sign that all was not as it seemed. But she'd found nothing alarming. There was no investment scam here. Conall Everard and Everard Hall were everything they claimed to be.

The idea was intoxicating and part of her wanted to believe in it. What if this place was truly impenetrable, truly a place where her husband wouldn't find her? What if she could be safe here? They were foolish notions. Conall would not tolerate anyone, not even her, putting Everard Hall in jeopardy. If he knew she was hunted, if he knew the magnitude of her husband's depravity, he would not allow anyone to draw such evil to this place. He would turn her out at once. It was one of the reasons for her haste. She wanted to leave with the illusion intact, not with Conall furious that her very presence had endangered his family and his home.

There was no sanctuary for her. There was an irony that her dream was to provide sanctuaries for others but there were none for her. What sanctuary she had was behind the flimsy protection of Barnham's name and the ability to run at any moment. Of course she couldn't stay in Somerset. She could stay nowhere for long, not with Il Marchese hunting her. A piece of paper declaring them legally parted would not stop him. Her husband would simply take her if he found her.

Chapter Ten

Giancarlo had been in no hurry to leave his bed, warm and full as it was with two rather talented women. As a result, he was in a better mood than usual when he finally sent for his secretary far later into the day. But what was the use of being a *marchese* if one couldn't take one's pleasures at will?

Giancarlo gazed out over the *piazza*, sipping his strong, hot espresso as he listened to his secretary's report, the contentment of his mood evaporating with each line. His secretary set aside the letter and waited while the news settled in. The bottom line was this: after two weeks of searching, Sofia was nowhere to be found. His man had lost her. Or perhaps she'd never been found. The evidence to the latter was starting to mount; she had not returned to her ruined home and she had not filed a complaint with the London constabulary. Both non-actions begged several questions: did she know about the house? Was she in London? Had she received his earlier letters? Did she even know he was hunting her?

Of all the questions raised, it was this last that bothered him most. He shifted uncomfortably in his chair. The only joy in this whole tiresome process of bringing her home was the knowledge that she'd be terrified. Now that was in question. She might be blithely going about her life in England, wherever that might be, oblivious to the trouble she was causing him. He thought about the studded crop in his wardrobe. It had a way of making a woman less oblivious to him. When he had her back, it would teach her the folly of ignoring him.

'She can't have disappeared.' He fixed his secretary with a sharp gaze. 'Was there an appointment diary at the house? A calling card from a friend? Notes? Letters? Anything that might indicate where she spends her time or who she spends it with?'

'I don't know, Marchese,' the secretary said with no small amount of trepidation. Good, at least one person had the sense to respect his authority. 'The letter doesn't say.'

The letter. Not a telegram like last time. Telegrams were so much faster, so much more immediate. A wave of anger surged. This was delayed news! 'When was the letter sent?' he snapped, reaching for the paper. Giancarlo scanned the report. It had been two-and-a-half weeks since this useless tripe was written. His grip tightened about the handle of his espresso cup. This was just another failure in a series of failures.

'Che palle!' Giancarlo swore loudly. How hard could it be to track down a woman alone, a woman in disgrace who had no one to support her? He'd tracked her this far, he wasn't going to lose her scent now when he needed to curry the monarch's favour. He had not necessarily liked the old King, but the man had been far more progressive than his son in regards to marital arrangements. His son did not favour divorce under any circumstance. Much had changed in the past three years.

He sighed and eyed the remaining pile of post with disappointment. 'Have we heard from her family?' It was long odds that he had, although he'd written to them immediately after Victor Emmanuel had issued his personal edict. Her family had been quite malleable the first time he'd approached them thirteen years ago with enough money to dazzle them. He'd chosen his quarry well: a family of landed gentry who lived far above their station and, consequently, struggled financially. He'd hoped they'd be malleable again. Sofia's father spent money at an alarming rate. No doubt the man would be eager for more by now, eager enough to return his daughter to her rightful husband if she was with them. The last was the gamble. Would Sofia go home to Yorkshire? Or had she finally taken her family's measure and washed her hands of them? He preferred the latter. Fewer people to deal with, fewer people to bribe. Even if her father was willing to turn her over to him, the greedy English bastard would want to use it to his advantage. Giancarlo would have no choice but to pay a second time for what he'd already purchased once at fair market value—a wife who'd caused him nothing but trouble.

Giancarlo rose and stuffed his hands into the deep pockets of his satin dressing gown. The solution to his situation was obvious and disappointing. He'd wanted to avoid this. 'Send for my valet and make the necessary arrangements. I will have to sort this out myself.' He was going to England. When he found her there would be hell to pay with interest. He smiled coldly to himself, feeling marginally better. He preferred immediate gratification when it came to his pleasures, but pleasure deferred had its merits, too, if one knew just how to extract them.

Sofia was procrastinating. She slid a guilty glance sideways on the gig seat, watching Conall at the reins, the early summer breeze pushing at his hair. He seemed happy and content this morning, but she knew she didn't have much time remaining. It had been over a week since the celebratory dinner announcing the purchase of the mill. She could have produced the contracts at any time. All she had to do was write them out and she had. She just hadn't told Conall they were done.

Now, here it was, day nine since he'd agreed to her partnership and the contracts still needed to be finalised. She kept coming up with details: a visit to the mill, another meeting with the mill's owner while she claimed one more day of peace.

This morning, she'd run out of legitimate particulars. Even now, the contract and other papers were drawn up and signed, lying safely in a drawer in the Dower House while she went fishing with Conall.

It was not plausible for the contract to be delayed any longer, nor was it fair. She was keeping too many secrets from him as it was. It wasn't only secrets and time that were running against her. For all his contentment this morning, Conall was getting edgy, too, although he tried to hide it. She saw the disappointment etch itself in small ways about his eyes and the tightness of his mouth each passing day that didn't bring the contracts to a close. She didn't want to cause him anxiety, yet she didn't want to go. *One more day.* She wanted one more day with his family, one more day in this beautiful world of his and, most of all, she wanted one more day with him. Why not take it? She hadn't had word from Giancarlo for over a month. She was starting to feel safe. Even as she allowed herself to think it, she chastised herself. That kind of thinking was dangerous. The one moment she didn't look over her shoulder was the one moment she should. She knew better than that. She had signed the contracts this morning and arranged to have them sent up to the house while she and Conall were out. They'd be waiting for him when they returned. She'd promised herself today would be the last.

The gig hit a rut in the road and she gripped the seat rail to steady herself, laughing as her other hand reached up to catch the brim of her hat. 'We're nearly there.' Conall chuckled at her efforts and pointed to the river, glittering in the distance.

Sofia slanted him a smile. Nearly there and still so far. What did she want from this man? He had not kissed her since their outing to the alpaca meadow. But he'd wanted to, she had seen as much in his eyes when they walked in the gardens of an evening after she and Freddie held their nightly backgammon game. Instead, he'd held himself in check. Perhaps out of respect for her, perhaps because he guessed at what lay beneath the surface of her marriage, or maybe because there was no point in kissing her again, as much as they'd both enjoyed it. She would be leaving soon. There could be nothing serious.

Perhaps the better question was what did she want for herself? *Was* she ready to pursue a sampling of intimacy? Marriage had not recommended physical intimacy to her. Giancarlo had been mentally and physically cruel to her. She was coming to understand, through Helena's marriage, and Conall's own innate courtesies, that what had passed for intimacy in her marriage was a false representation. She didn't know intimacy at all. Did she want to? Did she want to trust a man again? Her critical mind assessed the risk. If the opportunity presented itself, perhaps she should pursue it, especially if she could control it as she had the kiss. If it disappointed her, she was leaving anyway. And if it suited her? her conscience asked, already putting forth the idea that Conall would likely not disappoint. Well, she'd still have to leave, but at least she'd know.

Would Conall be open to that experiment? He was not the sort of man who would make love to a woman not his wife under his family's roof with his family in residence. But today was different. Today, they were alone, they weren't under anyone's roof, maybe not under anyone's codes but their own. Sofia sighed and smiled to herself. She'd wondered what it would be like to receive the affections of a good man. Now she knew—those affections were both generous and frustrating.

The Tone was a wide, placid silver ribbon that ran south-east after leaving Taunton. These particular six miles of its twenty-one-mile run, were, according to Conall, the best stretch of fishing on the river. 'There's carp, tench, grayling, sometimes even a salmon.' Conall gave her a wide grin, finding a shady place to park the gig. 'We should be able to set up our camp right over there.' He was all easy authority, gathering up their supplies from the bed of the gig with an alacrity that spoke of experience.

'You've done this before.' Sofia laughed, reaching for the basket. 'Let me carry something. I want to make myself useful.'

They were efficient and in a few minutes the camp was made, a small fire burning in anticipation of a fish lunch and blankets spread on the ground beside a hamper and two empty creels waiting to be filled.

'Are you ready?' Conall handed her a pole which she took gingerly.

Conall eyed her for a moment, realisation dawning with a healthy dose of incredulity. 'Have you never been fishing?'

'No...' She hesitated, feeling entirely at sea with the admission. Perhaps she should have disclosed that earlier before they'd left the house but if this was to be their last day together, she'd been determined to enjoy it to the fullest.

Sofia held out the pole for him to take back. 'I can watch you fish, though. That will be just as much fun.' Especially for her. She could look at him all she liked, storing up a hundred different mental pictures of him. He was clearly anticipating a day of fishing and she didn't want to ruin his excitement. He was boyishly handsome in his enjoyment. This was a different side of the handsome, well-dressed Viscount and she liked this earthy version.

'No,' he said simply. He cocked his head, studying her. 'Watching is *not* as much fun.' He thrust the pole back at her. 'You're going to learn to fish and I'm going to teach you. Are you game?'

He didn't wait for a response; perhaps he knew her well enough by now to know there was only one answer. He bent down and opened one of the creels.

'Lesson one, you have to bait the hook.' He held up a small piece of fish. 'Chubb pieces are perfect for this river.'

He did all the baiting, but she watched dutifully, admiring the deftness of his hands setting hooks and organising lines. Mental picture one, she decided, would be of his hands. He had wonderful hands, long and well-boned, competence mixed with elegance.

Hook baited, he turned to her. 'Now, we wade. You'd best get those shoes and socks off, miss.' He gave orders with a twinkle in his eye, his gaze moving to the river. 'And tie up your skirts. It's still spring and the water's higher than it is in the summer.' Conall was already pulling off his boots and rolling up trousers to reveal tanned well-muscled calves.

'This is highly unorthodox behaviour, my lord,' Sofia teased. She sat down on a log and removed her footwear, her gaze sliding to Conall's bare legs. Naughty assumptions flitted through her mind. Was the rest of his body as tanned and as muscled? Certainly there was evidence to support that from their dance at Cowden's. There was other proof, too. She looked away, blushing, remembering their kiss. His chest had been granite hard where she'd pressed against it.

Sofia gathered her skirts to one side and tied them in a knot, doubly glad she hadn't worn a gown requiring crinolines of any sort, and Conall reached out a hand. 'Ready to fish?' He grinned.

'Absolutely.' She gripped his hand and let him lead her to the water, which was cold, but it didn't faze Conall so she went doggedly in, refusing to back down from this friendly challenge. The cold water was worth it. Conall moved behind her, wrapping his arms about her, those competently elegant hands covering hers as they held the pole, the heat of him filling her.

'We'll start with a simple overhead cast,' he instructed, putting her left hand over the butt of the pole, drawing it against her body and positioning her right hand further up. The rod bent. 'It bends because it's baited. The chubb weighs it down. Now, we cast.' In a fluid movement, he directed the line over their shoulders and out into the river where the line and rod promptly straightened and the lure swiftly sank. 'Not bad. The trick to a good cast is to get the line out to where the fish are. It's not so hard in a river like this, but in a wider river where you can't go out as far as you'd like, you have to let the line do the work for you.' His voice was low at her ear, playing all nature of havoc with her senses. Good heavens, she'd not thought fishing could be so sensual.

'Now what?' Her voice was husky, a betrayal of how intoxicating she found this moment. He surrounded her in all ways: the smell of him, the sound of him, the touch of him. Had it ever felt this good to be with a man? This easy? She didn't have to please him, didn't have to flirt with him. She simply had to *be*. No games. It would be better if there were.

Games had rules, outcomes, clear winners and losers. She was off balance here.

'Now, we wait.' There was laughter and mischief in his voice. His hands flexed over hers. 'A fisherman might stand in the river all day waiting for the right fish.' She liked the sound of that. She could stand here all day with his arms about her. How novel, given that she'd never been this close to a man outside a dance, or outside her husband's bedroom. The old fear tried to grip her. This time, she pushed back. She would not let those thoughts insinuate themselves into this glorious day. Not all men were her husband. Not all touch was meant to denigrate. Conall had never pressed her.

'What do you do while you stand here and wait?' Her feet were either numb or they'd acclimated to the temperature.

'Hmm. I think. I sort through my thoughts. It's quiet out here. I cannot be disturbed, my thoughts cannot be polluted with contingencies and interruptions. Many fishermen are self-prescribed philosophers.' He chuckled. 'Do you think you can handle it from here?' She was tempted to say no, wanting to keep his body close, but that would be a lie. She was more than capable of standing in the water by herself.

He stepped apart from her, then, brandishing his own pole with an expert's relish. He cast out his line in a fluid motion that belied the notion anyone could fish. Anyone could stand in a river, she was proof of that, but he was something else: graceful, athletic, his movements smooth. He cast again, and again, a mesmerising dance of line and man. The act consumed him entirely like the Palio riders she'd seen once in Siena, at one with their horses, deaf to the cries of the crowd, to everything except the rhythm of their mounts. And sweet heavens it was…arousing…to watch him fish. It made a woman wonder what it would be like to be the recipient of such attention. Her earlier thoughts in the gig lapped at the shores of temptation. Did she dare take the experiment? To have him lose himself in her as he lost himself in the river. Where was his mind now? What thoughts claimed his attention today?

A tug pulled at her line. 'I've got something!' Sofia cried.

'Stay calm, we want to bring it in slowly,' Conall directed from where he stood. 'Turn the handle to bring in the line and let's see what we have.'

What she had was a beautiful, silvery iridescent carp that fought her efforts every tug of the way, its breathing laboured as its watery habitat gave way and its struggles grew more futile, but no less persistent. No matter how it fought, it couldn't free itself.

She couldn't do it. Sofia dropped the line and fell to her knees in the water, her hands groping for the carp. 'Help me, help me.' She was splashing aimlessly, making a hash of the line as she sought the fish.

In an instant, Conall was beside her in the water, splashing beside her. 'What are you doing, Sofia?'

'Freeing him. I have to save him.' Panic rose in her voice. She couldn't take its life. She knew what it meant to be forced, to know that all of one's efforts meant nothing in the end.

'I've got it, he's safe now.' Conall's voice was calm, his competent hands freeing the fish, the carp swimming off. Then he was lifting her out of the river, carrying her to the blankets and the little fire. She was starting to shake. 'He's safe, but you're soaked.' Conall reached for the spare blanket and wrapped it around her shoulders. 'There, that should help. You'll be warm in a moment.'

'I couldn't kill it. That's what reeling a fish in is, it's killing. All because they dared to grab the brass ring, because they dared to reach for more. They didn't know.' Her voice was a whisper now as she struggled not to go to pieces. 'They didn't know the brass ring was just an illusion.' Conall's arm was about her and she gave in to the temptation of his shoulder.

She really oughtn't to have done it. Every bone in her body knew it, screamed with the reality of it. Conall was an illusion, too. There were no brass rings, there were no safe havens. Not for her and, if he truly knew her, there would be none for him either. She'd lured Conall with lies and façades. She could not have him, could not keep him. She could only steal a few moments. Besides, even if she could have him, the price would be more than she wanted to pay.

She trembled against him. The enormity of the last six weeks caught up with her, overwhelming her. She'd entered society, however briefly. She'd faced her husband's threat to reclaim her, a threat juxtaposed against the awakening of her own unlooked-for desires for another man. The timing was beyond inconvenient. She'd promised herself she would never belong to any man again. Perhaps one day she would revisit that promise, but it could not be now. She could not break that promise when she was hunted by a man who would drag her back to hell, who would not free her from the hook, and another who teased her with glimpses of heaven.

There were no brass rings. There was no heaven if she fell, only hell. But for a while there could be limbo, that intermediate position where there was both nothing and something. In limbo, there could be kisses and maybe more as long as it led nowhere and required nothing, no promises, no revelations. She made a deal with her devils. She could have Conall to hold the demons at bay, if she left him in the end. That was the only way this could work.

Sofia lifted her head, her eyes finding his for a long moment before dropping to his mouth in the silent, age-old request: *kiss me.*

Chapter Eleven

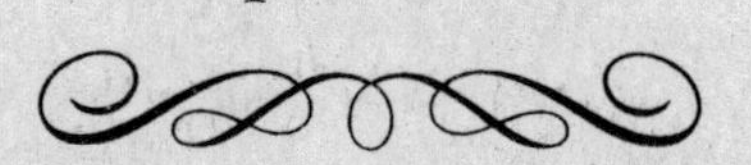

Y*es, this was what she wanted.* Conall's mouth took hers with eagerness, his hands tangling in her hair. He gave her his mouth, his touch, his kisses, his comfort and she gave herself over to him, to the reassurance that comes from being with another body, from the feel of another's touch. He would give her more if she asked. His own mouth was hungry, his own body wanting to feast. The tenseness of his muscles beneath her hands suggested he was keeping himself in check, waiting for her to set the pace, to exert her control on the interlude. He would not use her vulnerability to sate his own appetites, that she could trust him.

He sucked at her lower lip, his teeth sinking in lightly. A little moan escaped her. She pressed her body into his, an invitation to a kiss that encompassed not only mouths but bodies as well, and he took it. She let him lower her back on to the blanket, let him cover her with his length. She wrapped her arms about him, her own hands buried deep in the thick walnut depths of his hair. She could feel his own arousal rising; she could feel, too, that he was not ashamed by it. How she wished she could keep this moment for ever, where she wasn't a plaything for a man's gratification, where there was pleasure for her. And, oh, how she wished she was brave enough to ask for more of it.

Sofia moved her hips against his, her tongue licking the tender flesh of his earlobe, laughing softly when it elicited the catch of his own breath and a small, frustrated groan. Intuitively, she knew Conall would not disappoint, just as she knew asking for more would commit her down a path that might prove difficult to extricate herself from later for many reasons, not the least being simple want. She might not want to extricate herself. All her promises broken at her own behest.

Conall's hand shaped her breast through the wet bodice of her gown, pulling the fabric taut until she was sure he could see the outline of her nipple, and then his mouth descended, suckling and nipping until her hips arched and the chill of her body was chased away by the warmth of want. She wanted his mouth everywhere at once: at her breast, at her lips, at the very core of her where she was damp and burning all at once. It would be the work of a few words to direct his attentions there. If she dared, pleasure could be hers. Out here in the open by the river, she could claim what had eluded ten years of marriage.

No. She would not use him like that. Sofia forced herself to break off the kiss, the caress. She owed him better than that. He didn't know her. He *thought* he did. But that glimpse she'd allotted him was only a sliver of what lay beneath the surface. She would not take any more from him until he knew better, until he understood his choice.

'Would you like some warmed wine?' Conall rolled to his feet, his voice husky, but she saw the questions in his eyes. Why had she broken it off? Why had she stopped? 'I brought wine and bread. It will just take a moment to heat.' He was already reaching for the hamper and the straw-bottomed fiasco inside. 'A nice red from France.' He grinned as he held up the bottle.

'To go with our fish.' Sofia made a pout and gathered the blanket about her, the chill returning in the absence of his warmth. 'I've ruined your lunch.' She watched him pour the wine into a pan and balance it on the grill over the fire.

'Hardly. We have bread, wine, blue skies, sunshine and good company. One cannot ask for more.' This was the second time he'd cooked for her. Conall bent over the fire, checking the wine, his trousers pulled tight over the muscled curves of his buttocks, reminding her that his clothes were damp, too. A shiver went through her.

Conall noticed. 'You should get out of those wet

things. We'll lay them next to the fire and they'll be dry in no time.' As if to encourage her, he pulled his shirt over his head and hung it on a low branch, oblivious to the fact that her mouth had just gone dry. He was magnificently made, all elegant muscles and sinew, and *tan*. There wasn't a pasty white inch on him. He turned towards the fire and lifted the pan, presenting her with a glorious view of his back, muscles flexing with each motion as they tapered to a lean waist and buttock rounds. *They* would be white, she thought with a secret smile, her mind already imagining.

He poured the heated wine into a tin camp cup and brought it to her with a scold. 'You're still dressed. Wet clothes are the fastest way to a cold. Don't be stubborn for propriety's sake, Sofia. There's no one to see us for miles and I will not ravish you.'

More was the pity. It might be nice to be ravished by him, a mischievous portion of her thought; to have him decide for her how far things could go. No. Control was her only weapon, her only defence as she went tentatively down this new path of intimacy. Even so, the idea was quickly quashed by other more practical concerns. Even if she was in a position to entertain a consummated relationship, she wasn't going to undress in front of him. It would expose too much, would invite too many questions about a past she wanted to forget.

'I'll be fine.' Sofia took the wine, wrapping her

hands around the heat of the cup, but a sneeze belied her words.

Conall took back the cup. 'You're not fine. Take off your clothes or you'll have a fever by nightfall. I promise not to look.'

She humphed at that. 'You make me sound like a petty juvenile.'

'Well?' Conall arched an eyebrow. 'Perhaps you are.'

She sneezed again. Maybe he had a point. She could not risk a fever. It would leave her bedridden and weak, vulnerable. What if Giancarlo found her and she couldn't physically run? She rose and scouted the area for a discreet clump of bushes. She would keep the blanket close. She would be safe.

Conall spread Sofia's wet things near the fire and poured himself a cup of the heated wine, conscious that he was alone with a naked woman wrapped in a blanket and he was hot enough as a result. The woman was temptation for a saint on a good day. But the sight of her sitting beside the fire with her hair down took temptation to a whole new level. She was stunning and vulnerable and hungry for him. She wanted him or whatever she thought he could provide her. That much had been evident earlier and it had shaken him how much her desire had found an echo in his own. He sliced up the bread and toasted it over the fire to give himself something to do besides stare. He'd been with beautiful women before.

He was surrounded by them in London as *de rigueur*. The Season was full of them. But none like her, none who spoke their mind, who asked for what she wanted.

'Toast, too. I am impressed. You're quite the outdoorsman. Where did you learn to do all of this?' Sofia ran her fingers through the tangle of her hair, a gesture that was innocently sensual.

'My father.' Conall flipped the bread over. 'He would take me fishing and we'd build a camp like this one. Sometimes, in the summer, we'd stay overnight and sleep under the stars. He believed a man should be self-sufficient regardless of his title or station in life.' And yet, he'd left his family in debt, one too many investments gone bad in the pursuit of such self-sufficiency. He passed Sofia the first piece of toast. 'Some day I'll make you a slice with melted cheese on it.'

'Do you think I'll stay that long?' She laughed and gave him an appropriately coy look, but he detected a brittleness beneath. They were dancing too close to the subject of her nearly overstayed welcome and the contract's imminent arrival.

'You might,' he answered, not looking away from her, forcing her to acknowledge the current that ran between them. This was the third time that current had flared. They'd not talked about any of the kisses, the touches, the heat that was present whenever they were together. It would be dangerous to ignore it, to pretend it didn't exist much longer when it clearly did, and if it continued on its trajectory, they would reach a place where they did not stop at kisses and caresses through wet clothes.

She slanted him a teasing look. 'You do tempt a girl, Conall Everard.'

It was laughingly said, but Conall answered her gaze with a more serious stare of his own. 'Do I tempt you?' He thought he'd tempted her a few minutes ago, but she'd cut it off without warning. He was in deep waters now. What if they gave in to that temptation? Would it satisfy their mutual curiosity and be done or would it reveal something more? What was he angling for from her? An affair? What could he offer her beyond that? He knew the answer to both and it was no and nothing. She was already supporting his mill, a clear reminder that he had nothing to offer other than a title that needed propping up. But it wasn't just the practical issues. He could not offer her his heart. That was far too risky, especially if she claimed it. Then he could be hurt again, betrayed again, as his father's death had hurt him. Love itself was the greatest illusion of all.

Conall rose, feeling the need to create some distance. Things between them had a habit of becoming intimate so quickly. That day in the meadow, today on the river banks—both were evidence of just how fast things could escalate and of the headiness that came with it. She left him spinning until he hardly recognised himself. 'If you'll be all right, I think I'll fish for a while.' He made up some nonsense about his mother expecting fish tonight.

'I'd rather you sit with me.' Her words were bold. 'I should explain about this morning, about the fish…' Her words fell off, some of her boldness deserting her.

'You don't need to.' But the curiosity was killing him. Her words were stuck in his mind. *They dared to reach for more. They didn't know the brass ring was just an illusion.* She hadn't been talking about the fish. She'd been talking about someone else. He had understood that immediately. But who had she meant? Had she meant herself? Her marriage?

'I want to. Please let me.' She paused and looked away for a moment, suddenly nervous. 'No one ever lets me speak of it; often I don't even let myself think about it, but perhaps it would best if I did. Maybe I could move forward if I did. Consider it a favour? Of course, I'd understand if you felt it would be too much.'

Conall settled back into his place on the log. Some day she'd realise he would deny her nothing. 'Then I'd be honoured. Whatever you tell me, your secrets are safe here.' Her blue eyes said she didn't believe him, but she appreciated the gesture anyway.

'Be careful what you promise, Conall. You don't know what those secrets are.' She fell silent for a long while and then she laughed uncertainly. 'Now that I have someone to listen, I hardly know how to begin.'

'You wanted to tell me about your divorce?' Conall prompted.

She shook her head. 'No, I want to tell you about my *marriage*.' Her eyes locked on his. 'My husband was a sadist.'

Conall felt his breath catch. He wanted to stop her right there, to tell her she didn't have to say any more. But he saw the challenge in her eyes and he resisted. She was daring him to let her go on. Indeed, those five words already told him a great deal. He had to let her continue. This was where London had failed her. The ladies wouldn't want to hear such sordidness. They wanted the scandal without the details. It made condemning her that much easier. Details would create understanding, compassion, empathy, if not sympathy, and that would never do. So he let her go on.

'I married him at eighteen. It was a match arranged by my parents and Il Marchese while I was at finishing school. He visited me a couple of times that winter and that spring. I knew him, or I thought I did. He brought me flowers when he visited and small gifts. He said they were to make up for my not getting a Season. He wanted to marry me right away.' Her eyes took on the cast of one remembering the past instead of seeing the present. 'At the time, I didn't care too much. He was handsome, charming the way an older man can be when he gives his attention to a naïve young girl. All the girls at school thought it was terribly romantic and my parents were eager for the match. They were gentry and they needed me to marry well. They'd spent a lot of money for me to attend a school that was also attended by girls destined to marry ducal heirs.'

Girls like Helena Colbert-Tresham. An expensive school indeed. 'You couldn't have known what he was like,' Conall offered, feeling the words were entirely inadequate to the situation.

'No, I couldn't have. I was young, malleable, eager to please not only Il Marchese, but my parents and my older brother. Besides, his title was far grander than anything I could aspire to here in England.'

A suspicion took root in Conall's mind. 'How did your parents know him?' English gentry didn't rub elbows with Continental marquises.

'My father met him at a gaming hell in London.' She looked down at her hands. 'My father had a penchant for living beyond his means and Il Marchese was quite keen to cover his debts and more in exchange for marrying his daughter.'

'Ah.' The suspicion grew into a tight ball. 'Did your father have any inkling as to the sort of man he was?' Conall hoped not. It was the only saving grace that remained to one Mr Northcott, who had traded his daughter in marriage to a foreigner he barely knew, all to cover a rather extensive gambling debt.

Sofia's eyes were hard sapphires. 'No, he didn't. They gambled together and drank together, but for all his faults, my father is faithful to my mother.' She paused and Conall felt a measure of relief for the errant father. But her next words shattered that sense of relief. 'But my brother did. He and Il Marchese spent a few evenings carousing at a high-end brothel on the Strand where Il Marchese paid enormous sums for, ah, certain pleasures.' Her gaze slid away in her discomfort and embarrassment. 'A wife is a much more economical arrangement. She has to do those things for free.'

Anger ripped through Conall as the pieces came together. An innocent girl married to a stranger in order to clear a gambling debt no matter the cost—a cost her family had known and decided she would pay on their behalf. 'Where is your family now?' His hand flexed around a rock. He was of half a mind to call out the brother who'd knowingly sent his sister into sexual servitude. Northcott. Who did he know by that name? He would find out and when he was done with the brother, he'd call out the father for selling his daughter for his own comfort.

'At home, I suppose.' He noticed she didn't mention where home was. 'I haven't seen them since my wedding and I stopped writing after they returned none of my letters.' Which confirmed his other worst suspicions: that the family had done nothing to get her back, or to rescue her. They had simply left her to face her fate. Face it she had. The woman sitting beside him was strong. She'd survived. Ten years. Conall's respect for her ratcheted up another level, as did the need to defend her. Often it was the strong who needed protection the most.

'Life with him was horrible,' she said quietly. 'I fought as hard as I could. I tried to run, twice. But no matter what I did, I couldn't escape. Like the fish on the line, I was stuck. I'd consented to the marriage. I'd *chosen* this. I'd been dazzled by his wealth and charm, and the adventure of living abroad, seeing Italy. I only had myself to blame.'

'You had your family to blame.' Conall's words came out fierce. He would not sit there and let this woman censure herself. 'They should have had your best interests in mind. Your brother should have protected you.' Goodness knew he would have died for Cecilia before he saw her married to such a man. 'Your father should not have bartered you.'

'One cannot always count on others. I've become very good at looking out for myself.' She gave a wry smile. 'I hope you understand about the fish, now you see why I couldn't bring myself to reel it in. Freedom is everything. I wouldn't take it from any creature.'

He did see and he saw so much more than she might have intended. She needed control: to control the mill, to control their kisses. This was her way of warning him she would never trust a man again, never stay anywhere long enough to give a man dominion over her life, even if that man was him. And he wanted desperately to change her mind. Behind the hard sapphire eyes, he saw in her, too, the young girl denied a Season, a chance to be beautiful and admired, a chance to dance and be adored. There was so little he could give her, but he could give her this. He could admire her; he could adore her. He could show her real intimacy and that it wasn't to be feared or shunned, that she didn't have to control it.

Conall rose from the log. 'Come here.' He drew her to her feet amid her protests. 'I can't change the past, I can't replace all that you lost, but I can offer you a waltz, the sort we might have had if we'd met, if you'd had the Season you'd deserved.' He led her to the river bank, their bare feet sinking in the soft sand.

'We did dance, at Ferris's honeymoon ball,' she reminded him.

He shook his head with a smile. 'Not like this, though, not where I discovered you for myself from across the room and had to fight off suitors to claim you.'

She laughed at his story. 'Is that what would have happened?' It was an easy story to get swept up in, imagining meeting him at a debutante ball, being the girl who caught his eye. How different her life might have been.

'I would have put my hand, just here.' He gripped her waist, feeling the slimness of her through the secured blanket. 'And my mouth here.' He bent his lips to her ear, murmuring, 'And when the music started, I would have led you into a waltz.'

He moved them into the opening steps and she laughingly resisted. 'What are you doing, Conall?'

'Give over and dance with me, Sofia, like you did at Ferris's ball,' he whispered playfully and her resistance failed. He felt her body soften and comply, felt the current of the river lap at their feet. He gave her a hard turn and she laughed out loud. 'We are cutting quite a swathe through the ballroom, my dear,' he teased. He turned her again, bringing her up against him hard. Their pace slowed then to a quiet swaying, each of them aware of the other, their eyes lingering and sliding away, only to return.

'What are you thinking?' she whispered.

'That this might be the most perfect waltz ever.' He drank her in with his eyes: her blanket-clad form, the damp curls falling around her shoulders, the tentative enjoyment that sparked in her blue eyes as she struggled to trust him, to surrender to the moment. The sight of that battle woke the primal in him, an urge to protect her, this woman who was so used to protecting herself. Today, she was his. Today, he would ensure no evil could touch her.

Chapter Twelve

Conall took her mouth in an invitation to more, feeling the hesitation in her. It was not the hesitation of fear, it never had been with her, but the hesitation of caution and pragmatism. Would she let him continue? Kissing had always started with her and been an end in itself. Not this time. Kisses wouldn't, shouldn't, be enough. *Accept, accept.* The words beat in time to the rhythm of his rising pulse. *Accept the invitation, accept me. Let me show you the difference between what could be and what you know.*

His hand cupped the curve of her jaw, his kiss deepening, asking once more for her response and she gave it. He felt her open to him, felt her body relax against his, the tentative tension she carried with her leaving it. She whispered her assent against the rough stubble of his cheek. 'Conall, will you be my lover? Here? Now?'

Conall whispered back, 'Yes', with no illusions

as to the courage it had taken for her to utter those words, or what her request meant and how it would define them. He would be her exorcism and she would be his adventure. He would come to her this once, give of himself this once, dance on the edge of his fears. He would peer into the abyss of what might have been if he'd still believed he could trust another with his heart, his soul, and then he would withdraw. There would be no promises, no expectations beyond the river bank, and when they were through she would leave the next day or the day after that. There would be no revisitation, only now.

He took her hand and led her to their blankets spread beside the campfire. 'Shall I take your robe?' He played the gallant knight, but she refused to relinquish her blanket. Ah, Conall thought. Even within the boldness of her request, there were to be limits. Her courage had reached its boundaries. It was good to know from the start.

'But you should make yourself comfortable.' A spark flared in her blue eyes, the hint of a coy smile dancing on her lips.

'Are you inviting me to strip, my lady?' Conall teased. And why not? His shirt was already off and he'd been rid of his boots long since.

'I imagine wet trousers are not terribly comfortable,' came her rejoinder.

Nor necessary for what she'd asked of him, Conall wanted to remark, but thought better of it as he worked the fastenings. She might have reached the boundaries of her courage, but not the supply of it. There was plenty left. Good. He didn't want their lovemaking to be a hurried, embarrassed affair hidden entirely beneath blankets. Half the enjoyment was being skin to skin, an enjoyment he felt was heightened out of doors. They would have some of that today, but he would not push her for more.

Conall pushed his wet trousers down past his hips, an act that lacked his usual finesse. But he was determined to come to her naked and honest, unashamed.

Adam before the fall. Those were the words that ran through her head as she stared. He would have been glorious in a bedroom but here, outside in the nature he navigated so well, he was extraordinary—not just the obvious proud, jutting length that so easily drew the eye as it claimed the centre of him, but the setting for that manly jewel: the lean curves of muscle in his arms, his thighs, the sculpting of his torso would have been the envy of the early anatomists who sought to define the body and its parts. Those parts were all on fascinating display here, whole, healthy and well-defined. Giancarlo had excellent tailors, she'd learned. He had not looked like this after his clothes came off. Perhaps it was poorly done of her to think of the past at a moment like this, but how could she not? The whole point of this interlude was to defeat the past and to do that she had to acknowledge it.

Conall came to her, kneeling beside her on the

blankets and something warm started in her belly, reminding her the whole point wasn't only about defeating the past. There was far more to this than that. If not, she might have taken a lover before this. But that lover would not have engendered the depth of *liking* she felt for Conall. Soon, she was going to have to acknowledge that what she felt for him went beyond physical attraction.

She reached for him, drawing him down to her, along her length so that they lay side by side. 'I want to touch you.' Her hand skimmed the surface of his torso, running over the expanse of muscle, the tight buds of his nipples. 'You keep yourself in shape.'

'The country is good for that. City living makes a man soft.' He laughed softly and pushed back hair that had fallen in her face. His eyes stilled on her countenance and the demeanour of the interaction changed. 'I can give you pleasure, Sofia. Will you allow it? Will you allow me to run kisses up your legs, to trail my tongue along your thighs, to put my mouth on your sweet core?' She nearly wept with the realisation. He was giving her control of the game.

This was her seduction to design and, with a single word, she did. 'Yes.' It seemed she'd been reduced to such utterances since he'd carried her from the river. Rendering her speechless was another of his hidden talents, something she could file next to cooking over an open fire and protecting damsels in distress.

Conall's body shifted to the soles of her feet,

his hands running softly up her bare legs. Every gesture implied he understood the rules. He was to leave her torso, her breasts alone, and he asked no questions. His hands were warm on her river-chilled skin, his touch heated from the fire and the pan of wine.

He bent her leg, kissing the inside of her knee, and repeated the motion with the other, his mouth kissing its way along the tender insides of her thighs until he reached the warm, damp wetness of her. She sighed at the first stroke of his thumb, the gentle insistence of his hands, holding her steady as he found his target: a tiny nub hidden deep. He stroked it first with the pad of his thumb, his eyes holding hers, searching, perhaps? For permission, for proof of her enjoyment? She let him see both in her gaze and then there was only the dark top of his head against the white of her belly, her thighs, as his mouth took the place of his hand, his tongue where the pad of his thumb had been and the pleasure began all over again, only more intensely, deeply, until she arched her back, her neck, her face upwards to the sun above the trees. Her breath came in pants now, ragged and gasping, her mind no longer able to logically process the sensation. It was all just feelings now, animalistic and primal, and it wasn't enough. That was the only lucid thought emerging from the tangle of sensations. It wasn't enough to have his mouth, to have his hand. The experiment could not end here.

She gave an inarticulate cry, her hands in his hair,

tugging at him, wanting him up, over her, in her fully. Somehow he understood. He levered himself over her, matching his length to her, his hips fitting between the cradle of her thighs, his phallus at her slick entrance like a key to a lock. 'Now, Conall, now.' Only desperate strength wrung such coherency from her. At some point, she had outrun the past, outrun the future, she was simply here in this moment where nothing else mattered.

Conall slid into her, filling her, stretching her and then reversed until she clutched at him, legs wrapped about him, desperate to hold him to her. His lips bussed her forehead, his voice murmuring words meant to soothe, to reassure. He was not leaving. He thrust again and she was ready for him, body arching, hips finding the rhythm. She began to move with him, the motion new but instinctive. She was not a passive participant in this interaction, her body picking up the nuances of his: the tautness of his arms as he held himself above her, the clench of his buttocks as he thrust in, the ragged pace of his breathing which matched her own. She would soon reach the limits of her pleasure. An incoherent grunt, a further tensing of his body indicated his release approached as well.

Sofia gasped, rearing against him, her body hungry for release, too, yet reluctant to yield this known pleasure for the unknown. Once, twice more, and there was no choice but to yield, to give in to the unknown. It was not a release so much as it was a shattering. With a final gasp she broke, a wave against pleasure's rocks, and he broke, too, with a groan.

He gave her a final kiss and rolled to his side, the intimate warmth of him leaving her even as he gathered her to him. She felt the rapid rise and fall of his chest beneath her cheek, the sheen of a light sweat proof of his efforts. For her. All this glorious pleasure had been for her. The thought added to the contentment rolling over her in pleasure's wake. When had she ever been so revered? So honoured? Not just with pleasure, but with seeing this man exposed, vulnerable in his exhaustion. His breathing began to settle. She reached up to kiss him. 'Thank you,' she murmured, but Conall's eyes were already closed.

Sofia sighed and looked up into the trees, the blue sky filtering through green leaves. She felt powerful, knowledgeable, like an ancient druid. Now she knew one of the great secrets of life; the pleasure that could exist between a man and a woman. But knowledge had a price. This could not happen again. Now, she had to fulfil the other end of the bargain she'd made with herself. She had eaten from the Tree of Life and now she had to leave Eden. She would give Conall his contracts and set him free before he could even realise the danger he was in.

Dark thoughts hemmed the bright cloth woven of her pleasure. If Giancarlo should ever find her, ever discover she'd taken a lover, he would be furious. While his infidelities were manly achievements, any infidelity on her part would not be looked at so amiably, never mind it had occurred under the legal protection of a divorce. She snuggled against Conall, willing the darkness away. She was borrowing trouble. Perhaps Giancarlo had given up? She might never know. She would only know that she was free one more day. Because of that, she always had to assume he hadn't given up. It wasn't the easiest way to live, but in the last six months since the first letters had arrived, it was the only way she could live without giving up, without surrendering to the past.

Conall stirred beside her, his brief nap complete, and she pushed away all thoughts of tomorrow—where she would go, how would she reinvent herself? There would be time for that later. Conall's grey eyes opened, finding her immediately, and she traced a finger down his torso. For now it was enough to be with him, to collect memories for the lonely years of freedom ahead. She kissed him, long and slow, rolling astride him, hair falling forward as she whispered, 'Conall, I want you.'

Chapter Thirteen

He knew what she wanted the moment he opened his eyes, well before she'd mounted him like Godiva on her steed, and against his better judgement he gave it. She wanted something to hold against an uncertain future, not unlike himself. There was safety in loneliness even if that safety came with emptiness. This was farewell. Already the day had slipped past them, the afternoon cooling into evening, shadows lengthening.

It came as no surprise. Leaving had been implicitly acknowledged between them from the start. She would come, make her decision and go. Only, when all this had begun, there had been no acknowledgement of each other as more than business partners. They'd merely been a means to an end. He should be thankful. He'd had her far longer than he might have.

She slid down his length, taking him inside with a replete sigh, and Conall groaned. Had anything ever felt better? Ever felt more right than lying beneath the skies with her—Sofia Northcott, a woman of no substantial pedigree or fortune, none of the things he should look for in a bride? And yet this was the woman he wanted; he wanted her intelligence, her joy, the energy that radiated from her whenever she was in a room, the way she looked at him, not only now in the throes of claiming her passion, but from across the dinner table, or a desk.

She didn't see a title—she saw a man with ideas, a man with ingenuity, a man who loved his family. She saw him in a way the Olivia de Pughs of his world never would. Then again, the Olivia de Pughs couldn't see him any other way, they hadn't been raised to. But Sofia could. It had taken her own tragedies to strip away the lens English society had given her and replace it with a lens that allowed her to see and appreciate a man for who and what he truly was.

Sofia's hips began to move and he gripped the soft rounds of her buttocks, guiding his own hips into the languorous rhythm she set. Sofia was in no hurry and neither was he. They both understood what lay at the end of this: impossibilities and partings because her tragedies—the very things that had made it possible for her to appreciate him, to appreciate life—had also put her beyond him. There was simply no way to go on from here except separately. It was for the best. He would not have to risk disappointing her or she him. They could keep their illusions.

Sofia leaned forward, her mouth taking the nub of

his nipple, her teeth raking it with tantalising gentleness, and his body tightened, release finding him. She laughed, a sultry sound full of confidence and pleasure, He would hold that picture of her in his mind always: Sofia, her golden hair no longer forward, but streaming down her back in silky waves, her head thrown upwards to the sky, the ancient joy of joining with a man evident on her face as climax took them both. Conall knew without doubt that whatever else happened today or tomorrow, she had found a piece of herself even as he had lost a piece of him.

Conall held her as long as he could, as if by holding her, he could hold the sun in the sky for another minute and then another minute after that. As long as it was daylight, he could hold on to the fantasy that he could be loved for himself by a woman who truly knew him.

No, she doesn't. You've hidden things from her—important things. The whispers began at dusk. The fantasy began to weaken. *You've lied to her. She doesn't know how desperately you needed that investment. Perhaps she thinks you have money, perhaps she still sees the title and the fortune that's supposed to go with it. Test her, tell her that everything at Everard Hall is a sham concocted for her enjoyment and then see what she thinks.*

But he didn't tell her. Maybe he was a coward. Maybe he didn't have that kind of courage, not when it would cost him these moments of paradise and for what? She would leave anyway. Why ruin it when these moments clearly meant so much to her?

Because she's been honest with you, came the reply. *She's told you about her husband, about her marriage. Those disclosures were not easy for her. You have repaid her confidence in you with lies.*

But in the end, telling her could change nothing. So as the shadows lengthened, and the last sands drained from the hourglass of his fantasy, Conall said simply, 'Come, I'll take you home.'

They drove in silence—perhaps she was as busy with her thoughts as he was with his. Everard Hall, aglow with evening light, came into view. For the first time he could remember, the sight of his home caused a knot to form in his stomach instead of a rush of joy. Conall stopped the gig on the little rise and stared into the spring twilight. What if the contracts were waiting for him? A few weeks ago the thought would have filled him with elation, would have sent him speeding home. But that was before...her.

Sofia reached for his hand. 'You're thinking about the contracts.'

He nodded. He was thinking about the contracts, about her, about how everything was tied up together in a knot so tight he couldn't separate out the strands. The alpacas, the lies, the contracts, *her*—they were all inextricably linked in one unseverable Gordian knot. It wasn't supposed to be this way.

It doesn't matter, his conscience reminded him—*if those contracts are not there, they will come and soon. You knew you were on borrowed time.* Conall blew out a breath. This was the real danger of fantasies. They always ended and when they did, they betrayed those who participated in them because they weren't truth. Hadn't his father's death proven that? Up until last year, his entire life had been one long fantasy of wealth and comfort. He'd promised himself he'd never fall for such an illusion again. And here he was, already falling for a fantasy of his own making.

'Where will you go? Will you go back to London?' Conall set the gig in motion.

'I might travel a bit,' Sofia answered obliquely. 'Summer is lovely for travel and business is slow until October.'

'And then London?' Did he sound as desperate to her as he did to himself? Pressing her for a location, somewhere permanent where he might find her again? It would not be enough to have the occasional business letter as she checked in on the mill. 'I'll be up to London for the Michaelmas session of Parliament. I have to take my father's seat now that I can't claim mourning as an excuse.' He chuckled, but it was forced. It was an excuse. Any excuse to see her again and she saw right through it.

'Do you think it's wise? To see me again?' Even as she said it, she tucked her arm through his as if she, too, were reluctant to let the intimacy of the day go despite her realism. 'You will be a lord in Parliament, a pillar of society.' She paused. 'You needn't worry, Conall. I won't seek you out. I won't embarrass you with our association. I wouldn't dream of hurting Cecilia's chances. You've all been so kind to me during my stay. Kindness has been a rare thing in my world.'

Today, he'd learned just how rare: a family who had bartered her and a husband who had battered her for his own pleasure. Conall didn't need the details of that to know. Her comment validated he'd been right in not confessing the ruse to her, not now when she'd given her trust to him. Such a confession could only hurt her. His clean conscience wasn't worth the cost.

'Perhaps it doesn't have to be that way,' Conall said. There were only a few minutes left before they'd be in the drive of Everard Hall, surrounded by servants and family and reality.

'Yes, it does.' She cut him off with a sharp glance and severe words. 'Do you wish me to be your mistress? Because that's all I can be to you, if I were willing, which I am not. I promised myself when I left Il Marchese that I would not belong to any man again. Not even one as grand as you, Conall. I mean to keep that promise.' Then she softened. 'Even if I consented, such an arrangement would be short lived. You are not a man to bring a mistress into matrimony. I know men who would marry and keep their mistresses, but you are not one of them.' Heartbreaking proof that she indeed understood him too well.

They halted in the drive, the shadow of a groom moved towards them to take the horses. In the final moments of privacy left, Conall kissed her, hard and swift, letting the kiss convey in that short interlude all that his words could not. He did not miss Sofia's own desperate whisper as they broke apart. 'Goodbye, Conall Everard.'

It was best they'd said their goodbyes, such as they were, outside. The hall was bright with lights and there was a caged energy that greeted him when Conall stepped through the door. His mother, CeeCee and Freddie all appeared too quickly from the drawing room. They'd been hovering, waiting, with excitement. His gaze went to the dreaded pile of mail on the front console. There they were, in a brown envelope, larger than the rest of the usual notes and letters and newspapers. The contracts.

'Documents came today.' His mother nodded towards them, her own excitement barely under control. He felt a sudden twinge of guilt. How many hours had they stared at the envelope, knowing full well what it was while he'd been off fishing, seducing their houseguest and wishing the blasted contracts would never arrive? His mother's eyes caught his, grey like his own. They shone with pride and hope. Salvation was at hand for all of them. He was a cad for wishing it to be otherwise. This would be a great worry he could lift from his mother's shoulders.

Conall pasted on a smile and strode forward, prepared to put on a show. He picked up the contracts and sliced open the heavy envelope. He scanned the contents of the cover letter and smiled as he held up the deed. 'The mill is ours. We can commence shearing.'

Around him, everyone was laughing and clapping. Freddie whooped and grabbed Cecilia's hands, pulling her into an exuberant dance. 'We're going to make wool! The best wool in the world. We'll be famous everywhere!' His mother wiped away a subtle tear of relief. Servants smiled on the perimeter of the celebration. All would be well now, their positions secure. Taunton had done his job.

Conall slid his gaze towards Sofia. She smiled at him, the one person in the hall who could understand the bittersweet joy of this moment. He could not look at her for long without fear of betraying the bitter part of that sweetness and he would not ruin others' joy. He turned his attention back to the pile of letters, seeing one for Sofia. 'Here, this is for you. It looks like Helena has written.'

'Thank you.' Sofia tucked the letter into a pocket for later and nodded towards the celebrating family. 'I'll leave you to your family. I can walk myself down to the Dower House.'

'You'll come back for dinner.' It wasn't a question or even an invitation. 'Everyone will expect to see you. You're part of this.' His stomach tightened. She was really leaving. He could see it in her hesitation. He wouldn't make it easy for her. She could not slink away in the night. She would come to dinner and face everyone, one last time.

'Of course I'll come to dinner, but I won't stay

long afterwards. I have to pack.' She held his eyes for a long moment. She'd thrown down the gauntlet with those words, drawn the proverbial line in the sand that could not be crossed. This was the end.

Tonight was a new beginning. Tomorrow, she could go anywhere, do anything. She was entirely free. She could not afford to think of tonight as an ending or she would go mad. She would break down and cry, or worse, she would let Conall persuade her things could be otherwise. She was certain he would try. She'd seen the look in his eye in the hall when he'd pressed her to return for dinner. He read her far too easily these days. He'd been right. She would have preferred to hide with her packing in the Dower House. Instead, she had to wage battle with Conall.

Sofia dressed carefully for dinner, selecting one of her favourite gowns, a deep, almost navy-blue silk with creamy pink-tinged roses and matching cream lace that trimmed the scooped neckline and dripped from the short, puffed sleeves. The gown brought out the blue of her eyes and the ivory of her skin. The maid did her hair in a neat bun, fastened with a matching comb of silk roses, and she wore her pearls. Definitely festive, she thought, smoothing her skirt over the crinoline and taking an experimental twirl in front of her mirror. Tonight was for celebrating. Tonight she would pretend the perfection of Conall Everard's world extended to her. She glanced at the clock. She still had a little time before they expected her. Time enough to read Helena's letter. Perhaps it would be just the thing to lift her spirits. She could already imagine a letter full of news of the boys and preparations for the new baby. Maybe they had finally chosen a name.

She retrieved Helena's letter from the desk. Sofia slipped the letter opener beneath the seal. A newspaper clipping fluttered out from between the folds of the letter. An invisible, cold hand gripped her belly. Newspaper clippings didn't come with newsy letters about children and babies. Slowly, Sofia bent to pick up the clipping, time standing still as she read the damning five-line story that would change everything. 'A burglary in Chelsea destroyed the Margaretta Terrace house believed to be the residence of La Marchesa di Cremona. La Marchesa was not at home at the time of the break-in and has not been seen since. Anyone knowing her whereabouts should be in contact with the constabulary.' Hands shaking, she checked the date of the paper; it was recent, just four days old. Long enough for news to reach Helena in the countryside.

Il Marchese had done this. The break-in was weeks old and it had gone unremarked upon until now. A crime outside Mayfair was standard for London. If *The Times* reported on every minor crime, the paper would be full of nothing else. And no one she knew—not Helena or Frederick or Conall—would have made a public spectacle of the event, especially not so belatedly. Her hand shook. There was no question Il Marchese had done this. He couldn't know she had no friends. He was hoping someone would worry enough about her to contact him. Her hands clenched around the newsprint, the larger reality finding her. If he hoped someone would contact him, it meant he was here.

Sofia sank into the nearest chair, clutching the arm to steady herself. Her worst nightmare had been realised. Giancarlo was in London and he was asking about her, making no secret he'd come to take his wife home if only he could find her. Dear Lord, what had the new King promised him that would make him leave his comforts and travel to London, a city he detested, in order to claim her?

With trembling hands, she studied Helena's letter, forcing herself to go slowly. She needed all the particulars if she was going to be safe. Sofia drew a steadying breath, mentally listing each fact she acquired. Frederick had been in town and recognised the danger. He'd done his research and written to Helena immediately. Il Marchese was at the Coburg. He'd been seen at the theatre and at the opera, always with two women on his arm in an expensive box. He spent his nights at the high-end gaming hells losing good-naturedly at cards while he asked around for her. He'd made no secret of who he was and who she was and what he was here for—her—in the hopes of restoring them both to their formerly wedded bliss. Sofia read her friend's closing line.

Stay in Somerset.

And then the admonition.

Tell Conall everything. He will protect you.

Sofia gripped the arms of the chair, trying to quell the nausea rising in her stomach, the panic rising in her mind, clouding her ability to think. She fought back. Panic had paralysed her for years. She could not give in to it. Panic was her enemy, not Giancarlo. She found the usual litany deep in her mind, where she'd packed it away once she'd thought she was free. *Don't be afraid. You're safe.* Forewarned was forearmed. This was all to the good, a blessing, really. She could make decisions. She had choices. She'd known he was hunting her before this. This was not new. She had known for months now the danger was real. Only now the chase was so much closer, more personal.

He was slowly curtailing her freedom, methodically taking away her choices. He'd destroyed her home. He'd reported the news himself. Not just to flush her out through potential friends, but because he wanted the news to reach her so that she'd feel the net tightening. He could find her any day. *But he doesn't know where you are,* came the hopeful reminder. But that did little to belay the fear of knowing he might come upon her at any time. She wouldn't know if he'd found her until it was too late.

She had to think like him. If he didn't know how to come to her, did he think she'd come to him? Did he think the article would bring her back to London? That maybe she'd come for whatever might be left of her possessions? Maybe he thought she'd come back for the money and he could accuse her of having stolen it when she left. There would be many who would agree, men who believed whole-heartedly in coverture; that a woman was subsumed by her husband upon marriage, that all she had became his without the reciprocal being true under the law. Never mind that that marriage had been dissolved. Or maybe he wouldn't bother with a legal battle, after all. Perhaps he'd simply take her. That would be most expedient. She was doubly glad now she'd bought the mill. The money was spent, safe from Giancarlo's reach and it had its own protector. Giancarlo would not be able to take the dream, even if he managed to take her.

'Miss, it's time to go up for dinner.' Annie hovered in the doorway of the little office, looking nervous. It was past time, actually. She was officially late, but there was no question of eating.

'Send my regrets, Annie. I suddenly don't feel well.' Sofia rose on shaky legs. 'Then perhaps you could help me change. I want to lie down.' She'd managed to escape Giancarlo this long, she would manage to continue. Never mind that now he had a reason to find her.

Chapter Fourteen

She would not escape him so easily. Conall listened carefully to the message his footman delivered. Sofia was *not* coming to dinner. She was feeling suddenly unwell. Unwell? His foot, Conall thought. She'd been perfectly fine when she'd left here an hour ago. She was hiding, avoiding him.

Dinner seemed interminable. His family's spirits were high and it was only his desire not to dampen them that kept him in his seat, smiling and laughing. But he was restless and aware of his mother's watchful gaze on him. 'I should check on Sofia,' Conall said finally, laying aside his napkin only when the last of the dinner dishes had been cleared.

'I'll go with you, maybe she'll feel like playing backgammon,' Freddie offered, halfway out of his chair to fetch the board.

'No, Freddie, she needs to rest,' his mother intervened smoothly. 'Why don't you and Cecilia tell Cook to pack up a basket for her so she's not hungry down there on her own.' It was a neatly done dismissal, honed from years of practice in managing the balance of familial relationships. Conall would be impressed if he didn't know what it meant: his mother had something to say to him alone.

Cecilia and Freddie set off to collect the basket and his mother smiled. 'You've done well, Conall. You've eased the burden from all of us considerably. Your brother and sister are old enough to be worried.'

'We have the investment, not the success, not yet,' Conall cautioned. 'We still have to build a business.'

'Does she know?' his mother asked, pouring them each a drink. Sherry for her, brandy for him. A long conversation then, unlike the one in Cowden's study so many weeks ago, but just as telling. When a mother poured a drink for her son it meant she was acknowledging him as adult.

'No.' Conall took the brandy.

'And the ruse? She suspects nothing?'

'I don't believe so,' Conall replied, wary.

'She'll leave in the morning, then, none the wiser.' His mother raised her glass. 'Cheers to us, we've succeeded, against great odds.' She halted when he hesitated. 'You can't fool me, you know. I'm your mother. You put on a good act at dinner tonight and in the hall, but you're not as happy as you should be.' She paused. 'Does your discontent have anything to do with a blonde-haired, blue-eyed woman staying in the Dower House?' When he said nothing she set down her glass with a snort. 'I have eyes, Conall. I see how she looks at you and how you look at her. I am not blind. You were out late tonight, far too late for mere fishing.' She tapped a long finger on the table. 'What are your intentions?'

Conall swallowed. 'My intentions? I didn't think you were so old fashioned, Mother. It's 1854, after all.' Conall tried cajolement. His mother was a tolerant traditionalist.

She smiled at him, always with love even when he sensed she was scolding him. Apparently he would never be too old for that despite the fact that he was now thirty and she was fifty-one. The expression showed the creases at her eyes, her mouth, a reminder that time was marching for them both. 'What I believe, Conall, and the way the world actually works are often different things. I'm a realist enough to know that. Your father wasn't. He was an idealist and you are, too, especially when it comes to love. I don't want to see you or our family hurt. We know nothing about Sofia Northcott. We don't know her people, where she comes from. Those are no small things when one is a viscount.'

Her 'people' had sold her to a sadist. 'I thought you liked her.' Conall was surprised by his mother's reticence regarding Sofia, another reminder of how real the ruse had become for him. When had he forgotten that? A week ago? Longer?

His mother reached out a hand to stroke his cheek. 'I do like her well enough. There is much about her to be admired. But that was before my son stayed out late fishing with her and she came home with, ah, shall we say, dishevelled clothing?' She gave a soft laugh. 'I suppose no mother likes the reminder her son has become a man. We all miss our little boys. Perhaps we miss being the only woman in our sons' lives.'

'She fell in the river.' Conall attempted to assuage his mother's concerns.

His mother's eyebrows shot up. 'Then she probably had to take them off. I hope she didn't catch a chill. But they looked dry enough this evening when you returned.' His mother waited. But he would be damned if he was going blurt out into the silence that he'd made love to Sofia on the river bank.

'Does she mean to compromise you, Conall?' his mother finally asked pointedly. She held up a hand to stall his protests against the unlikelihood of that. 'If it hasn't occurred to you, perhaps it should. You're handsome, titled; you're polite, you have a good home, a good family. Those are very attractive qualities, especially to a woman who has nothing but the favour of Lady Brixton and apparently has to work for a living, running errands for a man who doesn't show his face in public.'

'She doesn't run errands, Mother,' Conall broke in.

'You're eager to defend her.'

'She's had a difficult life.'

'Marriage to you would certainly change that. She'd become Lady Taunton, a viscountess with two simple words.' *I do.* Two words Sofia was determined never to say to another man.

'I'm sure that's not what she's thinking.' He seldom quarrelled with his mother. In fact, he could not recall the last time they'd argued. But this was shaping up to be a fight he did not want to have.

'How do you know? Women are strategic creatures, more so than men give us credit for. I would wager she's hoping you'll come to the Dower House and check on her. Forgoing dinner is the perfect way to draw you to her in a venue where you'll be alone and where you can carry on from wherever you left things at the river.'

'Mother, I must ask you to stop.' Conall's tone was stern. He'd never spoken to her that way before and the newness of it took them both by surprise. Conall regretted it immediately. They'd been through so much together in the last year. She had been his bulwark and he had been hers. He did not want a rift between them. 'I am not a cad who would bed a woman not his wife in his family home.' Did his mother think he was a callous rake with no regard for propriety? He paused and drew a deep breath. 'Mother, I am certain Sofia Northcott has no designs on me. She is divorced from her husband, an Italian *marchese*. It was a poor marriage and she has no desire to shackle herself to another man.'

He waited for his mother to digest the revelation. 'How long have you known?' she asked quietly.

'Since London. We needed the money. I could

not be choosy once the Prometheus Club turned me down. But it has ceased to matter to me.' He reached for his mother's hands. 'Weren't you always the one who taught us that a person's mistakes should not define them? I think Sofia Northcott has proven herself to be more than the sum of her disappointing marriage.'

His mother patted his hand. 'Go to her, if you must. But be careful, Conall. You are Taunton now. You have responsibilities, not all of them economic. With your sister set to come out next year and Freddie's schooling to think of, we could do without the scandal, no matter how lovely the lady is and no matter how unfortunate her circumstances. I suppose it hardly matters. She's set to leave in the morning.' Beneath the approbation, Conall heard the warning. He was to make sure, for all their sakes, that they stuck to the plan. Her departure could not be delayed.

Apparently his mother and Sofia agreed on those grounds. He helped himself into the hallway without waiting for anyone to answer. The Dower House was a quiet bustle of activity. He knew the sounds of packing when he heard them. For a woman too ill to take supper, Sofia had found the energy to prepare for tomorrow's journey. Was this how it was done, then? Packing her trunks without a farewell? Annie spied him and stopped in mid-step on the stairs, linens in her hands. 'Milord, Miss Northcott isn't receiving. It's practically the middle of the night!' She looked scandalised.

'Annie, it's ten o'clock, and I wouldn't need to be here if Miss Northcott and I had settled our business earlier. Now, you can either ask Sofia to come down or I will go up.' Between Sofia missing dinner and his mother's misplaced concern, his patience was running thin.

There was movement at the top of the stairs. Sofia emerged on the landing. 'Annie, it's all right. Go on up and finish, I'll talk to Lord Taunton.' Sofia sounded weary. Defeated. Her energy was gone. She wore a satin dressing gown, her hair a loose cloud at her shoulders. Whatever recriminations he might have rehearsed on the way down faded in the wake of the obvious. She would have been lovely but for the telltale signs of crying.

'Sofia, what has happened?' His mind sorted through options. What could have occurred in the time since she'd left him to bring on tears? Then he remembered the letter. 'Is it bad news? Is Helena all right? The baby?'

'They're fine,' she assured him, coming down the stairs. 'What has happened is none of your concern. I need you to accept that without question and you need to let me go in the morning.'

Conall folded his arms across his chest. 'What do you think the chances of that are going to be?'

Next to none. 'This is why I didn't come up to the house for dinner,' Sofia said sternly. She had too much fighting to do, she didn't want to fight Conall as well.

'Because I would want you to explain why you

were leaving without saying goodbye? That's what you intended, isn't it?' Conall prodded bluntly, grey eyes like charcoals. Now he would press and she very much feared she would give in to the temptation to lay this latest disaster at his feet like she had the night of the break-in, although this was so much more.

Conall nodded towards the basket. 'Freddie and Cecilia packed up dinner for you. Freddie wanted to come down and play backgammon.'

The thought of Freddie and Cecilia brought the sting of tears. He did not fight fair. She didn't want to think about all she was leaving behind. Instead, she would think of all she was protecting. If Giancarlo was going to find her, he wasn't going to find her with this family. She would not have them used as leverage against her.

Conall moved to the basket and began to set out cold chicken pie and a bottle of wine, a sure sign he was entrenching. She had to prevent that. Sofia moved to the table. 'I'll eat later, I promise.'

Conall angled a speculative dark brow at her. 'You also said you would come to dinner. Forgive me if I doubt your word on that.' He poured a glass a wine.

She tried again, hands on hips this time. 'Don't ignore me, Conall. I want you to leave.'

He poured a second glass in direct opposition to her request and then sliced into the pie. 'I will leave, once you've answered my questions.'

'I am trying to protect you, Conall. You and your family.' If he wouldn't listen to reason out of respect for her, perhaps he'd listen to caution on behalf of those he loved.

He pulled out a chair and sat, crossing his booted feet at the ankles before fixing her with a grey stare that brooked no rebellion. 'Then tell me the truth, Sofia. What was in that letter that has you running like a frightened rabbit?'

She was going to have to tell him. She recognised defeat, but she also recognised a chance to turn the situation into victory. Once he understood, he would also understand there was no choice for him but to let her go.

Sofia tightened the belt of her robe and sat, taking the plate of chicken pie before she said with all the calm she could muster, 'My husband is here in England. He wants me back.' She willed back the panic the words engendered. Saying them out loud made them more real than they'd been in the last three hours. But she could not let Conall see the depth of reaction they wrung from her. He could not be tempted to fix this, to wade in where his efforts would be useless. He would only endanger his family and himself.

Conall's body stilled at her words. 'Why does he want you back?'

'Why does he do anything? There are two reasons he does anything: the promise of more wealth and to torture me.' She looked down at her barely touched pie. 'In this case it's both. The new Piedmont King has offered him great wealth if he restores his marriage,' she explained dispassionately. She couldn't let herself think about all that return would entail. She would be utterly destroyed if she did.

'The new King will not recognise the divorce?' Conall asked.

'He does not wish to. It cuts against the grain of his personal beliefs.' She played with her fork. 'My husband is hunting me, Conall. He's been hunting for a while. At first by letter and then by proxy. Now, he has come himself and my husband will not leave England without me.'

'Don't call him that. He is *not* your husband, not at the moment, nor at any time in the last three years.' Conall's voice was harsh, perhaps with the desire to protect tinged with a bit of jealousy. 'Proxy? How do you know?'

Sofia bit her lip. 'The burglary. It was a warning to me. You commented on it as well. Nothing was taken. Common thieves don't break in and not take anything.' She reached into the pocket of her dressing gown and took out the clipping. 'This was in the letter from Helena.' She paused and sipped at her wine, giving him time to read.

Conall looked up, eyes sharp. 'He doesn't know where you are. He's all but begging for information. This is the act of a desperate man.'

'Yes. It's why I must leave. He cannot find me here. You cannot be put in jeopardy.' This was the argument she needed to win with him. Any other man would be more than willing to put her on a train and gladly see her far, far away.

But Conall would disappoint in that regard. He was not any other man. 'I disagree, it's precisely why you must *stay*. Here you can be protected. Out there…' he made a gesture to indicate the whole of England '…you are in the open, exposed.' Conall's hand covered hers where it rested on the table, warm and strong, lending her his strength in a single touch. 'Look at me, Sofia,' he commanded softly. 'I will not let him take you. We can have men posted at the house. We can make sure no one approaches the house without permission. I am a viscount. I am not without resources.'

Sofia gave a sad laugh. It took all her willpower not to fall into that strength, to take the offer. He made it sound so easy to stay. 'No, I don't want more jailers, even benevolent ones. I don't want to live my life surrounded by guards.' But the temptation was there. The lamp limned his face, calling out its strength and masculine beauty in its flame.

'Those guards stole your freedom. These guards would protect it,' Conall argued. 'Don't be stubborn about this, Sofia.' Her glass was empty and he filled it, a subtle reminder that he looked to her needs even in the simplest of things.

The most perilous whisper of all started in her mind: *What if you trusted him? What if he could prevail against Il Marchese? What if you sent him to fight...? With his words, his resources, his title... what a champion Conall Everard would be.* She had to stop. That was not the deal she'd struck with herself when this day had begun.

'It's not only that,' Sofia said, tamping down the temptation. 'I can't allow it. It's too dangerous. The last thing I want is for you to be hurt, for your family to be hurt. You don't know him the way I do. He will use anything and anyone for leverage. I am not worth risking Freddie or Cecilia. He's made me a poison.' Her voice trembled. 'I destroy everything I touch.'

In her heart she knew she was better off alone, where no one could be leveraged against her, where there was nothing that could be destroyed. *That* was the deal she'd struck. She would come to this glorious man once and then she would leave before the poison could claim him, too. Even if Giancarlo caught her, even if she was somehow forced back to Piedmont, she would have a memory Giancarlo could never touch, never take, never destroy.

'Sofia,' Conall said. 'I can protect you, even without guards.'

She shook her head, her gaze wistful and sad. 'Oh, Conall, if only that were true.'

'It could be, if you married me.'

Chapter Fifteen

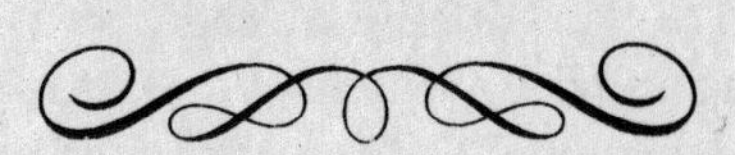

Sofia froze. Dear God, one look at Conall's unwavering grey gaze and she knew he was serious. 'I don't need a hero, Conall. What I need is to get on the train and re-invent myself.'

'Until the next time he finds you?' Conall answered smoothly. 'You said yourself he wasn't going to give up.' She'd meant for those words to be her defence, her weapon for driving him off, but he'd managed to turn them to his benefit. 'Maybe it's time to stop running and stand and fight. It would be much harder for him to claim you with a marriage certificate in your hands and a husband beside you.'

'Paper won't stop him.' Had Conall missed that part?

Conall laughed. 'It might not stop him from an outright kidnapping, but I hardly think the King of the Piedmont would want to see your lawful husband show up in his court crying that one of his noble courtiers is now a bigamist.' He sobered, slipping his fingers between hers until they were interlocked. 'I would come for you, Sofia. He would not have you for long if it came to that.'

'And your family? Would you sacrifice them as well? Viscounts cannot think just about themselves.'

That got a rise out of him. Anger flashed in his eyes and the leash of reason slipped just a fraction. 'And don't I know it? Everything I have done this past year has been for others! Can't there be one thing that is for me? Can't my marriage be for me? Because *I* want to? I want to do this for you, Sofia.'

The realisation came hard and fast: she wanted to do it, too, for herself, if things were different, if she was different. If she wasn't afraid of losing her freedom, if she wasn't afraid of what Giancarlo might do to Conall, to his family, maybe then she would have said yes. 'I've already told you I won't marry again.'

'I would not take your freedom. Do you think that I would?'

'No. But I would take yours. You can't imagine what society might do,' she said. She'd lived with the ostracising for three lonely years. She'd overheard the girls at the ball, seen the way the women and the men looked at her.

'They might forget,' Conall cut in. He came around the table and knelt before her. 'They've forgotten before. No one seems to remember how early Helena's first baby was. No one recalls that the Duchess of Cowden's father was a notorious gambler who lost his estate in a card game. Shall I go on? There are more examples. The *ton* can polish any diamond they choose. They will choose to polish you once you're my Viscountess. Helena and the Cowdens will champion you, my mother will champion you, although it's hardly needed. Once people get to know you, get to hear your story and understand you had no choice, all will be forgotten.'

Might it? It wouldn't happen overnight, not even Conall could promise that. But what if Conall was right? A little seed of hope, of possibility, began to sprout, watered by the image he painted.

'Think what you could do, what *we* could do. You are not the only woman trapped in or escaping from a bad marriage. We can advocate for changing the marriage laws, for more equality in marriage for women. It's high time those archaic codes were revisited. You are the woman to lead that fight and I will lead that fight with you.'

Did he know how potent his argument was? How much she longed to make the world a better place for women, for children, those with no voice of their own under the law. All she had to do was say yes and she would be protected from Giancarlo, she would have a family, a real family, and access to real change. It was too good to be true… The thought brought her up short. *When something sounded too good to be true, it probably was.* Where was the flaw? When she looked into Conall's eyes, when she felt the eager, assuring pressure of his grip, saw his face shining with anticipation, she couldn't find flaws.

'Why would you do this for me? What do you get out of it?' she asked. 'A good man who could do better than a ruined woman doesn't throw himself away without cause.'

'I get you. I get a wife who looks at me and sees me, Sofia, not my title. How could I endure a London Season, picking through debutantes who only see my assets, after being appreciated for so much more?'

Sofia smiled at that. 'At least you aren't offering protestations of love. Then I would have known you were lying.'

'Those may come in time.' The solemnity of those words sent a warm trill down her spine, her body recalling the intimacy of the afternoon on the river bank. 'We may not start out as a grand love match, Sofia, but we do start with respect and hope between us. We'll have the mill and the alpaca, we'll have our political cause. I think those are good starting places. We can build a meaningful life from those things.'

'It would be a marriage of convenience, then?' Sofia prompted softly.

His eyes were steady on her. 'There is more than convenience between us, though, isn't there? We proved that today.' He smiled. 'There is plenty to build from and plenty to look forward to.'

'You should have been a barrister. You never would have lost a case,' Sofia hedged. She was running out of reasons to object. Only one reason remained. 'It may not be necessary, this grand sacrifice of yours. Giancarlo may never come. He may never find me and you risk much on that gamble.'

'Maybe I would want to marry you regardless of Giancarlo.'

'Maybe you should test the waters first.' She was thinking fast, looking for an option that could satisfy him without ruining him, that left him an option if he changed his mind once this fit of gallantry passed, once he truly understood what this would cost him, even if he were right.

Conall nodded. Perhaps he sensed he had to concede something to her, that she had to control something, that his plan was overwhelming to a woman used to making her own decisions, used to trusting no one. 'What do you propose?' His eyes crinkled at the pun.

Sofia held on tight to her courage. She had not trusted another the way she was trusting Conall right now. 'An engagement. If Giancarlo poses a real danger, we can wed. But if he does not find me, you will not be shackled to a ruined woman without good cause.' The engagement could be broken. Society would support him in jilting her if something sordid were to come out, something he could claim to having not known beforehand. Divorced women were expendable and handsome, marriageable viscounts were easily forgiven.

Conall looked down at their hands joined together in her lap and his words nearly broke her heart. 'My dear Sofia, I think you just said yes.' She could have wept with joy, with a sense of being complete with this man. He understood in the most intrinsic of ways what the compromise had cost her. After thirteen years of distrusting men, it was as close to yes as she could get. She'd trusted Conall with the shame of her divorce. If they were to marry, they'd at least start with honesty between them. He could not accuse her of coming to him with secrets.

He'd not been honest with her. The thought kept Conall awake. Yes, he'd offered a convenient marriage to keep her safe. Yes, he was willing to sacrifice whatever needed sacrificing to protect her from her husband. All of that was true. But he'd not told her about his financial situation, that the coffers were all but empty except for her investment.

It wasn't supposed to have mattered. She was supposed to secure the loan and leave. It was supposed to have been business only. His conscience could live with that arrangement. As long as the mill was successful and her loan was repaid, his personal finances were not relevant. But it had become more than business. In fact, business and money had not factored into his rather unplanned proposal tonight. Yet, if she were to discover that omission, she might misunderstand his motivations. He'd seen the way she'd looked at him, with a rare consent of trust in her eyes. He knew how hard won that consent was, what a struggle it must have been for her to give it.

He would tell her tomorrow. After he explained

this latest development to his mother, after he went in to town to arrange a civil licence at the registrar's office so that he was prepared on a moment's notice. Tomorrow would be a prickly day. There would be nerves to navigate and feathers to smooth. But in the end, Sofia would be protected. And he would be, too. This marriage of convenience would protect them both, she from a dastardly ex-husband and he from the blinding illusions of romance.

He would not fall into his father's trap of being motivated by love and blinded by sentiment to the realities of living. His mother thought he was an idealist. But she was wrong. He might have been at one time, but he was a realist now. He would have a marriage built on respect and shared interests. There was room for intimacy within those parameters as he'd experienced today. There was room for feeling, too. He was not without emotion where Sofia was concerned. But it was not all-obscuring. It did not obliterate his good sense. There would be no illusions.

Giancarlo was under no illusion. Finding Sofia was going to be difficult. Even if she was in London, the city was a sea of people during the Season. He eyed the pile of newspapers on his desk in his suite at the Coburg with distaste. He was down to this: reading *gossip* pages searching for any mention of his errant wife. It was dismal, really. He was much smarter than this. Giancarlo took a seat behind the desk and gestured to his secretary. 'Ring for breakfast and we'll get started.' She was the sort of woman who could not go unremarked for long. If she'd gone out even once society would have noticed.

He was right. A pot of coffee later, he crowed in exultation. 'She was here! She went to a wedding, the hypocrite.' His eyes riveted on the three lines. So little and yet it told him so much. She'd not only gone to a wedding, but a man had sat beside her, a man who'd deliberately come up the aisle to join her. 'Bring me *Debrett's Peerage*. I want to know who Viscount Taunton is. Then, get me invited to the Hammersmith ball tomorrow night. Everyone who's anyone will be there.' With luck, that would include Taunton. If that English bastard had touched his wife, he'd cut his balls off.

The waltzing at the Hammersmith ball had been disappointing, the card rooms had been far more instructive. Giancarlo poured another round of his host's fine brandy into the tumbler of his new best friend, a young, blond Viscount by the name of Hargreaves who had better tailoring than sense. The young man was an open book, telling him every piece of *ton*nish gossip under the pale, elusive London sun as they played cards. One might admire Hargreaves's stylish élan, but the man had no appreciation for discretion, which was fine with Giancarlo. After two weeks in London chasing dead ends, he'd finally found gold.

'I am wondering if you know Viscount Taunton?

I was told to contact him when I was in England.' Giancarlo led the conversation around to the topic he wanted to discuss most.

Hargreaves gave a wide grin and nodded. 'We're good acquaintances when he's in town. We have the same club memberships. I saw him at a wedding just a few weeks ago.'

That was better luck than he'd had all night. He'd discerned early in a dismal waltz with a gossipy widow that Taunton was not in attendance, much to his disappointment and hers, it seemed. Now, he'd found someone who didn't just know of Taunton, but was something of a friend. 'Is he in town at present?' He kept his tone casual. 'I should like to see him during my visit.'

Hargreaves frowned. 'I wish he was. We only meet up during the Season. Our estates are on opposite ends of the country. Goodness knows he *should* be. The man needs to marry. He inherited last year and now that mourning is behind him, he has to get busy with his nursery.' He winked at Giancarlo. 'This year's crop is a good one, if you know what I mean. If I had to marry quickly, this would be the year for it. There are four heiresses out this Season, twenty girls with respectable titles and another fifteen with notable dowries, and that's not counting—'

'Yes, I've noticed. A spectacular crop,' Giancarlo broke in quickly, not wanting his quarry getting sidetracked. 'So, he's at his estate?'

'Likely. He prefers the country more than I do.'

Hargreaves chuckled. 'I haven't seen him since the Tresham wedding, Duke of Cowden's second son, don't you know?'

No, he didn't know and didn't want to know. If he wasn't careful, he'd have to listen to the details of a wedding that was only significant to him because it was the last place Viscount Taunton was seen sitting next to *his* wife. 'Where did you say his estate was?'

'Somerset…' Hargreaves waved his hand to indicate he thought Somerset the end of the world '…just outside Taunton. Everard Hall. It's the family seat. He adores it there, loves to fish. He had some harebrained scheme when he came up to town to invest in alpacas and farm them.'

'Alpacas? Really? Hmm…' Giancarlo wondered what the chances were his errant wife had gone with the Viscount. On the surface, it seemed unlikely. A viscount who needed to marry wasn't exactly in the market for a divorcee. Then again, his wife was very beautiful and the gossip rag had indicated the Viscount had been taken with her—taken enough to leave his seat and join her in the back of the church. Giancarlo worked out the timing. His letter would have arrived by then, she would have been present for the burglary, after all. That meant she would have been feeling desperate. Perhaps she had persuaded the Viscount to take her with him.

Hargreaves looked on the verge of launching into another story Giancarlo had no need of. He swallowed the rest of his drink and stood up, checking his watch. 'If you'll excuse me, I have someone to meet. Thank you for the enjoyable conversation.' Hargreaves looked disappointed at being robbed of his eager company, but Giancarlo did have someone to meet, a lush widow waiting for him in the library who wasn't against a little rope play. He also had a decision to make. Did he go to Somerset himself and risk missing her if she wasn't there, or did he stay, guarding the lair, as it were, and send Andelmo, his trusted body servant, to scout the terrain? The latter might be better. If she was with the Viscount, she had protection. That decided it, he would send Andelmo. He'd consult the train schedules. The man could be there tomorrow.

Chapter Sixteen

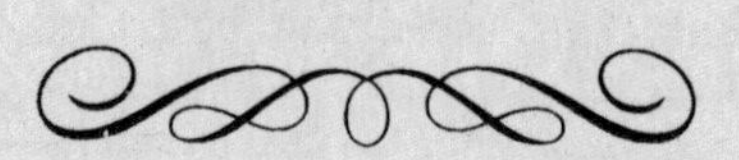

There was a certain euphoria to going into town. It was a market day and the weather was good, he was driving the gig with a light breeze in his face and a pretty woman by his side. Conall pulled the gig into the livery and helped Sofia down. She looked fetching today in a white-and-yellow walking ensemble with a straw hat trimmed in the same primrose ribbon. She had a market basket slung over her arm and 'Every intention of shopping,' she warned him with a wide smile.

'I want to look for some pencils and art supplies. Your mother and Cecilia mentioned they wanted to teach the tenants' children drawing this summer. I'd like to help. I miss my work from London.'

She looked up at him from under the brim of her hat, her smile genuine, her eyes sparkling and something warm blossomed in his chest. This was what goodness looked like; this woman who had overcome her own adversities and was intent on making better futures for those around her. 'I can recommend a shop that carries art supplies,' Conall offered as they stepped out into Canon Street and headed towards the market.

Conall manoeuvred them through the vendors' stalls, past vegetables and breads, past goods made with Taunton wool, stalls with ribbons, toys and fabrics. The diversity and importance of Taunton as a market centre in Somerset was on display today and it made him proud. Soon, his own contributions would be in evidence. Maybe not in a market stall—they had to seek a larger outlet for their goods, but it would be present in the coins people had to spend in the market.

There was already employment on the alpaca farm for the men and work in the house for those interested in entering service. His mother would be able to staff the house and the grounds fully, to say nothing of the jobs that would eventually come as the alpaca project grew and the mill began. There would be mill jobs, shearing jobs, shipping and transport, sales, bookkeeping—the list was endless.

Sofia tugged at his arm, urging him to stop at a booth selling ribbons. She held up two lengths of silk, one in a pale-green, the other in sky blue that matched her eyes. 'Which one do you like?' She looked utterly enchanting with the ribbons, her smile wide, and he wondered how long had it been since she'd been happy? Was she truly happy now?

'They're lovely, get them both.' He would buy her a thousand ribbons if they brought her a smile. His words came out strangled as the realisation sucker-punched Conall in the gut. He *wanted* to be responsible for her happiness. He cared *deeply* that her happiness was genuine, that it wasn't forced or an artifice she employed to hide herself. He wanted to remove the threat of Giancarlo Bianchi.

'Your head was in the clouds back there,' Sofia whispered with an elbow nudge to his ribs as they moved on.

'Just happy, just planning,' Conall admitted. 'Are you happy?'

She gave him a thoughtful stare as if the question was worthy of weighty consideration and maybe given her background it was. 'I think I am, for the first time, in a long, long time.'

'Then we should celebrate.' Conall stopped by a pastry vendor. 'We must have some of these. I love Bath buns.' He grinned at the woman working the stall. 'We'll take two to eat now and a dozen to go.'

'You have a sweet tooth!' Sofia teased.

'No. My family would be severely disappointed in me if I failed to bring any home for them.' Conall put the wrapped buns in her basket and passed her one to eat. 'Let me take this.' He put the basket on his arm and took her arm with his other, letting the moment wash over him. This was what it could be like—enjoying the market with a wife, stopping for treats along the way. 'In the autumn there are apples,' he told her. 'Taunton is known for its cider. We have a special cider apple, the Black Taunton, and the cider is delicious. Autumn is beautiful here. The leaves turn colour, farmers harvest their orchards, there are cider-press parties. It's very festive.' He was being shameless, tempting her with ideal images of country life in the hopes that she'd be here in September, that she would want to make the marriage regardless of the need for it.

She laughed and licked sugar from her lips. It was not meant to be seductive, but a bolt of yearning shot through him none the less. 'You live a charmed life, Conall Everard. You have a beautiful home, a lovely family and Midas's own touch. Whatever you turn your hand to becomes a success.'

Charmed? Guilt pierced his yearning, a reminder that he'd succeeded thus far by employing a certain level of deceit. He'd done his job well if she believed all she'd seen. But it was an illusion—except for the family, he did have a good family. The quality of his home had been tricked out with smoke and mirrors. If she went upstairs she'd see a different story in the bedrooms where curtains were faded and carpets worn thin with age. As for his success, well, that had been a near-run thing and still would be until the first alpaca wool products were ready.

They were out in the sunshine now, away from the crowds as they ate their buns. 'May I tell you something?' He should at least attempt to disabuse her of some of her notions. She'd make him out to be a god otherwise. 'Today is the first day I've felt even remotely close to Midas since my father died.'

He finished his bun, trying to find the words to explain. 'Being an heir is an awkward position. I don't think people fully understand how morbid it is. You spend your life being trained by your father to take his place, to anticipate his death. Perhaps even to hope for it because you cannot fully come into your potential without it.' He shrugged, trying to shake off the emotions. He'd never shared them out loud before for fear people would think he was crazy. 'Secretly, I think second sons have it better. They are free to develop themselves, to explore their interests in a way an heir is not. Our lives are one long morbid waiting game. I wouldn't want that for my children. I didn't want my father to die. I would have been willing to wait years if it meant more time with him.'

'You loved him. He was a good father,' Sofia offered softly.

'Yes, he was,' Conall said slowly, letting the realisation settle around his mind. Amid the grief and the feeling of betrayal that had accompanied his father's death, it had been easy to forget that. He'd spent a large part of the year being angry at his father for leaving them, for lying to them about the disastrous situation of their finances.

What had he said to his mother last night? That a person shouldn't be judged by their single failing? But he had done just that. He'd allowed his father's one failing to weigh against the good. His father had *loved* him, played with him, taken a hand in raising him, taken him fishing, taught him about the outdoors, while Sofia had had the very worst of fathers, a man who'd sold her into marriage to a wicked, corrupt man in order to cover his sins. 'I'm sorry,' he said simply. She would know all that was entailed in those words. Sorry for being maudlin on a sunny day, sorry that she hadn't known his father, sorry that she hadn't had a better father herself.

Conall smiled, working hard to restore the earlier levity. 'Here I am. The local registrar's office, the place where I can apply for a civil licence. Do you want to come?' Usually only the groom was needed for the allegation.

She paused, her eyes wary. He sensed her reticence return. 'It's just a precaution.' Conall reminded her, 'We want to be prepared.' Thank goodness for the new marriage act that allowed people to marry legally outside the Church of England. He wouldn't have to go into London for a special licence, or wait three weeks to have banns called.

'Might I look around? Perhaps I'll visit the stationer's for art supplies.'

Conall put a steadying hand on her arm. 'It's just a licence. We don't have to use it.' Although the thought of not using it left him hollow. In that moment, he knew the truth. He was lost, despite his attempts to convince himself otherwise, that he had this relationship well in hand. It simply didn't matter that she was the divorced Marchesa di Cremona, the woman who had made a poor foreign marriage, the woman who'd slapped Wenderly for his salacious offer. Unless he could rewrite the rules of society, there would *never* be a time when Sofia Northcott would be a suitable choice for a man such as him. But he could not shake the idea there was no one *more* suitable.

She straightened her shoulders. 'I'll meet you afterwards. I will meet you outside the Black Horse Tavern.'

Sofia wandered the stalls, making her way towards the stationer's store on St James, her mind replaying the day: each conversation, each touch, each smile, a pearl of its own. She'd never had a day like this, strolling around a market on a good man's arm, whose wish was to make her happy, to *ask* after her happiness. And he'd shared part of himself with her today, speaking of his father and his feelings. Had she ever been that close to anyone before?

Oh, she had to be so careful! If she wasn't, she'd have herself falling in love with him and the fantasy of their sham marriage. She'd forget all the reasons she couldn't really go through with it. She could play at the engagement, she could even let him get the licence. But she prayed he wouldn't have to use it. She could only disappoint him no matter how hard he argued to the contrary, no matter how much she wanted to believe those arguments.

Lost in her daydream, she'd not paid attention to her surroundings. Her skin prickled and Sofia paused at a booth selling wooden toys, pretending to admire a carved doll. Someone was watching her. Surreptitiously, she looked about the market to quiet her jangled nerves. But she found only the usual array of people: a man slouching against a booth, a woman with a basket full of produce, customers haggling over prices. The sights and sounds were to be expected. It was an act of appeasement. No one here knew her and no one knew she was here. She was just another customer at the market.

Still, she'd feel better if she moved. Sofia hurried away from the stall, crossing the street and taking refuge in the stationer's shop. The shop was quiet and she lingered over the assortment of pencils and papers. But her gaze strayed out the window, the sensation of being watched remained, suggesting she had not only been watched in the market—she'd been followed. Which meant someone knew who she was. That list was short.

Cold fear made her stomach churn even as she sought to reason with her runaway imagination. She rapidly made her purchases, trying to keep a sense of normalcy about her actions. If she was imagining the stalker, she would look silly and paranoid for running. If she wasn't imagining it, she didn't want to alert her stalker to the fact that she was aware of them. She gathered up her purchase and fixed her mind on one goal: getting to the Black Horse Tavern. If she could just reach Conall, all would be well.

She stepped outside, looking left, then right before hurrying on. Just two streets to go. She was nearly there. She breathed deeply, repeating the mantra she'd concocted since stepping out of the stationer's: there was nothing to fear. She was safe. She could see the sign for the inn from here, everything would be…

A man bumped into her from behind, causing her to stumble. She fell, going down hard on her hands and knees, the impact of the fall making it hard to breathe. The contents of her basket spilled on to the pavement. Instinctively, she reached for the children's pencils, gasping for air. A man's dirty boot came down on the pencils, snapping them inches from her hand, his hand tangling in her hair and jerking her head back to look him in the eye as she choked on fear and recognition. She couldn't get her body to co-ordinate its effort, couldn't find enough air to scream, couldn't find enough strength to fight him as he dragged her into the alley, away from prying eyes, eyes that might bring help.

'My pardon, Marchesa.' The man leered, showing off a dirty face and a mouth missing teeth. She trembled with shock, the brick wall at her back the only thing holding her up. She could not faint. It would all be over then. He would carry her off. She'd thought never to see this man again, this man who'd been her jailer, entrusted by her husband never to let her out of his sight. It was a duty he'd done exceedingly well. He'd made her life a living hell.

'I've been missing you, my pretty trollop. Il Marchese will be glad to know you're safe.' He put his face close to hers, close enough to smell the garlic on his breath. 'Aren't you tired of this game yet? I always find you.' He yanked more forcibly on her hair, causing her to make a choking mewl of pain. 'Maybe you like it, though. Maybe you like what we do to you afterwards, hmm, my pet? Il Marchese is planning a special welcome for you this time. I'm to give you a taste if I found you.' A knife flashed in his free hand.

'No, please. No cutting.' Too late, she'd forgotten not to beg. Three years of freedom had made her forgetful. He gave an evil growl and she shut her eyes tight. But the cut never came.

She heard the snap of bone and the meeting of fist with flesh. Her eyes flew open. Conall was there, standing between her and the henchman, the henchman grabbing his nose in pain, blood spurting between his hands. But Conall wasn't done. His fists struck the man again, once to the stomach, once to the face and repeated until the man was doubled over, the knife clattering away. Conall took a final swing at the man's face, rendering him unconscious.

He turned to her, breathing hard, his body bristling with fury, his face filled with rage. She'd never seen a man so fierce on her behalf. 'Sofia, what happened? I'll get the constable.' His eyes raked her form, searching for signs of injury.

'He broke the children's pencils,' she stammered, shock taking her. 'No constable, please.' She gripped the lapels of his jacket, pleading. She didn't want to give explanations, didn't want to create a scandal. Good Lord, that seemed to be all she did. Even when scandal didn't follow her, she managed to create one.

Conall's hands bracketed her face, forcing her to focus. 'Sofia, are you hurt? I saw him drag you into the alley, I came as fast as I could. I was at the other end of the street. Dear Lord, Sofia, when I saw him knock you over and put his hands on you…'

She shook her head. 'I'm fine. I'm all right,' she assured him, desperate now not for herself, but for Conall. She did not want him embroiled in this. She could only imagine what he would have done if she had been hurt. Her jailer would be dead. She knew that with a painful, stunning clarity. Conall would not have hesitated to kill him. Conall had been her warrior and it could not happen again. She could not risk him. Giancarlo was here, somewhere near. His minion was his warning just as the burglary had been his calling card. Giancarlo was closing in and he would stop at nothing, not even a chivalrous viscount. Giancarlo would kill Conall to get to her.

Conall would not die for her. She began to shake in earnest now, the seriousness of the attack and its aftermath overwhelming her. She collapsed in Conall's arms, finally giving in to shock, her body cold, her mind numb. Giancarlo had found her in the most personal of ways. He was tightening his net. The last few moments had changed everything.

Chapter Seventeen

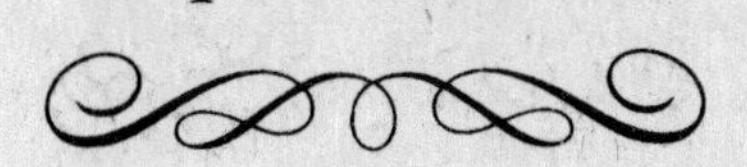

They must marry right away. It was the one thought that had run through his mind since the attack. Conall paced the length of the Dower House parlour, all his agitation and pent-up anger taking up residence in his strides. He'd brought Sofia home and promptly called for reinforcements against Sofia's protests that she was fine. She was far from fine and in no condition to be on her own. He knew from experience it was times like these when one needed to draw one's family close about them.

She'd barely spoken a word on the drive back, staring blankly at the passing scenery. He'd allowed it, choosing not to press her on the details of the episode immediately. He was already regretting his decision not to call for the constable. But Sofia had been insistent she didn't want the attention and, in his desire to see her home safely, he'd let her have her way on the subject. Now, Sofia sat in a chair by the window, dressed in a clean gown, her hair loose, his sister beside her, his mother in the opposing chair and Freddie at the cold mantel.

Conall went to the decanter on the sideboard beneath the window and poured himself a drink. He had his own nerves to settle. Sofia had been assaulted. The episode was imprinted on his mind. He could see the incident happen in slowed motion. He'd begun to run the moment she'd fallen, prepared to fight when the man dug his hands into her hair and yanked her into the alley, making it clear this was no accident, but a targeted attack. Which led Conall to a troubling conclusion: the man had known her, had been following her, waiting to make his presence known.

'Who was he, Sofia?' The man looked more like a street thug, the kind hired to retrieve a gambling hell's unpaid debts, than an Italian marquis's servant. Conall toyed with his glass, his mind full of recriminations. He shouldn't have left her alone.

'A man who works for my husband.' Sofia's hands were clenched, white and tight in her lap, evidence that shock and fear still lingered.

'You knew him, then?' Conall pressed gently.

She looked down at her hands. 'Yes, I knew him. He is in Il Marchese's employ. When I was married…' She hesitated over the word, her gaze coming up and darting to his family.

'We know, Conall has told us everything.' Cecilia took her hand in a sweet gesture of feminine alliance. 'You are among friends here and family,' Cecilia added with a modest blush. 'We'll be sisters soon.' Conall was never more proud of Cecilia than he was in that moment. It was exactly the support Sofia needed.

Sofia offered Cecilia a faint smile. 'His name is Andelmo. He was my bodyguard, at least that's what my husband called him. I was never without him.' A jailer, then. He understood the unspoken words she could not share, not even in front of family. She transferred her gaze to his, a hot flush staining her skin, her eyes warning him not to ask for more. She was remembering difficult times. He felt like a cad to poke at memories she so obviously wanted buried.

'So, the Marchese is here.' The word carried a more dangerous, more explicit meaning than it had just a day ago with the arrival of Helena's letter. Il Marchese was not simply here, as in England, or even here as in London. He was in Somerset, or soon would be. Andelmo was his harbinger. He shared a look with Sofia. They'd been lucky today; he'd meant to take her. Instead, he'd merely warned her, merely tipped his master's hand.

'I can pack and be gone by morning,' Sofia spoke with fierce determination. 'If he means to come, he cannot be here sooner than tomorrow afternoon.' Assuming Andelmo caught the afternoon train to London. 'La Marchesa di Cremona can vanish.'

'Damn right she'll vanish,' Conall growled, not caring if his family heard. Despite Sofia's word to the contrary, he'd expected one last opposition from her, one final but misguided attempt to protect him and his family. 'But not on the train. By tomorrow morning, La Marchesa will become Lady Taunton. Only marriage can protect you now.' He turned to Freddie. 'Perhaps you could persuade the vicar to come after supper, we can do it in the drawing room.'

His mother rose to her feet. 'I will hear of no such thing, Conall Charles Everard.' For a moment the intensity of her glare startled him. He did not need one more fight on his hands. Then she softened. 'No daughter-in-law of mine will be married in such indecent haste. We need at least the evening to make *some* arrangements. Cecilia can see to flowers and I can see to a dress. Cook will need time for a cake and Freddie will need to ride out with invitations.'

'I don't need all that fuss,' Sofia began to argue, but his mother had her well in hand, too.

'Perhaps not, but you deserve it.'

'Mother, really, it's not necessary.' But Conall's argument got no further than Sofia's.

She put a firm hand on his arm. 'It *is* necessary. *You* are Taunton now. Your people need to be included. Your wedding is for them as much as it is for you.' She winked. 'And I still know how to throw a party, even on short notice.'

Conall's mother was as good as her word. Even the weather obeyed her dictates, Sofia mused as an open-air landau pulled up in front of the Dower

House promptly at eight o'clock the next morning beneath blue skies.

Cecilia disembarked, waving up to her, a pair of maids piling out of the carriage behind her with a box in tow. 'I've brought the dress!' Cecilia called up exuberantly. 'We've only got an hour, so we'll have to hurry.'

An hour. Before she married. Her stomach was a ball of knots this morning, not all of them bad. Much to her surprise, the thought of marrying Conall was not a thought that filled her entirely with fear or worry or anxiety. It should—wasn't this what she'd vowed never to do again? Never to give a man control of her life? And yet, not to do this thing would give another man a type of control she did not want him to have: the ability to control where she went and how she lived. Conall was right, if she did not stand and fight now, she would never have the type of control she wanted, never have the life she wanted. She could have that life with Conall.

Upstairs, Cecilia was a whirlwind of orders. Maids laid out white-silk petticoats and satin slippers. They unearthed a gown from layers of tissue that took Sofia's breath away. 'Wherever did you find this?' The dress was elegant simplicity itself, done all in white after the fashion set by Queen Victoria. The bodice of heavy white satin tapered into a deep vee at the waist, the décolletage off the shoulder with tiny puffs of sleeves banded around the arm with a delicate drip of lace.

'It's mine,' Cecilia said over her shoulder, busy laying out brushes at the vanity. 'It was meant to be my come-out gown next year, but I thought you could make better use of it. I am sorry it's not a wedding dress, in truth. It's a bit plain for a viscount's bride, I suppose. We altered it last night.'

Sofia drew a finger over the soft satin of the skirt. 'I can't accept this. It is too much and I have other dresses I can wear that will do.' She would not take this sweet girl's debut gown. Her throat tightened at the thought. Perhaps Cecilia believed there would be no need for it, if her brother married her. 'Have I ruined your chances, Cecilia? Will you not go to London next spring?'

'Oh, my dear, I did not mean to imply—' Cecilia broke off and came to her side, taking her hands. 'No, of course you haven't ruined my chances. In fact, you might just make me interesting enough to notice.' She laughed.

But Sofia had to be sure. 'Do you mind terribly, me marrying your brother?' She'd come to care deeply for this passionate young girl with her ideas and ideals. 'I don't want my happiness to be at the expense of yours.'

Cecilia shook her head. 'Nonsense. We'll worry about next year, next year. Today, we worry about you. Besides, if alpaca wool takes off as Conall expects, he can buy me another gown. But now we need to get you dressed.'

Sofia had taken precautions against that occasion

already. She had her undergarments and corset on and was decently covered. There were only the petticoats and the gown to see to. Her last secret would be safe a while longer. At least until her wedding night. The butterflies fluttered again as the maids helped her with the petticoats. There would be no crinoline today. The gown came next, the satin slipping over her head as her thoughts focused on that one idea and all it meant: her wedding night *with Conall.* She would be his wife. She would be safe from *him.* She would have the chance to live out her dream of making a safe place for those with no voice in society. *If it sounds too good to be true...* No. She didn't want to think about that today.

'You look lovely,' Cecilia breathed in awe beside her. 'Conall will just die when he sees you!' She paused, her eyes shining. 'I think you make him happy, and that's something he hasn't been in a long while. I think he'd want to marry you even if it weren't for the situation with Il Marchese.' She sighed. 'I do so want to see my brother happy again. He's different since our father died.' She shrugged, shaking off the darker thoughts. 'But you will make him better, I just know it.' Sofia hoped Cecilia was right.

They did her hair next, braiding it up in a coronet before settling a long, filmy veil crowned with a wreath of fresh summer flowers on her head. When she saw herself next in the mirror, she looked like a bride in truth, no longer just a woman in a pretty gown. The enormity of what she was about to do settled on her shoulders in a new, profound way after Cecilia's words. This wasn't just about her and her old life. It was about Conall and the new life they'd make together, marriage of convenience or not.

Cecilia retrieved her pearls from the vanity. 'These should do it. Something borrowed—that's my dress—something blue—that's the ribbon on your corset—or…' she giggled '…your eyes. Something old—these pearls—and something new…' She frowned. 'What's new?'

'The slippers?' Sofia suggested. 'Even if they're borrowed, they're new.' But the old rhyme had different meaning for her as she took a final look in the mirror. Today she exchanged the old life for the new. She would not have to rely on the borrowed graces of the Treshams, kind as they were.

'Ready?' Cecilia asked as the clock downstairs chimed ten.

'Yes.' For the first time since Conall had insisted on this marriage, she was ready to accept it. Ready to be his bride in truth and in trust. She indulged in the wave of elation that swept her. *This* was her wedding day. For a moment, a happier bride had never existed.

He was as ready as he'd ever be. Conall stood with Freddie in front of the carved, oak mantel in the drawing room, in his best morning suit—a blue superfine jacket, white linen and slim, dove-grey trousers, every inch of him brushed to sartorial splendour until he positively *gleamed*. He looked out over the 'crowd' gathered in their Sunday best: the squire and his wife, the squire's son's family, the doctor who lived in Taunton, neighbours like the Withycombes and the Hardwickes, all country families he'd grown up with. It might not be St George's in London, packed to the roof, but these guests were sincere. They wished the best for him no matter how hastily arranged it might be.

Although the hastiness was not in evidence outside the arrival of the invitations last night, written in his mother's hand as if they were ordinary letters. His mother and Cecilia and the entire household had outdone themselves—as a way of thank you for bringing jobs to the estate, one maid had told him this morning when he'd complimented the decorations. There were large urns of fresh flowers on the mantel, a beautiful mantel cloth of old lace his mother had found somewhere in the attic and long white tapers. Even the banister of the staircase was dressed in a garland of summer flowers and greenery, lending the house a festive atmosphere.

He was glad his mother had insisted on the effort. He wanted the day to be perfect for his family, for his people, for Sofia, in the hopes that perhaps this wedding day would put the other wedding day behind her. This was the start of their life together and he would make it as good for her as he could so that she would never regret the decision of putting her life in his hands.

Outside, the landau drew up and Conall felt his pulse speed. She was here. Sofia. His bride. Did every bridegroom feel this way? He'd not expected to. He was not marrying her for love. He respected her. He wanted to help her. He was physically attracted to her, but he'd promised himself that those things, while they could equate to feelings for another, did not have to equate to love. And yet here he was, sweating, pulse racing, palms clammy as the vicar's wife played an old, familiar hymn at the pianoforte.

Sofia appeared at the doorway and breathing became difficult. Beside him, Freddie whispered in adolescent awe, 'You're so lucky, Brother.' Lucky was indeed the right word. Sofia was stunning as she walked the short distance to him, satin skirts swaying softly, the gauzy veil over her face, the bouquet of summer flowers he'd sent down this morning in her gloved hands. He would take those gloves off soon enough to put a ring on her finger.

Conall lifted back the veil. Sofia's hair was shining like the sun itself, her eyes glimmering with bridal tears. '"Thou burning sun with golden beam..."' he murmured the lines of the familiar hymn.

'"Thou silver moon with softer gleam,"' she whispered with a smile. 'Your grey eyes have always been my steadying point.'

After that, Conall remembered very little of the service. He supposed it was a beautiful service, but in truth he was focused only on Sofia, only on the promises he made to her and the ones she made to him, the tremble of her hands when he slid the ring on. He remembered the words pronouncing them man and wife, and he would remember that kiss for as long as he lived; the warm response of her lips as he claimed her. Their first kiss *together.* A kiss of hope. Then it was done. La Marchesa di Cremona was no more.

Outside on the back lawn white tents full of trestle tables and food welcomed guests from town. A country orchestra played reels at a makeshift dance floor, games were set up, races for children and contests for adults. Servants had been up since dawn erecting those tents and everyone had contributed to the food, from the butcher to the baker.

Hand in hand, he and Sofia moved from table to table, greeting everyone, talking to each guest and, above all, thanking them. The effort made on his behalf was overwhelming and Conall was touched, often beyond words.

'Thank you for bringing the jobs to the estate, milord.' He heard it over and over as men shook his hand and women hugged him. The words differed but the message was the same:

'We won't have to leave, thanks to you.'

'I was afraid we'd have to go and live with my brother.'

'I can support my family now.'

'Your people love you,' Sofia commented softly as their circuit through the tables ended. 'I imagine rumour of this party will spread far and wide.' She said it laughingly, but Conall heard the question beneath it. They had not been discreet.

'I am counting on it,' he replied, squeezing her hand. He wanted Il Marchese to hear of it, to know that Sofia could never belong to him again in the eyes of the church and the law. With luck, it would drive the man away without him making an appearance in Somerset. He smiled at his bride. 'But that's not what this party is for. It's for you, for my family, for my people.'

Sofia's soft hand stroked his face. 'Is it for you as well?'

He captured her hand and kissed her palm. 'Tonight is for me,' he whispered wickedly. 'For us.' He'd given her all he could: his name, his body, his material possessions such as they were. She had her own limits. Surely, she would understand that he had his.

Chapter Eighteen

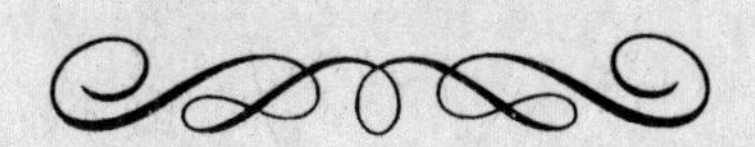

Tonight there would be no limits. Sofia trembled with the knowledge of it as her husband led her up the festooned staircase to the lord's bedchamber. *Her husband*—something she never thought she'd have again, let alone welcome. But she did welcome him. She already knew this. Her body welcomed him and her heart welcomed him, this brave man who was willing to stand in the breach between her and society, between her and Il Marchese, this man who was willing to build a life with her. But tonight, there was one last secret to show him.

They'd said a formal farewell to the guests gathered on the lawn and now, for the first time all day, they were alone together. But even in the lord's chamber they'd not been forgotten. Candles had been freshly lit by a stealthy maid, the bed turned down and sprinkled with rose petals. A bottle of champagne stood sweating and cold on a small table by the window accompanied by a bowl of the largest, fresh-picked strawberries, red and ripe. The scent of a summer night quietly filled the air: sweet, direct. It carried a type of innocence with it. So unlike... She didn't want to think of another wedding night. But how could she not compare them?

Conall moved to the champagne and popped the cork. He poured her a glass. 'Some day, you will lay those ghosts, Sofia. For now, it is enough that you see the difference between then and now, between what you were and what you've become.' He picked up his own glass. 'Cheers to the future, my beautiful wife.' They drank, the champagne cold on her dry throat. Conall set aside his glass and began to strip, slowly, deliberately, much as he had on the river bank, a man comfortable in his skin. Naked in the candlelight, he did not disappoint. 'Now it is your turn—shall I help?' He took her nearly empty glass of champagne.

She hesitated. 'I'm not so beautiful, Conall.' She was not ready to let go of the illusion that had been today; the illusion of a perfect wedding created so skilfully by his family; the illusion of being a bride Conall Everard would have chosen on his own if his honour hadn't prompted him. He would see now that her divorce wasn't her only flaw, that even the superficial beauty of her was an illusion as well.

Conall began to work the laces of the gown. 'Let me be the judge of that,' he murmured softly at her ear, his hands competent and swift, slipping the satin from her shoulders. 'I want to see you, all of you, naked, Sofia, every beautiful inch of you.' But of course, he didn't know, couldn't guess what was beneath her clothes.

The exquisite gown fell to her feet in a cloud of white satin, her corset, her chemise, her pantalettes, joining it as Conall stripped away her last defences. The breeze from the window caressed her bare skin and she trembled. Behind her, Conall's body was a delicious contrast of warmth and male heat. He ran his hands down her arms, his voice a husky whisper. 'Don't be afraid.'

He drew her to him then, her buttocks against the heat of his groin where his desire was evident, her back against the strength of his chest, his arms wrapping about her, his hands skimming upwards from the flat of her stomach to the fullness of her breasts, filling his hands with her, learning her with each caress in ways he'd not learned her before at the river. She closed her eyes, savouring the moment, because it couldn't last, her body poised for the inevitable.

She knew the moment he found it. His warm hands froze. His finger traced the ridges. 'Dear God, the bastard branded you.' Conall's voice cracked. With revulsion? With distaste? Sofia swallowed. He would not want her now. She stepped away from him, turning slowly to face him, to show him.

'Now you know I am not beautiful.' Even her beauty was an illusion. 'I have a lovely face, nothing more.' Giancarlo had seen to that. *This will stop anyone who seeks to cuckold me. I should have done this long ago.* Sofia squeezed her eyes shut, pushing back the memory of the searing heat, the smell of burning skin, her skin, as the R pressed into her, Andelmo holding her down as she'd screamed. It was the type of brand given to runaway slaves. She moved her hands to cover herself and waited for the rejection.

'No.' Conall's voice was firm, firm enough to make her eyes open. 'You don't need to cover it up. You don't need to hide it, not from me.' His eyes met hers. His horror had been *for* her. Not in reaction *to* her. 'The Marchese did this because you ran away?'

'Twice.' Her voice sounded small.

'Twice? You're very brave, my dear girl.' Conall's finger traced the R anew and she saw something new in his gaze, not the revulsion she'd expected to see, but respect, admiration, mingled with deep sorrow. Real sorrow, not pity. 'Someone should have stopped him. Someone should have protected you.' He danced her back to the bed and they lay down, length to length as they had been at the river. There was comfort in the familiar, in the notion that she and Conall had an intimate ritual all their own. His hand was warm at her hip, his light stroke encouraging. 'Tell me? Sometimes the best way to exorcise ghosts is to confront them.'

Here in this little candlelit cocoon of theirs, she could tell her story, needed to tell her story perhaps in order to let it go, to be rid of its power over her. 'There was no one I could turn to. I was an outsider. I barely spoke any of the language. No one was willing to risk Il Marchese's wrath to help a foreigner. So, I learned to help myself.' It had been another reason why he'd been so keen on an English bride. The language barrier, the new culture, being an outsider had all been restrictions of their own. Prisons without walls, without locks. She'd been entirely reliant on him.

Conall's grey eyes were steady. 'And your wedding night? Was he cruel then, too?'

'He brought ropes and a blindfold to our wedding chamber,' Sofia confessed. 'He felt it was important to initiate his virgin bride to his tastes immediately. Later, he had other games. Many were physical, not all of them. I made the mistake of thinking humiliation only existed in the physical variety. It didn't. There were the clothes, the places he took me, the things he'd ask me to do.' Sofia shook her head. 'I don't want to remember him tonight. I don't want him to have a place here.'

'And now he won't. Here, in this room, in this bed, with me, you are safe. Always.' He put his mouth on the brand, tracing it with kisses. 'R is for redeemed, Sofia.' And then the loving began. He came astride her, straddling her body with his long, muscled legs, his head lowering to kiss her mouth, her throat, her breasts and the valley in between leading to her navel. 'Will you let me be in charge tonight? Let me show you that it can be good even when you are not in control?'

How easily he'd divined the secret that had sustained her courage on the river bank. He slid down her body, his hands framing her hips as he kissed her abdomen, the nest of her mons and, lower still, finding the seam of her. Kisses turned to licks, her sighs of delight to begging mewls. *More, more, more.* She was deliciously out of control, this mix of the new with the old. They had done this before, but tonight was different. They were naked, both of them entirely exposed, and she was giving him his lead, putting herself into position as the recipient, not the director of the pleasure, and it was a heady difference indeed even knowing what came next.

Conall raised up over her, his eyes dark with unrestrained desire, his arms bracketing her head, as he levered his body between her thighs, already wide, taking her in a swift thrust, her body ready for him, eager for him. *Yes, this!* her body cried. This was how it was supposed to be: a lover who was energetic and thorough, dedicated to mutual pleasure.

Sofia picked up his rhythm, hips rising in time with his; thrust and slide, thrust and slide, until the pleasure came again, claiming and receding like the tide with each pulse, each movement pushing her closer to the brink again. Only this time she was not alone, this time it would not be pleasure for only one, but for both. She could feel it in the gathering tension of his body, in the ragged inhalations of his shortening breaths. Climax was coming. And when it did, they shattered together, bodies slick, breathing laboured, desire satiated.

* * *

Sofia floated in the aftermath, savouring the moments of bliss in no-man's-land where no fear could reach her, no doubts. She snuggled against Conall's shoulder, his arm draped across her hip as he dozed. She was drowsy, too, she could feel sleep coming for her on the wings of lovely, impossible dreams. She would fall asleep in this man's arms every night; passion was hers for the taking as long as she conquered her fears. But before she let sleep claim her, Sofia reached up a hand to push an errant strand of hair out of Conall's face and smiled at her sleeping husband and whispered the impossible words, 'I love you.' He'd given her a great gift tonight in ways that went far beyond the physical. She loved him, as much as she could allow herself to love a man.

She'd married the Viscount, the cunning bitch! Anger coursed like wildfire through Giancarlo. A lesser man would leave on the nine-fifty to Taunton and confront them both, but Giancarlo Bianchi liked to think he was not *un elefante in un negozio di porcellane*, charging in with no finesse. There was no game in that. No pain in it. Giancarlo gave his cigar a hard, satisfying snip and lit it on the balcony of his Coburg suite. Emotional castration, that was what he sought. He let out a long exhalation of smoke.

It had been a week of shocks. His man, Andelmo, had returned with a black eye and sore ribs, claiming he'd barely been able to drag himself to the train on its return to London. The Viscount was serious about her, then. Serious enough to follow a man with a knife into an alley unarmed. That level of seriousness had been borne out in *The Times* days later with the announcement of the marriage. Taunton was indeed serious about protecting her. But if Taunton thought a piece of paper would stop him, Taunton had misjudged. Possession was nine-tenths of the law. If he could drag Sofia back to Piedmont, he would let the Catholic King and the Pope sort out the legitimacy of a civil-licensed, Protestant marriage and see what Taunton had to say about that then.

Giancarlo blew out smoke. Of course Sofia had married. She knew he was coming. She must be very scared indeed. She didn't know when, however. That was what made the game delicious. Now, he could claim a dilettante's pleasure in the planning, knowing that every day he delayed was a day of agony for her. Did she realise yet she was the proverbial sitting duck? Marriage had not set her free, it had trapped her. She could not run now. Which meant time was on his side. He knew where she was and where she'd be when he chose to make his move. He would do so when her guard was down, when she thought the Viscount had made her safe. There was just enough trust left in her to believe such a fairy tale one last time. He would have to go through the Viscount, though. That was an unplanned circumstance, but it was easily done. Everyone had an Achilles heel and he already knew Taunton's. Hargreaves had told him:

that damned alpaca project. But it also gave him the perfect opening.

He'd enjoy taking her pet project and turning it against her just as much as he'd enjoy making her a widow. That would certainly cut through the marital paperwork. Perhaps he'd shoot the Viscount in front of her to make sure she understood he meant business. Giancarlo took another long drag on the cigar and leaned on the wrought-iron railing. 'Ah, my dear. I am coming for you and this time I will never let you go.'

Chapter Nineteen

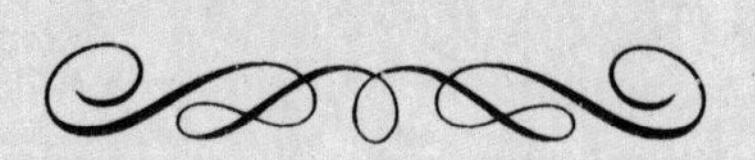

He was never going to let her go. It was Conall's first thought upon waking, Sofia's warm body in his arms and sunlight streaming through the window curtains. It was the perfect morning, as had been the last week of mornings and only a fool wouldn't want more of them. By all accounts, it had been an unorthodox honeymoon. Under other circumstances a man of his stature would have taken his summer bride to the Lake District and a quiet, charming country house, but he had alpaca to shear and a mill to oversee, so they'd settled immediately into the rhythm of daily married life, splitting their time between hiring for the mill and overseeing the shearing. Their days were full and dinners were served late in order to maximise all the daylight possible. But after the dishes were clear and the business of the day was behind them, the nights were theirs. As a result, the alpaca were sheared, the mill was staffed. They had a competent overseer in place and they could begin to relax at least a little. *They.*

So many of his thoughts and sentences these days started with that word and it filled him with a terrifying happiness. How long could it last? Part of him embraced the happiness, but the other part was cautious, waiting for the moment when the bottom would fall out of the fantasy. Helena and Frederick had written, sending their congratulations and news. London had taken the announcement of their marriage with a mixture of mild neutrality and outrage.

Some simply hadn't cared. There were other, more interesting scandals happening right under their noses. They didn't need to beat the brush of the countryside for gossip. But others had cared greatly, mainly mothers with daughters who'd fancied themselves the next Viscountess of Taunton. Those hostesses would not make life easy for Sofia or perhaps for his family when the time came. He'd understood that risk from the start, they all had, and they'd chosen to accept it. That wasn't necessarily the fantasy he was focused on losing. He'd never cared overmuch about London life. It was the fantasy between them, between him and Sofia. That was the fantasy he didn't want to lose. He was holding a small piece of himself in collateral against that moment. Was she?

Sofia's body stirred against him, implicitly answering his as she slowly came awake. Did she feel the same? Partly happy, partly fearful? He kissed her neck and nuzzled her ear. For her sake, he wanted to quash those fears, to give her an entirely fresh start.

That was his mission today: to secure that happiness, starting right now. He pressed another set of soft kisses to the back of her neck, a smile taking his mouth when he felt her stir. Her derrière wiggled deliciously against his groin as she stretched, a little mewl of delight indicating her willingness to play.

Her soft bottom bumped the hard length of him in invitation and he took it, entering her from behind in a long, lingering thrust, taking his time as he filled her and as she stretched to accommodate him. She made him feel as if he'd finished a long journey and arrived at the one place where he knew he belonged. How fantastic and strange to find that place with a stranger he had not known seven weeks ago. His hands cupped her breasts in a gentle holding. He listened to her sigh and he began to move again. As languorous as the joining was, it did not take long to bring them to a slow, boiling climax that left them both lazily soporific in its aftermath.

He played with her hair as he held her close, watching the sunlight turn it platinum and gold in shifts. 'Spun gold, that's the colour of your hair. Do you know the children's tale of Rumpelstiltskin? The little man who spun straw into gold? I always imagined this was the colour of it.'

'I like that. I carry a fortune in my hair.' She gave a soft laugh.

'Shall we ride out for a picnic today? Just the two of us?' he cajoled quietly at her ear. She smelled like sage and love in the morning and he was already stirring for her again. 'We can dance barefoot in the grass, fly kites and pick wild flowers. We can hunt for strawberries.' There would be blankets and a hamper of food, and time to make love under the blue sky.

'What about work?' She hesitated with practicalities.

'Beautiful days in England should not be wasted. We never know when we'll get another,' Conall joked. 'Tell me you'll come for a proper English picnic. Well, at least an *improper* English picnic. Proper ones aren't nearly as much fun.'

She turned in his arms and wrapped her arms about his neck. 'I suppose the mill can do without us for a day.'

It was to be a holiday in truth, a break from all that populated their days. They drove out to a weir, away from town, away from the mill, away from the pastures full of big, brown-eyed alpaca, away from the house with its constant bustle of people. For a woman who had lived three years quietly and mostly alone, it was a welcome change of pace. Not that she minded the constant companionship of her new family and station in life, but it did take some getting used to.

She was finding, much to her surprise, she didn't like sharing Conall *all* the time, yet part of what she adored about him was the way he selflessly gave of himself to others. There were other surprises, too, in these heady midsummer days. Her mantle of fear was slipping. Each day she waited for the bottom to fall out of her happiness and each day, when it didn't, the horror of Andelmo's attack receded, the belief growing that she could be safe here. The most wicked whisper of all took up residence in her conscience: maybe Conall was her reward. She had suffered and now she was entitled to some happiness of her own.

Not the least of the surprises was her personal happiness. She *was* happy. *With* Conall. *Because* of Conall. She had not expected happiness and she'd certainly not expected to find it with a man, in marriage. And yet, somehow, she had. Or most of her had. Part of her clung to the old admonition: when something sounded too good to be true…but each day the admonition faded just a bit more, overwhelmed by this new sense of freedom without fear. She laughed out loud for the pure joy of it. There was only light now.

A pleasant breeze blew at the blanket in her hands as she tried to spread it on the ground. 'Did you bring those kites? The wind is picking up.'

'I found Freddie's old ones in the stable.' Conall held up a furled bundle. 'Shall we give it a try?'

He let out the string and motioned for her to join him. 'Come hold the string.'

They got the kite aloft and Conall wrapped his arms about her, hands on hers where she held the ball of string. She was warm against him, smelling of sun and sage. This was all that mattered, being here with him. He wished it was that simple.

'Let the string out a little, it wants to soar,' he coached her gently, but the wind gusted, tugging hard at the kite, and Sofia gasped, the string slipping out of her hands. 'Oh, no! It's getting away, Conall!'

He was after the kite in an instant, running hard to grab the trailing ball of string as it unravelled. At last, he grabbed the string and brought the kite back to the blanket. 'My offering, dear lady.' He knelt on one knee, giving the kite and string to Sofia like a knight of old, and she laughed, watching him sprawl on the blanket beside her. He propped himself up on an elbow, head in his hand. 'I haven't done that for ages. When we were younger, Freddie and I would let the kites go on purpose and run after them.'

'Did you catch them?' Her hands deftly sorted through the tangle of string.

'Usually. I'm a fast runner, in case you didn't notice.' Conall laughed and lay back, his hands tucked behind his head.

'You're a good brother to have flown kites with Freddie when he would have been so much younger than you,' Sofia said softly, imagining Conall nearly full grown, on the cusp of manhood, out in the fields still flying kites. 'How much younger is Freddie?' Sometimes she marvelled at how much she felt for this man when she knew so little about her husband and his family. And then were days when she felt like she knew all she needed to know.

'Fourteen years. But I was glad to have a brother and a sister. Being an only child is lonely. I played with Freddie every chance I had when I was home from university. I missed him those years I was in America. I didn't want *him* growing up without a brother, especially when *he* didn't have to. He had Cecilia, of course, they are only two years apart, but it's not the same.'

'Your family makes me envious,' Sofia admitted with a sigh. 'My brother and I were close in age, but never close otherwise. I was simply…trouble…an expense to be borne in the pursuit of having another son, a calculated risk. But there wasn't another son.' Her hands stopped working. 'There was another boy after me, but he died and then my mother couldn't have any more children. My parents wished I had died instead. I think that's when I first knew I was nothing more than a commodity for them to broker. But I never really believed they would, until they did.' She shook her head. 'Even then, it took me a while to admit to myself what they had done.' She paused. 'That's my great failing, I think. Even when I know better, it takes a powerful amount of evidence for me to believe the worst of someone. There's a part of me that just can't imagine evil even when I know it exists.'

Conall rolled to his side and propped himself up on an arm. 'I think it's called optimism, Sofia. And it's not a weakness, but a great strength. It's been your phoenix, not your albatross. We are married because of it.' He reached for her then, drawing her down to him so that she lay alongside him on the blanket. 'We'll have a family of our own one day, you'll have children to lavish all that optimism and love on and you will be a spectacular mother.'

The words took her breath away. Not because they conjured an image of sitting with children—*Conall's* children—a blond-haired boy and a dark-haired girl on a blanket like this one, tablets on their laps, pencils in their hands as they practised their letters. It wasn't because the words were an approbation of her attributes, or an absolution of her past, but because the words spoke of the future, a private future she and Conall would build together outside the mill and the alpaca and all the people who counted on Taunton for their welfare.

She stroked his face. 'We've never talked about a family before.' She gave a tremulous smile that belied how deeply his words had touched her. All their plans had centred on the good works they'd do externally for the greater good. Never had they spoken of their private life and how that life would be built between them.

'You promised me an improper picnic, Conall Everard. What exactly did you have in mind besides flying kites?' She moved into him, sliding a hand up one long leg to where his body quickened for her.

In a swift move, Conall rolled her beneath him. 'I envisioned this: a slow loving beneath the sun, a light breeze caressing skin and you beneath me, skirts falling back, thighs bare.'

He kissed her hard as he entered her. She moaned

beneath him, her back arching, her eyes fluttering shut as she gave herself over to the pleasure. This was what she wanted to believe in—pleasure and peace always, with Conall. She felt his body gather as she climaxed against him in a soft spasm and he followed her moments later.

Sofia hummed softly to herself as she sat behind Conall's big desk in the estate office, patiently looking through drawers. Cook had brought her the receipts from the market shopping and she thought to enter them in the household ledgers while Conall's mother was out visiting a neighbour with Cecilia. Eventually, the transition between Dowager and the new lady of the house would be complete. For now, Sofia was happy to let her mother-in-law run the house while she focused her efforts on the mill. Still, Sofia felt it was important to do her domestic part whenever possible so that the servants would come to respect her authority as well as the Dowager's. It was a good sign today, she thought, that Cook had sought her out instead of waiting for Conall's mother to return.

Ah ha! Success! Sofia drew a long, brown ledger out of the drawer and opened it, flipping to the most recent page only half-filled with receipts and purchases. She began to write down the day's entries when a something further up the page caught her eye. A minus sign, an indication of a deficit. She furrowed her brow and flipped back a page. Another deficit. Then an entry marked: sale of china and an addition of funds; sale of upstairs painting. She ran her finger up the ledger, finding the pattern. The household was running in the red, only the sale of items kept the accounts balanced. She traced back to March and then rose and combed the bookcases for another. The ledgers were quarterly records and she wanted to see the rest of the year. A suspicion was taking root. She hoped she was wrong.

She pulled the other ledgers down from the shelves and settled at the desk, horror growing with each turned page. The Viscountcy had run in the red for over a year. *A year spent in mourning.* That triggered another thought. Conall's father's death. She pulled the previous year and then a sampling of the earlier years, a sense of panic giving speed to her fingers as they ran through the columns, her mind assimilating the facts at lightning speed.

Sofia sat back in the chair, her heart pounding. Two facts were clear: the Taunton coffers were empty, far emptier than she might have guessed on her own, and they had been for a while, long before Conall had inherited; second, everything that could be leveraged had been for the purchase of the alpacas back in November. She did the maths; the purchase would have been arranged over the winter, the alpacas transported when the winter seas stilled, arriving the end of March, perhaps. In April, Conall had come to London to seek funds from the Prometheus Club for his mill, for his syndicate.

She sighed and closed her eyes, remembering that first walk in the garden. He must have been desperate by then, knowing he had no resources left and no place to make the wool. He needed that mill. He'd taken an enormous gamble and he'd been out on a limb and unable to crawl back to safety. Her heart wanted to weep for him. How difficult it must have been for him. And how strong he'd been, not letting on at all how he must hurt, how he must have panicked. And yet, he still found time to dance with her, to take care of her when her house had been burgled, when she'd sat alone in the church amid her enemies.

But her mind had other ideas about what she should feel. Logic taunted her. *Of course he found time for you. You were eager to invest, you had money, piles of it. Silly girl. When it sounds too good to be true, it probably is...*

Sofia gripped the edges of the desk, her knuckles white as she tried to push back the rampaging thoughts. He'd taken a gamble large enough to countenance the trade-off of marrying her. So large, in fact, he'd risk Cecilia's Season against his ability to win over society with his success and perhaps his charm in order to make others forget the inappropriate history of his new wife. Marriage certainly suited him far better than merely arranging for the mill.

The full import of that took her like a punch to the stomach, nearly winding her. Why stop with a mill, when he might solve all his problems by marrying her for *all* the money? Her rational brain laughed at her. All this time, she'd been so sure he hadn't been seducing her. It was a most crafty seduction with those manners and courtly gestures of restraint all the while making it clear he wanted her. He'd been stoking her curiosity—how would it be to be with a good man, to be cared for by a good man? But he wasn't a good man, was he? Not entirely. For the greater good of his family, his Viscountcy, he'd lied to her in the worst of ways. He'd made her believe he cared for her, even loved her, that they would build a life together. *Our children, you will be a spectacular mother.* He'd been building that fantasy even yesterday as they'd lain together on the picnic blanket. Giancarlo had never pretended *that*. But who else had pretended? Cecilia? His mother? Freddie? Had all the warmth and acceptance been an act?

Another wave of horrible thoughts came to her. Now that Conall had what he wanted, would he still protect her if Giancarlo came? Or would he step aside and wash his hands? What would be the greater scandal? Would Giancarlo simply buy him off with enough money to make the loss worth it? Conall had already proven, hadn't he, that he had a price.

Her fearful mind came to life after so many dormant weeks. She had to leave. She had to go before she found out the answer to the horrible question. She didn't want to know the answer. The optimist in her wanted to hold on to at least a shred of memory, a shred of what happiness felt like, even if it was feigned, so that sometimes she could take out the shred and pretend that perhaps for moments the happiness had been real.

She steadied herself, forcing deep slow breaths into her lungs. She would just concentrate on the next step and then the next. She would turn her attention away from the big picture. She would go upstairs and pack. She might even make the evening train if she hurried. It didn't matter where it went, only that it did. She had to be away from here. Conall wasn't due back from town until supper.

Sofia only made it halfway across the room before the door opened and Conall blew in, his hair windblown. 'Sofia!' Excited energy radiated from every pore, a grin on his face, a paper in his hand. Damn, but she didn't want to remember him this way, looking as if she was his world.

At the sight of her face, though, the excitement faded. His gaze scanned the room, his own energy dampening. 'What is going on?' The exuberance was caged now, replaced by wariness.

'Perhaps I should ask you that.' She'd not wanted this confrontation.

Chapter Twenty

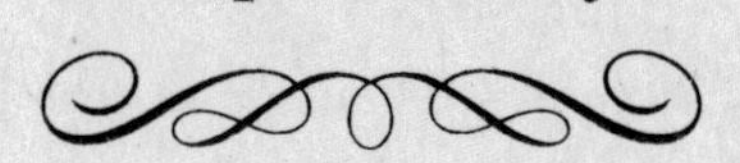

He did not want this confrontation. One look at the room told him all. She knew. Sofia had discovered his one guilty secret. He'd convinced himself telling her didn't matter any more. They were together now in all ways. There was no need. He'd been wrong there. There was every need.

'You saw the ledgers.' He folded the letter in his hand and put it in his pocket. His news could wait. From the stricken look on Sofia's face, this was far more important.

'Yes.' Her voice was polite, cold. He'd heard that tone before in the rail car on the journey from London. They were going to be civil and do their best to talk about the situation in business terms devoid of emotional attachment. 'It seems the Viscountcy was facing financial hardship and had been for quite some time. You needed my support badly.'

'Yes. There had been a series of poor investments, but my father had said nothing. We only discovered the state of the books after his death.' The old anger surfaced, anger that had nowhere to go, no one to direct it at because that person was gone.

'Thankfully, you're twice the businessman your father was.' Sofia's eyes were hard sapphires again, the way they'd looked when he'd first met her. 'Why stop at a mill partnership when you might have so much more.'

Conall's brow furrowed. 'What are you implying?'

'You married me for my money and you put on quite a show to get it, you and your perfect family.' Conall froze. The depth of her anger showed through those words. The ruse that had so long ago ceased to be a trick was coming back to haunt him.

'It's not like that, it hasn't been like that for a while.' Would she believe him? Conall could feel the threads of his new marriage unravelling.

'Ah ha! But it was like that in the beginning, wasn't it?'

'There was never any intention to force you into a marriage,' Conall argued. 'Do you want me to admit to needing the money? Yes, I needed it. Yes, we arranged for you to see the best of us, the best of Everard Hall in the hopes it would influence a favourable outcome. But that was all and it didn't last long.' He paused, slowing his words. 'We came to like you, Sofia. I came to like you, to respect you, to admire your fight, and that admiration grew into something much more. What I feel for you is not a ruse. I proposed marriage for your protection because I could not imagine you in the hands of that bastard again.'

The debate in her eyes nearly broke him, her sharp businesswoman's mind against her optimist's heart. 'You still don't believe in me.' This was not her tragedy alone, but a tragedy for their marriage. He hated being the one who had put the doubt there, hated the realisation that for how far they'd come together, they still had not come far enough for her to trust him. At the first sign of trouble, it was easier for her to think the worst of him, instead of what they were building together. 'I have always thought the best of you, Sofia,' he said solemnly. 'I wish you would do the same of me.'

'How can I when there is evidence to the contrary? The ledgers don't lie. You need money and I had it to give.'

'You needed protection and I had it to give,' Conall answered. 'This was a marriage of convenience from the start, your terms, your preference, and now you are angry over the truth.' He had her there. A hot blush crept up her cheeks. 'Your own anger should be proof enough I speak the truth, the *new* truth between us, that there is more than convenience between us now. What might have started as a trade of services, if you will, has given birth to true affection. I think that's what scares you. If you can't be angry with me, you might have to love me and you're afraid to do that.' He clenched his fists at his sides, his own emotions roiling. He'd never wanted to throw something so badly in his life. The shattering of a crystal vase against the hard marble of the fireplace would be most satisfying right now. As would taking Sofia in his arms and kissing her hard and senseless until she saw the nonsense of her fears.

'I'm not the only one who's afraid,' Sofia retorted. 'You're scared, too.'

'Yes, I am. I am afraid you'll run, Sofia. That you won't believe in me enough to let me keep you safe, to let us build the life we could have together.' After the bliss of yesterday, he should have expected some kind of resistance like this. She'd flown so close to the sun on that picnic and now she was warning herself to beware. He wanted her to stop looking over her shoulder and live in the present fully. 'If you don't let go of the past, Sofia, I cannot save you. I cannot save *us*.'

'And I cannot save you.' Something in her was letting go, was relenting in the wake of his words, and she feared it. She would lose this battle if she stayed much longer. 'I am not the only one living with the past.' She'd seen it in the ledgers, the ghosts he fought against. 'Do you think I don't see the grief, see the anger behind your efforts? You love your father and you hate him, too. You haven't forgiven him for...something.' She groped for a word there. She hadn't figured that out yet. It wasn't the debt that angered Conall. It drove him, but it didn't anger him.

'The illusion,' Conall said tightly. 'He created a

world that didn't exist and he built it on money that didn't exist either.'

'We are not so different then.' Sofia swallowed. 'We've both been chasing illusions and we created one between us.' The anger was gone out of their fight now, leaving the ash of shredded emotions. As always with them, they had started with business and meandered into the intimate. 'I will leave and that will be one less illusion for you to worry about.'

She moved to pass, but he would not allow it. His hand gripped her arm. 'Damn it, Sofia. It's not supposed to end this way. You are my wife.'

Her eyes flashed. 'I am sorry to spoil your idea of a happy ending.' But he did not let her go.

Instead, he tugged her to him, his mouth hungrily finding hers and the madness broke out between them. Her cool reserve was gone. Her hands were in his hair, her body pressing hard against him as a sob escaped her, her hands at the waist of his trousers, fumbling in their haste with the fastenings. He lifted her then, pushing back her skirts and balancing her against the wall. This would be swift and powerful.

She was all gasps and moans as he entered her, his name a cry on her lips and he thought for a moment as they surged towards an abrupt, overpowering climax, that he might have a chance, that *they* might have a chance. She felt a shudder run through him. He buried his face against the arch of her neck as release took him. She dug her nails into his shoulders, their grip raw and strong. She fantasised he would have marks even through the fabric of his coats. Raw desire took her. She wanted nothing more than to mark him, a reminder that he'd marked her, too, in ways not visible.

Still rooted in her, he carried her to the sofa near the fire and sat with her astride him. He kissed her softly then, the storm of their passion receding in the wake of something gentler. He kissed her eyelids, her cheeks, the puffiness of her lips, his hands framing her face and tangling in her hair. 'I have one last secret and then all will be out in the open. I love you, my sweet Sofia. Whatever you believe about me, believe that.' His words were coming fast now and his voice was thick. 'You don't have to go. We can make our illusion real.'

He reached for his discarded trousers and took out the paper he'd folded away. 'I was coming to tell you about this.' His grey eyes moved over hers. 'We have an investor. It's the beginnings of our syndicate. Others will come, I am sure of it. His name is Peter Sullivan, he heard about the alpacas in London. He's passing through on his way to Exeter tomorrow and he wants to come for dinner, to see the animals and to talk about investing. We are so close, Sofia. Stay, believe in me, believe in us just a while longer.' He paused. 'Let me prove myself to you. No matter how this thing between us started, it is not that any more, it is far deeper, far more than the convenience either one of us imagined. Say you'll stay.'

'It seems I am always saying yes to you, Conall Everard.' She smiled, but they both knew that what had happened against the wall and what was happening now didn't fix everything. Something between them had been tested today and, while it had survived, it was not entirely intact. *Yet.* And despite the fact that he roused within her, hungry for her again, and that she would slake that need once more here in the office, there was a chance it might never be. She might have to face the reality that she was too broken to fix.

The next evening, the family gathered expectantly in the drawing room, waiting to welcome Peter Sullivan. Sofia smoothed the skirts of her evening gown, keeping her nerves under control as she smiled at Cecilia and Freddie. This was a big night. For them, it was about the hope in meeting a potential investor. Beneath that, there was more at stake between her and Conall. This was about Conall showing her he meant for her to be his partner in all ways. Not only as business partner, but as his wife. *I love you*, he'd whispered yesterday. Tonight, he was acknowledging that by presenting her to his guest.

It was a public and sincere apology for yesterday. Perhaps there was hope for them after all, perhaps Conall was right and they could make a life between them. Her heart ached for that, even after yesterday's discoveries. But she knew, too, that not all of her had quite forgiven him for the deception. Her mind had not been quiet all night with the doubts. She couldn't simply pretend his ruse didn't matter. Neither could she pretend she'd been taken in by that trick, that her guard was not as staunchly established as she liked to believe.

'Did you and my brother quarrel?' Cecilia whispered, coming to stand beside her while they waited for their guest. 'You've hardly looked at one another since we've gathered and I swear the tension between you is almost palpable.'

Sofia smiled. She'd not wanted the family to know. 'It's nothing, just a misunderstanding. Newlywed things,' she offered vaguely. 'It will be fine.'

Cecilia was about to press for details when Sofia was saved by the crunch of carriage wheels in the drive. She patted Cecilia's hand, redirecting the girl's attention. 'Our guest is here.'

There was noise at the front the door, footsteps coming down the hall. The footman intoned, 'Mr Peter Sullivan.' A dark-haired man with olive skin stepped into the room, sweeping them an expansive bow, his eyes locking on hers as the hairs on her neck prickled.

Chapter Twenty-One

This was not Peter Sullivan. Instinctively, she stepped in front of Cecilia, shielding the girl as her worst fears were realised. Giancarlo was here, in this very house where she was supposed to be safe. Her throat tightened. She needed to speak, needed to warn everyone, but she couldn't make her voice work. Conall stepped forward to shake the man's hand. She found her voice. 'Conall, no.' But it was too late.

Giancarlo had come up from his bow with a long-nosed pistol in hand. From her angle, she saw the confusion on Conall's face as he tried to make sense of a guest with a gun. Why would an alpaca investor have a pistol? 'Stand down, Viscount.' Giancarlo waved the gun. 'Sofia, *mi cara*, why don't you introduce me properly?'

'Sofia, what is going on?' Conall's eyes darted to hers, his mind starting to register the answer on its own.

'Shut up, or I'll shoot you now instead of later.' Giancarlo trained the gun on Conall. 'Sofia can decide how long I'll wait to shoot you. Introduce me, *mi cara*.'

She swallowed. She knew this game. Her compliance in exchange for an act of mercy. She'd thought never to have to play it again and certainly not here in the haven of Everard Hall surrounded by people she cared for. 'This is Giancarlo di Bianchi, Marchese di Cremona.' She fought to keep the tremble from her voice. She could not show any fear, nor too much defiance. Too much of either would set him off.

'And?' he prompted as if she were a silly child who didn't know her manners. 'Who are these fine people, *mi cara*?'

'This is the Dowager Viscountess of Taunton, her son, Mr Alfred Everard, and her daughter, Miss Cecilia Everard.' Sofia could feel Cecilia tense beside her and Freddie was bristling from across the room by his mother. She hoped Freddie wouldn't try anything gallant. He was no match for Giancarlo's games.

'Your new family, I hear?' Giancarlo made a mockery of small talk. 'Felicitations on your marriage. I should offer those good wishes now, before it's too late. I'll be offering condolences before long.' He chuckled. 'Married, divorced, remarried, widowed, remarried again. You will have quite the reputation.'

Cold settled over her. In her worst imaginings, she'd pictured Giancarlo taking her. Hurting Conall in the effort. But not this. Not murder. With Conall dead, there would be nothing, no paper, no law, no marriage, no man, to stop Giancarlo from claiming her again. A glance slid between Freddie and his mother. Giancarlo caught it, too.

'I do mean business, although not alpaca business. I am sure that is disappointing for you, it was just a little trick to get an invitation. No one can ever say Giancarlo di Bianchi was an uninvited guest.' Giancarlo laughed at his joke. 'I wouldn't try anything, you two. Let's keep this simple. I am here for what is mine and that is La Marchesa. If you will just come with me, Sofia, we can let these people get on with their dinner.'

'She is not yours,' Conall spoke forcefully. 'She is my wife and she will not leave this house against her will.'

Giancarlo's face turned up into a wicked leer. 'I don't think that will be a problem. As a gentleman, I will give her a choice, of course. You insult my honour.'

Conall's next words were for her. 'You are not to go with him, Sofia, no matter what. Promise me.'

'If she loves you, if she loves *any* of you, she cannot possibly promise that and she knows it.' Giancarlo smirked. 'Don't you, *mi cara*?'

'You can't win. You have one shot,' Conall reminded him. 'You might shoot me, but there are four others in this room and a house full of servants who will bring you down.'

'I can see why you like him, *mi cara*, he's a gallant fool. You always had a sweet spot for those sorts.' Giancarlo laughed. 'Willing to die for her, Taunton? She's that impressive in bed, isn't she? And for your family? That's quite noble. I have yet to meet anyone I'd die for.' He shrugged, his glittering dark eyes hard on Conall. 'As for the odds, you're wrong. Not much of a gambler, are you? I did not come alone. While we've been passing the time of day, my men have rounded up your staff and secured them. They will not be harmed if everyone co-operates, but neither will they be coming to your assistance.' Heavy boots sounded in the hall. 'Ah, here they are now.'

Sofia felt chilled as the hulking form of Andelmo entered the drawing room while a group of men loitered in the hallway. All hope was leaching away. There was real danger here that they would all die and quite horribly.

'Andelmo, if you would keep a gun on this fine gentleman? Taunton seems inclined to honourable sacrifice. I'll see to my wife.' Giancarlo advanced on her. She stepped towards him, shaking off Cecilia's hand. She wanted as much distance between her and the girl as possible. She would wield her beauty as a shield, a chance to keep all the focus on her. With luck, Giancarlo would forget about the dark-haired girl.

'Ah, Sofia. *Molte bene.*' His cold eyes raked her. 'You look as beautiful as ever.' His arm was about her, drawing her against him as a shield, a wicked blade to her throat, his mouth close to her ear, the smell of brandy strong on his breath. He'd been drinking in the carriage. 'What have you told the Viscount about us? Does he know all the things you did for me? Does he know what a naughty little runaway you are? Did you show him the brand? Perhaps he doesn't mind a used whore.'

He tried to march her towards the door, but she dug in her heels. He would not slice her throat. She had a certain latitude there. But he would not hesitate to carve out some retribution of his own, or to throw the blade, finding a target in another of the victims in the room. 'Andelmo will shoot Taunton, I promise you,' he spoke at her ear. 'Don't take it personally, Taunton,' he spoke beyond her. 'I need her for an heir and for my own standing in the court. Divorce is no longer acceptable in Piedmont. The King's son has the throne now and he's done away with his father's liberal leanings. If I don't bring her back, I shall be reduced. Surely, as a man who was recently in need of funds himself, you can understand.'

Sofia was breathing hard now, fighting back the panic his words brought on. She would not go back, she would not…and yet what choice did she have? Conall would not die for her, no one in this room would die for her. She'd brought ruin on them just as she'd always known she would. She would never be free of Giancarlo. The old fears, the old worries, were back in full force now. She could never be free, but Conall could, his family could. She could give them that.

'Don't make it hard on yourself, my dear. I dare say there is punishment enough waiting for you as it is.' He paused and put on an exaggerated show of thinking. 'How about this—come with me peaceably and I won't let Andelmo exact retribution for the drubbing Taunton gave him in town.'

'No, Sofia, don't listen to him,' Conall growled in his corner, a caged bear trapped by a hunter.

Giancarlo forced her forward. 'I will not ask you to walk out of here with me again. Do you remember that boy on Sardinia? The one who flirted with you?' The one he'd shot in the knee, who would never walk right again. 'You know I'll do it. Start walking. The moment we're down the drive, Andelmo will lower his gun. You are the only one who can stop the bloodshed, who can keep your Viscount alive.'

She knew he was right. Sofia began to walk. Conall made a move, brought up short only by her words. 'Don't, Conall. I am not worth it. Let me do this for you.' She willed him to stay still, to stay quiet, to do nothing that would cause Giancarlo and his dubious code of ethics to change his mind.

'You see, she's not leaving unwillingly, just as I promised,' Giancarlo taunted Conall one last time before he hauled her down the stairs and stuffed her into the dark carriage.

It was all falling apart; her world, her heart. Tears were wet on her cheeks. If she broke down now, she might never recover, might never put the pieces of herself back together. Giancarlo had threatened her in Conall's home. The fear she'd so recently released came back in waves, smothering her, shrouding her. The weight of it settled on her shoulders, heavy and familiar, a dark cloak she couldn't shake off as she faced Giancarlo in the carriage, helpless as he bound her hands. 'I can't take any chances with you, can I?'

She'd been ten kinds of a fool to think she could walk in the light, that she could escape. Giancarlo would have killed Conall if she hadn't complied. 'Don't cry, *mi cara*, you'll forget him soon enough. I'll personally see to it. It will be in your best interest.'

Giancarlo settled a hat with a thick veil on her head. 'Just a precaution in case anyone recognises you. We can dispose of it when we reach the ship.' He drew the veiling down, the first of many barriers that would separate her from Conall, from the life she'd so briefly had before the day was through. By this time tonight, England would be behind her, happiness would seem a lifetime ago when she was someone else.

'Do you think he'll come after you?' Giancarlo settled against the squabs with a jeer. 'Or will he decide you are more trouble than you're worth?' She stiffened. She knew this game, too. It was meant to sow doubt, to remind her she was worthless.

Giancarlo fingered his knife, testing the blade. 'It's an interesting litmus test, isn't it? If he comes, then you'll know he's truly besotted. He'll be dead, of course. I have my guns, my knives, I have Andelmo and so many ways to kill him, but at least you'll know he loved you and not your money or your looks. How would you like me to do it? Would you like me to gut him in front of you or just shoot him? If he dies, it will be your fault. You should at least get to choose how. Then again, he might not come at all and you'll know it was all a sham. If so, you should thank me for showing you his truth.'

'You're despicable.'

'And you're still beautiful.' He leaned forward and lifted her veil. 'We're safe enough in here, I suppose. Just you and me.' The blade tickled its way down her jaw. She watched him rub himself with his other hand. 'You still arouse me despite how bad you've been. You are even more beautiful than I remember. When I walked into the drawing room, you looked like an angel with that pale cloud of hair, those pearls at your neck, you dressed in cream silk, like a damned virgin.'

He pulled the pins out of her hair, vicious and rough until the strands fell about her shoulders. 'There, now you look the young girl in truth. Do you remember my favourite fantasy with you: the virgin and the dragon; you bound to the altar, or tied to the stake? Of course, you're not a virgin any longer, or even exclusively mine. How many lovers have you taken since you left? We'll have to have you purified first before we can play those games. There are purgatives that guarantee you don't come to me with the Viscount's babe in your belly.' That brought on an additional sense of panic. It was too early to know, but what if? What if she carried Conall's child? Would that innocent pay for her, too?

He smiled. 'Because of you, I'll be obscenely rich. If you're nice, I'll be generous. I'll have the opportunities promised to me by the King.'

She forced herself not to look away, to show no fear as the bulge in his trousers grew. 'You cannot claim my heart. You never could.' But Conall had claimed it. She knew that now, despite her anger yesterday, despite that doubt. She knew that she loved him and he loved her. She knew it only when it was too late to do anything about it but save him.

Giancarlo chuckled cruelly. 'I never wanted your heart, just your body and your obedience.' He stretched out his legs. 'Get comfortable my dear, we'll drive through the night. We sail at dawn. Andelmo will meet us in Bristol. How nice, the three of us back together again for the duration of our voyage. Who knows what entertainments we'll come up with? Just like old times, don't you think?'

Dawn was just hemming the edges of the sky when Conall rode into Bristol. He couldn't afford to rethink his choices. He'd bet it all on Bristol as Giancarlo's destination. Searching the roads at night had slowed him down considerably, that and the fact that Andelmo had overstayed his welcome. The thug had not followed his master's orders and left when the carriage reached the end of the drive. Instead, Andelmo had held them at gunpoint for a nerve-racking half an hour beyond that, and then bound them up to keep them from following. If it had just been him alone, Conall would have launched himself at the man and taken his chances with the gun, but the presence of his family and the servants effectively held him hostage against such heroics.

By the time he was free and mounted, over two hours had passed and Sofia was further and further from him, in the clutches of a man who terrified and tortured her. It was exactly what Conall had promised her would never happen. He'd also promised her that he'd come for her and he intended to keep that promise at least. He hoped. Right now, that was all he was living on, hope that he'd guessed correctly. There were many roads out of Taunton. Giancarlo might have gone to Exeter, or Bristol, or any of the other coastal towns. Conall was betting on Bristol after none of the other usual carriage routes turned up any sign of a man meeting his description passing that way.

Freddie had wanted to come, but Conall had emphatically insisted he stay behind to look after his mother and Cecilia, both of whom were visibly shaken from the ordeal. He didn't want to worry about Freddie when there was already Sofia to protect and Giancarlo was as cruel and as twisted as they came. He would need all his wits to bring her home safe. And he would.

He loved her. Sofia had been his hope, then a lifeline for a failing estate. But she'd become so much more—the woman he loved, the woman he wanted to build his dreams with, his own family with. He would not fail. To fail would doom her to Giancarlo and the unthinkable. He surveyed the busy port and swung off his lathered horse. He had to act fast. Boats would sail on the tide. If she was on one of these ships, he would miss her. He tossed the reins to a boy waiting to earn a penny. He'd start at the shipping offices, that would be faster. If that wasn't successful, he would throw his title around and search each ship personally.

Conall was in luck at the shipping offices. There was a ship leaving for the Mediterranean on the tide. It was a merchant vessel. A man by the name of Carstairs and his wife had taken the cabin. The names didn't match, but Giancarlo's description did. Conall was sure it was them. But he had to hurry. Morning had broken and the ship would sail. Conall broke into a run. He had only a matter of minutes.

Chapter Twenty-Two

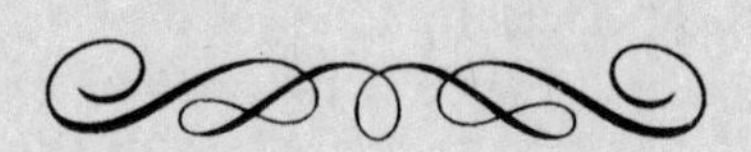

Just a few more minutes and the ship would cast off. Conall would be safe. Sofia repeated the words again and again, holding herself together up the gang-plank. She stumbled, Giancarlo jerking her roughly upright. She fought the urge to look back, to hope ridiculously that Conall would somehow be there. Giancarlo would make her pay if she did. It would be a futile effort. Conall wouldn't be and she didn't *want* him to be. To be here put him in danger. It had to be this way.

There was no choice, her conscience reminded her. This way was the only guarantee. As long as she was on this ship, it would take Giancarlo away from England and those she wanted to protect. Her best energies now were spent on looking to her own redemption. Perhaps there would be a chance to escape later. She would try, she would never stop trying as long as her efforts risked no one but herself. Andelmo arrived, presenting another obstacle she'd have to overcome. She tried to keep her fears in check. She focused on the activity around her. Crew scurried everywhere with last-minute preparations. Surely, there was some chivalry among them if she could make her plight known once they sailed.

She felt safe on deck, surrounded by others, but Giancarlo did not let her remain. He took her below to their cabin and shut the door firmly behind him, calling for Andelmo to join them. His ever-present blade was naked in his hand. *'Il gioco es fini, mi cara.'* The game is finished. 'And you lost. You know what that means. You led me on a merry chase and now you must be punished for it. Those are the rules of the game.' He nodded towards his thug. 'Andelmo, hold her.' To Sofia he said, 'Will you submit? It will go easier for you and we can be done with this.'

No! She was not going to submit. Not ever again, not when the memories of Conall's love was still fresh. He would want her to fight. Her submission could protect no one, not even herself. Sofia got an elbow into Andelmo's ribs, a foot down on his instep, causing enough sudden pain to wrench away from the big man. She struggled hard, pushing past Giancarlo to the door. She had the handle in her hand, she turned it, shoving it open. It opened, but not fast enough. Giancarlo tackled her from behind, she fell, half in, half out of the cabin. She screamed, hoping one of the sailors would hear her. She clawed her way forward, but Giancarlo had her ankles. She grabbed for purchase, clinging to an iron grip in the deck used for coiling rope, anything to prevent being hauled back into the darkness of the cabin. Her efforts only forestalled the inevitable. Giancarlo dragged her inside, but not before she let out a scream again.

The door shut ominously, Giancarlo breathing hard as he threw her on the bunk, his body heavy astride her, pinning her down. 'We'll be having no more of those antics, *mi cara*,' he growled, malevolence in his dark eyes. 'Light the lamp, Andelmo. Once this ship lifts anchor we'll have need of some heat.' The tip of his blade pressed against the fabric of her bodice, slicing the gown apart. 'While we wait, let's see what we have to work with. It's been so long, *mi cara*...ah, your beautiful skin, such a lovely blank canvas to work with.' He traced the outline of the brand. 'Well, almost blank. Might be time for a mate.'

Sofia heard the rumble of the anchor lifting, stripping away any illusion that there might be a rescue if the ship stayed in port. There would be no help now. No one would even know she was in here, trapped with this mad man until it was too late. Not that it would matter when they did discover her. Giancarlo would have excuses; his wife's poor health kept her to the cabin. She knew too well how this worked.

He ran a hand over her breast. She squeezed her eyes shut, trying to find the blackness, some place where she would be safe, some place where her mind could hide. She tried to remember the old litany. She would live, he wouldn't kill her, he wanted her alive, needed her alive. This *would* end and when it did, she would pick herself up and put herself back together. Again. She could feel the heat before it found her. R was for redeemed. She held on to that in her mind and screamed once more.

Conall heard the scream, a miracle really, given the noise of the wharf, but perhaps not considering the state of his mind, all of which was fixated on finding Sofia. He was fixated on her and the reality that time was slipping away. The high cry of a woman pierced through the masculine tones of the dock and he launched himself up the gangplank, not bothering to think about the consequences or about what he'd do when he got there. It only mattered that Sofia was in trouble. Instinctively, he knew the cry could have come from no other.

'Sofia!' he bellowed, pushing past guards at the wharf who protested the intrusion. If she could hear him, she would hold on, she would know help was coming.

'Sir, you can't go that way, the boat is leaving!' one of them called after him.

'Stop the ship! Stop the ship!' Conall yelled, waving his arms frantically to attract attention, anyone's attention, his legs pumping up the gangplank as the ship inched away from shore. The lip between the ship and the dock spread to become a gaping maw of a hole dropping into dark water. He wouldn't think about that now. Consequences simply had no meaning at the moment. There was only action. Conall eyed his destination, the stern of the ship. A sailor saw him and tried to wave him off. But Conall kept coming. At least now if he fell, someone might pull him out, might pull him on board. Getting on that ship was all that mattered. Conall hit the end of the gangplank and leapt.

He missed the deck, hitting the railing instead. His hand reached out blindly, grabbing a rail as he fell. His arm wrenched painfully from the jolt and for a moment he dangled precariously from the ship. Then he gathered himself, swinging his body to get his second hand on the railing. The sailor who'd warned him off raced over, hauling him aboard.

'I'm Viscount Taunton,' Conall panted, hoping to establish credibility and authority. He'd need both to search the ship. 'There's a madman on board.' Conall shouted abrupt explanations as he scrambled to his feet, not at all sure the sailor wasn't thinking *he* was the madman. 'He's got a woman trapped in a cabin. She came on board probably veiled.'

Recognition flickered in the man's eyes. He gestured below-deck and Conall sprinted past him. 'Sofia! Sofia!' Let Giancarlo hear him coming, let his voice distract the bastard from Sofia. His boots pounded down the narrow corridor. It would not be the best place to fight. This would be about fists and knives, close combat and closer quarters.

A door burst open, a pistol flashed, Conall veered left, hugging the corridor wall, the bullet missing him by fractions. There was little room for ducking. He charged Giancarlo, taking advantage of the empty gun. He caught the man in the midsection, charging like a bull. Conall took him down, pummelling relentlessly with his fists. His only thought was that the sooner Giancarlo was rendered senseless, the sooner he could get to Sofia.

He could hear sounds of a struggle in the cabin, bodies thrashing. Andelmo dragged Sofia out in pantalettes and the torn shreds of a chemise. She fought him for every inch, refusing to be used as bait. Andelmo hauled Sofia up against him, a knife to her throat, her neck extended and exposed. 'I'll cut her this time,' he growled in low tones.

Conall rose slowly from Giancarlo's prone body, hands in the air, his eyes steady on Andelmo, cautioning his temper to be careful at the sight of Sofia, her clothing torn. Giancarlo moaned behind him. With luck, the sailor would arrive with assistance and all this would be over. But before they arrived, Conall wanted Sofia away from Andelmo. 'You wouldn't want to hurt your master's pretty wife. He wouldn't like that,' Conall cajoled the big man. If there was a time he needed his persuasive skills, it was now. If Andelmo felt threatened by the arrival of assistance, there was no telling what he might do.

'There's no need to harm anyone, I've surrendered.' Conall put his hands in the air, sure to keep them at the level of his eyes. 'You can put down your knife.'

'Do you think I'm stupid? I've tangled with you before,' Andelmo grunted. 'If you want this knife, you come and take it.'

'Let her go and we can have another round.' Conall made a come-on gesture with his fists. He'd love nothing better than to land a few punches in revenge for Sofia. 'But I don't think there will be time.' In answer, the knife jabbed Sofia's neck and Conall launched himself at the henchman, forcing him to choose between defending himself and holding on to Sofia. Andelmo let go of her.

'Sofia, run!' Conall's guttural cry reached her as she fell against the wall. A blur on the periphery of her vision warned her Giancarlo was up, moving and unsteady on his feet. Conall couldn't help her now. He was in a deadly wrestling match with Andelmo for control of the knife. She staggered to her feet. The motion of the ship made speed difficult. Giancarlo reached for her, had her, she pushed, kicked, broke free and stumbled down the corridor, Giancarlo behind her. If she could make it to the deck, there would be sailors, there would be help. She scrambled up the ladder to the deck, kicking Giancarlo in the jaw with her foot.

'Bitch!' She felt his hand swipe against her leg and miss.

She ran past stunned sailors and heard the cry go

up behind her, 'He's got a gun!' The second pistol. The second shot. He wouldn't shoot her. He couldn't. But he could shoot the sailors. It was enough to deter immediate action. The sailors froze. Giancarlo kept coming. She kept running, barefoot over the wet deck. She slipped, fell, got up and kept going, but she was running out of ship.

She reached the prow and clambered up on the barrels, one hand grasping the rigging for balance. The ship had not left the harbour entirely. Shore was still visible. Hard to know how far it was, though.

'Get down, or I will shoot.' Giancarlo raised the gun.

'You won't. You need me,' she called his bluff. In the distance she saw Conall's dark head emerge from the hold, saw him begin to run.

'Do I? Being a widower isn't a sin, only suspicious.' The hammer went back on the pistol.

Conall was yards behind him. He wouldn't make it in time. She would be dead before he reached her. There was only once chance. Sofia didn't think. She jumped. She heard Giancarlo's pistol fire as she fell towards the water. The bullet found her halfway down.

If bullets were fire, then the water of Bristol Harbour was ice. The ice numbed the pain. But it couldn't make her arm operational. The water closed over her head again. She couldn't stay afloat with one arm. Around her the water was pink. The wound was probably better than it looked. Water had a way of making injuries look worse than they really were. Not that it mattered. She couldn't swim. Not like this, wounded and cold. Consciousness was starting to slip. This time she'd barely found the strength to kick to the surface and each time she went under she fell deeper into the ocean and had further to go to swim to the top. Conall was up there, though. If he could see her, if he could find her, she thought sleepily. If she could just hold on long enough to give him the chance...but she'd already been holding on for so long. She summoned her strength one more time, pushing to the surface one more time, but this time her strength didn't come. The last thing she remembered were the arms of a merman wrapping around her.

She'd always thought dying was supposed to be pleasant, a peaceful passage into bliss. That was completely false. Dying was uncomfortable. Painful at the worst of times, hot at the best, and that was when she was conscious of feeling anything at all. There was darkness and sleep and nothingness. There was only floating on the rim of frustrated awareness where consciousness taunted her just out of reach. But the harder she tried to reach for it, the more she hurt. It was easier to stop trying. There was relief in that. She didn't hurt when she stopped, she was only warm. But always she was lonely. Sometimes she could hear loud voices. Sometimes shouting, but she didn't understand what was being said.

She tried to talk to the voices, but that hurt, too. Her voice didn't work. Her throat was raw and sore and hot like the rest of her.

Then came a day where there was only one voice. A soft, sibilant tenor that sounded like a spring creek running fast over agates. She liked the sound of that. Sofia sighed in her darkness. She knew this voice; she had memory of it. What did that memory belong to? The voice was telling her things…things they'd done: fishing, a campfire, wet clothes, a quilt, backgammon, moonlit walks, a picnic in a meadow. *Artiodactyls. Conall.* The word came again, stronger, more insistent in her consciousness now. *Conall.*

I love you, Sofia. You can say you've married me for convenience, but I have married you for love.

There was light now about her, the darkness greying, now glowing and the sibilant tenor persisted, calling her towards the light. 'Just a little further, Sofia, you can do it, today is the day you wake up, you have to. The alpacas want to see you. I know you're in there. I know you're scared, you have every right to be after what you've been through, but you have to wake up. The doctors say…' The beautiful voice cracked. 'I don't give a damn what they say, Sofia. Wake up. Our life is waiting and I can't live it without you.'

Yes, she would wake up. She wanted to see the voice, wanted to see Conall. Wanted to see the alpacas, wanted to see love. Conall loved her. And then she remembered. She loved him, too. She loved him enough to give him up. She was running towards the light now, running to Conall. She was pushing against something, something that wanted to stop her, but she didn't let it. She gave a mighty shove.

Her eyes flew open, the effort taking an inhuman amount of strength. 'Conall.' The word was a rasp, a faint whisper that made her throat ache. But there was a face that went with the name. That face had bloodshot eyes and dark circles from lack of sleep, it was pale and lean, but at the sight of her eyes, it broke into a smile that obliterated all else. She was home.

Chapter Twenty-Three

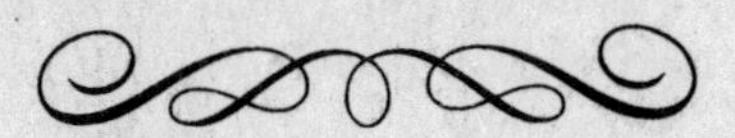

Conall was crying. 'Sofia. You've come back. I hoped you would,' he said softly, tears falling from his grey eyes as he pressed her hand to his lips—her good hand, she realised. Her other arm was heavily bandaged, immobile.

He gave her water and that helped her throat. He felt her forehead and gave a sigh of relief. 'The fever's broken at last. It's been nearly a week, far too long.' A week? A whole week? How could that be? She'd been in the water, she'd been shot. Oh, yes, she'd thought she was dead. That was where the week had gone: playing dead. Only she'd been alive the whole time.

'What happened?' She couldn't remember any more than foggy images.

'I jumped in after you, only it took me for ever to find you. The harbour doesn't seem that big until you have to find one small person in it, then it seems endless. But I found you and you scared the life out of me. You were limp, unconscious. I didn't really know for how long. Time had become meaningless. I thought I'd been underwater for ages, but the crew assured me it had been a matter of mere minutes. We hauled you aboard the ship. There was blood everywhere. I've never seen so much blood. I got a bandage on your wound and when the captain got the ship back to shore the ship's doctor was able to get the bullet out. By then, you were so far gone, you'd lost so much blood, no one thought there was much of a chance. The great fear was that fever and shock would finish you off.' Conall paused here, overcome by emotion. 'It nearly did.'

She looked around, her eyes the only part of her fully capable of moving without hurt. 'We're not on the ship now.'

'No. I brought you home to Everard Hall. There seemed no harm in it. Moving you couldn't do worse than already had been done.' She heard the unspoken words in that. She'd been that close to death, where it hadn't mattered one way or the other what happened to her. 'I carried you on the train. Everyone looked at me as though I was crazy. I held you all the way home. If you were going to get better, you needed happiness around you.' He paused, perhaps remembering their last quarrel. 'I fancied you'd been happy here. Cecilia, Freddie and my mother have all taken turns nursing you. You were never alone for a moment.'

'Ah, the voices. I heard them.' She smiled, a precarious act with cracked lips. She stifled a yawn. Conall stretched out beside her, his body a comfortable presence. She wanted to rest, she was feeling sleepy again, but there were more questions to answer. 'What of Giancarlo? What happened to him?'

Conall stroked her hair. 'You should sleep.'

'*After* you tell me about Giancarlo,' she insisted.

'He cannot trouble you any more. He is on his way to Barbados, under cabin arrest, courtesy of our Captain. When he arrives, he will be informed he is not welcome in England again, or in any other British holding outside of the island. The King of Piedmont has been notified of the arrangement and what led to it, by the Queen's special envoy to the Italian Kingdoms. What he might decide to do is anyone's guess. But it's hardly our concern.'

'His very own Elba.' Sofia sighed as Conall drew her gently against him. 'An island prison.'

'Where he will be watched closely. He won't hurt anyone again,' Conall assured her, but the better assurance was the warm presence of his body.

'Then all has been taken care of,' she murmured.

'All but one question, Sofia, and only you can answer it. Where does that leave us?' His voice was a raw husk, the scrape of his unshaven jaw rough against her cheek. She wanted her strength more than anything, strength enough to make love to him, to show him all she felt. 'You already know where I stand.'

I love you. 'Those words were spoken before you

knew how much trouble I was, before Giancarlo stormed into your home. I would not hold you to them.' But her heart was breaking to say them. Had she survived simply to leave him again? Was leaving the only right thing to do?

'I want you to hold me to them,' Conall whispered, kissing her. 'I jumped into Bristol Bay for you, I faced down guns and knives for you. What makes you think I don't want to be held to those words?'

She knitted her brow. 'I don't know, it's just that…'

He silenced her with another kiss, this one more insistent. 'It's what people do when they love one another. They believe. They trust even when the way isn't always clear.'

She did reach for him then with her good arm and pulled him close as best her strength allowed. 'If that's what love is, then I love you, too.'

'Yes, I think you do.' Conall smiled. 'You gave up the one thing that meant the most to you for me and I never want you to do that again.'

She made a protesting pout. 'That's what people who love each other do.'

Conall grinned. 'Welcome to happy ever after.'

Epilogue

Conall looked up from the last of the shearing and wiped a hand across his sweaty brow, enjoying the sight of his wife sitting on a hay bale feeding a bottle to the newest baby alpaca. Sofia's arm was healed, but she still had to be careful not to overexert herself. Despite the doctor's cautions, she insisted on being part of all the work. Conall allowed it, as long as he was the one who could keep an eye on her.

He came to kneel beside her, stroking the sweet fuzzy baby. 'I've decided to call our first run of wool the "Sofia". It will be the softest, silkiest, most durable of wools, able to withstand great pressure, flexible enough to adapt to a wide variety of circumstances.' He was flirting with her, loving the blush that crept over her cheeks. His desire started to simmer. He'd been hungry for her since breakfast. 'When people ask me how the wool got its name, I'll tell them it was named for…' He paused.

'Don't you dare say it, Conall Everard,' she warned playfully at his naughty nuance.

'A woman I once knew,' Conall concluded. 'What did you think I was going to say?'

'Well, one never knows.' Sofia laughed. He might have kissed her and more, if hooves hadn't interrupted. A rider approached and Conall hoped that he didn't bring bad news. Sofia's eyes mirrored his concern. 'I hope it's not Helena, it's too soon for the baby,' she worried.

'A letter, milord!' the rider called out, dismounting from the sweating horse. 'It's from Piedmont.' The messenger handed it to Conall. 'I thought you'd want to know right away, milord.' Conall dug in his pocket for some coins. The messenger gave a smart salute and remounted, wheeling off to make other deliveries.

Conall passed the letter to Sofia. 'You should be the one to open it.' She did so with nervous fingers. He waited patiently while she scanned the contents, a smile breaking out on her face. 'What is it?'

'The King apologises for Giancarlo.' Her hand fluttered to indicate all that was in the past. 'As reparation for anything I might have suffered, he would like to bequeath the wealth of his estates to me as a wedding gift.' She named an exorbitant sum. 'Do you know what this means?'

'You tell me.' Conall smiled. He knew what she'd say. She would be right and wrong.

'We can buy another mill. We can expand the

alpacas by purchasing another herd. We can build the school.' Her mind was racing with possibilities. Conall put a hand on her arm, laughing. He'd guessed right about his generous wife. She'd had a fortune for mere moments and already she was planning on how others could share in it.

'It means all of that, Sofia, but it also means the past is done, for good this time.' He drew her to him and kissed her soundly, his desire too insistent to be ignored. He wanted his wife. 'Come with me, there's something I want to show you in the meadow.'

They walked out to the pastures, hand in hand, in no hurry. 'Are we going to see the other babies?' Sofia asked. Three of the females had been pregnant, an extra blessing for the herd. Now, three new alpaca babies graced the fields.

'They're growing fast.' Conall made a clicking sound and the babies trotted over, eager for treats.

'You spoil them,' Sofia scolded with a laugh.

'I think they're the cutest things I've ever seen,' Conall freely admitted.

'Hmm.' Sofia gave him a knowing look and drew his hand low on her abdomen. 'I wonder, then, what you'll think about your son or daughter when they arrive?'

It took a moment for Conall to process the words. 'Are you sure?' The full magnitude of it caught him hard. He couldn't speak.

'It's early, but I am sure. Are you happy?' Sofia asked, her eyes worried.

'Happy? I am ecstatic.' He cleared his throat against the rising emotion. 'The last year has been full of death and loss and tragedy at every turn, but it is ending with life. You don't know how much it means.' How did he make her understand? She was not the only one putting away the past, putting away fears.

She moved into him, her eyes dark with invitation. 'Then show me, Conall.' Sometimes, bodies were better than words.

'Right here?' he asked, only partially shocked.

'Right here. I have it on good authority there's nothing quite like making love out of doors on a sunny summer day in England.'

Conall's eyes darkened. 'What did you have in mind?'

She knelt before him, her hands on his thighs. 'Something I've been saving for a special occasion.'

Her hands moved to the waistband of his trousers, her tongue running slowly along her bottom lip, a promise of other pleasures to come. Conall's body went hard in anticipation. Dear heavens, to have her hands, her mouth on him would be the stuff of fantasy.

Her eyes teased him with their blue flames. She undid his trousers, sliding them past his hips, freeing him to her hands. She cupped the weight of him, stroked the length of him, tested the hardness of him, learning him anew with every intimate osculation and all the while his desire grew until his mouth was dry and his hands dug into the depths of her hair for an anchor.

Lord have mercy, she was a temptress with those hands that touched him, those eyes that held him. She knew exactly the effect she was having on him. He would come right here in the field. But there was no mercy. With a final, lingering gaze on his face, she put her mouth on him. It was the most wicked, the most wonderful thing a woman had ever done for him, an act of true intimacy.

She sucked hard on his head, her tongue licking the little pearl of moisture at his tip, and Conall groaned, a carnal primal sound somewhere between animal and man. Her hand reached between his legs for his sac, squeezing with delicate aggression until he gasped, his body gathering for release. He tightened his hand in her hair in warning. She sucked hard one last time and rocked back on her heels, taking him in her hand, her eyes locking on him with the wicked whisper, 'I want to watch you come, Conall. I want to watch you fall apart in your pleasure.' And he did, far past the point of being able to do otherwise.

It might have been the most intimate moment of physical pleasure he'd ever shared. He wanted to remember her the way she was right now: eyes glowing, her skin translucent in the sunlight, her face tinged rose from her efforts, the fabric of her gown straining against her breasts, proof that she was aroused, too, having found pleasure in the pleasuring. It was a rare lover who delighted in the giving as well as the receiving, perhaps even rarer for her, having come so far in her own sensual journey where pleasure was no longer one person's to control, but something to be shared, given and received.

He leaned forward, tipping her head up to meet his, taking her mouth in a slow kiss as he knelt beside her, his hands at her skirts as he laid her down in the long summer grass. He would show her what she was worth to him one more time, he would honour her with his touch, worship her with his body just as he'd promised before God and witnesses. Most of all, he would show her what was possible when two people put their faith in each other.

* * * * *